ALSO BY MARY YUKARI WATERS

The Laws of Evening: Stories

The Favorites

A NOVEL

Mary Yukari Waters

SCRIBNER
NEW YORK   LONDON   TORONTO   SYDNEY

The majority of my thanks goes to two people: my editor, Alexis Gargagliano, for her invaluable help and vision, and my agent, Joy Harris, for her many patient reads. I am also grateful for the support and encouragement of family, colleagues, and friends.

SCRIBNER

A Division of Simon & Schuster, Inc.
1230 Avenue of the Americas
New York, NY 10020

First Scribner hardcover edition June 2009

For information about special discounts for bulk purchases, please contact Simon & Schuster Special Sales at
1-866-506-1949 or business@simonandschuster.com.

The Simon & Schuster Speakers Bureau can bring authors to your live event. For more information or to book an event contact the Simon & Schuster Speakers Bureau at
1-866-248-3049 or visit our website at www.simonspeakers.com.

Designed by Kyoko Watanabe
Text set in Garamond 3

Manufactured in the United States of America

1 3 5 7 9 10 8 6 4 2

Library of Congress Cataloging-in-Publication Data is available.

ISBN 978-1-4165-6107-1
ISBN 978-1-4165-6113-2 (ebook)

For my mother

Part 1

I t was an early morning in June 1978, and the Ueno neighborhood was just beginning to stir.

This was an old neighborhood, far enough north of the city's center to have the feel of a small village. It lay in the shadow of high green hills that surrounded the city of Kyoto like a giant horseshoe, trapping the moisture from its four rivers. A century ago, before the emperor's seat had moved to Tokyo (and before smog and pollution made their appearance), this moist climate had been considered ideal for the refined senses of the nobility: it captured the subtle fragrances of each season and fostered the most delicate complexions in the country. The downside, of course, was that Kyoto summers were brutally humid.

Fortunately the air was still cool and crisp, laced with the smells of moss and verdure that had sprouted so lushly during this month's rainy season. The walls and fences, their planks aged as soft and dark as velvet, reflected the pink glow of sunrise. Within cool pockets of shadow, the smell of dew-soaked wood still lingered.

At the open-air market, behind iron shop grates not yet rolled open for customers, rubber-booted fish vendors arranged the morning's catch on beds of ice. Several blocks away, a procession of shaved, robed priests from So-Zen Temple clip-clopped on geta through the crooked, narrow lanes. *"Aaaaa . . . ,"* they intoned. *"Ohhhhh . . . Ehhhhh . . ."* They performed these vocal exercises each morning to develop stamina of the lungs, and indeed their deep, resonant voices rose up from their diaphragms and into the morning air like the long aftermath of a gong. All throughout the neighborhood, produce peddlers were beginning to make their appearance. These farming women, brown from the sun, came in each morning from the surrounding country-side. Noticeably shorter than their urban counterparts, they padded through the lanes on old-fashioned *tabi* shoes made of cloth, leaning their weight into wooden pushcarts and grinning up at customers from beneath the shade of white cloths draped under their straw hats. "Madam . . . ? Good morning . . . ," they called out every so often, as a gentle signal to housewives in their kitchens.

None of this registered with fourteen-year-old Sarah Rex-ford, who slept soundly after yesterday's long plane ride. She didn't hear her mother rising from the futon beside her, or the priests' distant chanting as they headed down Murasaki Boule-vard on their way back to the temple complex, or the murmur of women's voices directly outside in the lane—among which the excited tones of her mother and grandmother were mingled—as they gathered around a peddler's cart.

The house in which Sarah slept had a gray tiled roof with deep eaves; its outer walls were left unpainted in order to dis-play the wood's aged patina, which had deep chestnut under-tones like the coat of a horse. This had been her mother's childhood home, but only her grandparents lived here now. The house stood on a corner, where a narrow gravel lane intersected a slightly wider paved street that fed into Murasaki Boulevard.

Each summer the Kobayashi house attracted attention because of its morning glory vines, whose electric-blue blossoms blanketed the entire eastern side of the house. The locals—housewives walking to the open-air market, entire families strolling to the bathhouse after dinner—often altered their routes in order to admire the view. As Mrs. Kenji Kobayashi liked to tell people, she had nurtured these vines from a single potted plant that her granddaughter Sarah had given her eight years ago: a first-grade science project, grown from seed. The younger generation of adults would nod, remarking fondly that they'd had the same assignment as children, that they could remember documenting the seedlings' growth in sketch journals. Under Japan's public school system, all schools used the same government-issued text-books.

Sarah Rexford hadn't attended a Japanese school since she was nine years old. That was the year she and her parents had moved away to America, after selling their home up in the Kyoto hills. There were various reasons for this move, one being that they thought it might be easier for Sarah to be with "her own kind," meaning children who wouldn't stare at her on the street or bully her after school. She was a mixed child, or as they said in Japan, a "half." Her features, however, were predominantly Western: straight nose, light gray eyes, dark wavy hair with brown highlights instead of blue.

The marriage of her mother, Yoko, to John Rexford, an American physicist almost old enough to be her father, had shocked everyone back in the early sixties. The match was particularly unusual because Kyoto was a traditional inland city, far removed from the seaports and military bases where such unions (euphemistically speaking) were known to occur. Fortunately Mr. Rexford was a civilian, a physicist at NASA. If he had been a military "GI," with all the unsavory connotations of that label, the Kobayashi family would not have been able to hold up their heads.

As the years passed and Yoko was neither abandoned nor mistreated by her American husband, the Ueno neighbors gradually came to accept the marriage. Some even suggested, as a graceful way of putting the scandal to rest, that the match had been ordained by fate. As they pointed out, it seemed prophetic in hindsight that the temple astrologer, on whom local parents relied for auspicious Chinese characters when naming their babies, had chosen for Yoko's name an unconventional hieroglyph associated with the Pacific Ocean.

And the neighbors agreed (how clear it seemed, looking back!) that Yoko Kobayashi had always been destined to lead a bigger, bolder life than her peers. Even as a child, there had been a larger-than-life quality about her—a striking air of confidence, bordering on effrontery, that was apparent in her firm step and erect posture. This wasn't the result of wealth or privilege. The Kobayashis had no money, although like other families with good crests who had been ruined in the war, they still held remnants of their old status. Nor was Yoko unusually beautiful, although her features were above average. In fact, her face had been memorable for its expression of mature comprehension, better suited to a grown woman, rather than the limpid, innocent gaze that was so highly prized in Japanese children.

A more likely explanation for Yoko's charisma was her range of accomplishments. All throughout her academic career, with the exception of one year, she had been ranked first in her class. She was captain of the girls' high school tennis team. Twice, she won a certificate—a fifth-place and a third—in the annual municipal haiku contest held for adults. She passed Kyoto University's notorious entrance exam, the nemesis of ambitious young men from all over the country. Long after she married and left home, she continued to hold the record as the youngest pupil ever to have performed a solo at one of Mrs. Shimo's autumn koto recitals. She had been six years old.

Despite her achievements, Yoko Kobayashi was down-to-earth and *shomin-teki,* "of the people." The only time she abused her powers (although she preferred not to see it in quite that light) was when she defended the weak: a classmate bullied on the playground or, as she grew older, an adult belittled in "polite" conversation. Then Yoko's killer instinct arose and she was at her cruel, cutting best. As a result, some of her staunchest supporters belonged to the social classes beneath her. They were former schoolmates who had grown up to become silk weavers, vendors, or shopkeepers.

Over this past week, Mrs. Kenji Kobayashi had used her daughter's history to her advantage, enlisting the shopkeepers' expertise in choosing uncharacteristically expensive cuts of fish and the choicest slices of filet mignon. Although Mrs. Kobayashi was not as socially democratic as her daughter, Yoko, she was nonetheless admired for the cool elegance of her etiquette and poise. It was widely known that before her marriage, she had grown up in one of Kobe's most exclusive seaside neighborhoods. Perhaps it was the cosmopolitan sophistication of her birthplace—not to mention her pleasing height—that gave Mrs. Kobayashi the flair for carrying off, to such dashing effect, those Western-style clothes that almost everyone wore nowadays. "I'll take some of this Kobe beef, for Yoko and her daughter. They're coming to visit from America," she told the butcher, and in the same breath wondered aloud—almost as if talking to herself—whether it would be at all possible to adjust the price.

"For you, madam, certainly," he assured her. He could hardly say no.

"It's their first time back in five years . . . ," Mrs. Kobayashi explained, and it was understood that today's favor would be balanced out by increased sales over the course of the visit. The butcher remembered the little "half" girl, wheedling her elders to buy this or that in an impeccable Kansai dialect that was completely at odds with her Caucasian features.

Mrs. Kobayashi's purchases now lay, shrink-wrapped and waiting, inside her tiny icebox. Some of them, like the sweet bean condiments and slices of teriyaki eel (for restoring strength to tired bodies), were already laid out on the table along with the usual breakfast staples: sweet omelettes, hot rice in a linen-draped wooden tub, julienned carrots and burdock roots cooked in mirin and soy sauce, a tall tin of dried seaweed, umeboshi with *shiso* leaves. A stack of lacquered bowls awaited the miso soup, which would be prepared at the last minute with skinny enoki mushrooms and tender greens. Mackerel steaks, sprinkled liberally with salt and broiling on the grill, filled the house with their savory aroma.

At the opposite end of the house, Sarah slowly awakened to the low, liquid burbling of pigeons in the lane. She had forgotten about the pigeons—there weren't any back home in Fielder's Butte, California. Their contented bubbling struck a deep chord in her memory; suddenly she was a little girl again, half-asleep, cradled by the sounds and textures of her early childhood. She listened, eyes shut, cheek unmoving against the buckwheat-husk pillow. Other long-lost sounds emerged: the kitchen door sliding open and shut, its glass panels rattling softly in the aged wooden frame; a newly hatched cicada starting a feeble *meen meen* in the garden. Years later, when she listened to pigeons as an adult, their sound would be overlaid by the magic of this moment, as she wavered in time on a Japanese summer morning.

chapter 2

Although Sarah Rexford had been sitting at the low-level breakfast table for less than an hour, her brain was already overloaded. For one thing, the Japanese conversation was fast. For another, there was an unexpected strangeness about all the things that should have been familiar. Her grandmother's traditional table setting, for instance, struck her for the first time as something exotic. Over the last five years, Sarah had grown used to the plain white Corelle back home in California. Now she was fascinated by the toylike arrangement before her: tiny porcelain bowls for rice, tiny lacquered bowls for miso soup. In the center of the table was a cluster of artfully mismatched bowls, each holding a different condiment that everyone picked out with chopsticks and placed on individual dishes that were one third the size of saucers. Sarah picked up each dish as if it were a museum piece, cradling it in both hands in order to savor its shape and heft. One was a rustic, pitted ceramic glazed with summer hues of ecru and blue; another was a paper-thin porcelain of misty lime, upon which a single bamboo stem was etched in white brushstrokes.

"Mother! This takuan is amazing!" exclaimed Mrs. Rexford,

munching vigorously on a slice of pickled daikon radish. "Where did you *get* this?"

"I made my own this year," Mrs. Kobayashi said. "You should take some home with you." Her expression brightened, as if she was about to discuss the pickle making, but she stopped herself. Her husband was about to speak.

Mr. Kenji Kobayashi was a handsome man in his sixties, permanently browned from years of tennis and golf. He designed avant-garde jewelry for a living. While extremely social in public—he was popular with both men and women—he was absentminded at home, as if conserving energy for his outside pursuits. When conversing with children, he often gave the impression of being slightly irrelevant, slightly off the mark. "So how many slices of bread," he now asked his granddaughter, "does an American person eat in a single day?"

"*Saa*—at least four," Sarah said. "Two slices of toast for breakfast, a sandwich for lunch . . . dinner's usually something else, like noodles or potatoes. But some people eat dinner rolls too, along with the main course." She glanced at her mother for confirmation, which was out of character for her. Back home, Sarah was a know-it-all; she was quick to correct her mother's English mistakes, or her gaps in Western knowledge, with contemptuous finesse. But this switch in turf had wrought some change in Mrs. Rexford, giving her the relaxed authority she lacked in America. The girl sensed this, as dogs sense the subtle ups and downs of their masters, and already the balance of power had shifted between them.

Mr. Kobayashi continued his interrogation. "So do you eat breakfasts like this in America?" he asked.

"Sometimes. But not very often. Mama usually makes eggs and toast and orange juice. And sometimes pancakes, because my father and I like pancakes."

"Pancake . . . ?" said Mrs. Kobayashi.

"She means hotcakes," Mrs. Rexford explained.

"Aaa, hotcakes!" Mrs. Kobayashi nodded her understanding. "How tasty!"

Sarah wished her grandfather would stop asking these questions. She felt the old, familiar shame of being singled out for her foreignness. She remembered her early childhood here in Japan, how it had felt to board a streetcar or walk down a street: the baleful stares of children, the frank curiosity of vendors or those weaving people who lived on the other side of Murasaki Boulevard. Such people, of course, were the minority; their social graces were less polished than the rest of the population. But they betrayed the truth behind everyone else's tactful facades of indifference. Young Sarah, who had grown up among Japanese faces (with the exception of her father, the only foreigner she knew), felt taken aback herself each time she passed a shop window and caught a glimpse of her own reflection: a pointy nose sprinkled with freckles, a sharp chin that was severe, almost foxlike, compared to the softer, more pleasing contours of those around her.

To shift the subject away from America, she announced to the table at large, "Granny Asaki waved to me from her balcony this morning."

Mrs. Asaki, or Granny Asaki as she was known in the neighborhood, was Mr. Kobayashi's elder sister. A longtime widow, she lived kitty-corner down the gravel lane with her daughter, her son-in-law, and her two grandchildren. The two houses, while bound by close ties, had something of an uneasy relationship. It had never occurred to Sarah to wonder why; she simply accepted it as the nature of her family.

As Sarah had anticipated, her mother and grandmother turned toward her with an air of sharp interest that, in the presence of Mr. Kobayashi and herself, they attempted to disguise with expressions of kindly disinterest.

"You saw her already? How nice," said Mrs. Kobayashi. "Did she happen to be hanging up something on the clothesline?" The two women exchanged a brief, sardonic glance.

Sarah nodded importantly. This had happened less than half an hour ago. She had folded up the futon comforters, stowed them in the closet, and was heading toward the dining room when she was struck by a sudden urge to see the garden where she had played so often as a little girl. Hurrying over to the wall of sliding glass doors that opened out onto the garden, she had thrown open the heavy, floor-length drapes. The metal rollers slid back with a *shhh,* like a receding wave, and the room was suffused with green light.

The garden was pleasantly unchanged—although smaller than she remembered—with the same four-legged stone lantern in one corner and the familiar stepping-stones spaced at artistically irregular intervals. The roof's extended eaves cut off the sky, intensifying the effect of mass foliage: maple and yuzu and bamboo and camellia, all at the peak of summer lushness.

From a slightly stooped position Sarah could peer up, under the eaves and over the wooden fence and the dwarf yuzu tree, and get a good view of Granny Asaki's second-story balcony. Mrs. Asaki was pinning up handkerchiefs and socks on the clothesline. She, too, was unchanged: small and spry, with the faint beginnings of a hunchback, and dyed black hair slicked into a small bun at the nape of her neck. Immediately spotting the girl's face at the window, the elderly woman leaned over the wooden railing and vigorously waved a wet handkerchief, causing a large crow to flap up from a nearby pine branch. Sarah waved back.

"It was almost like she'd been watching our house," Sarah

now reported to her mother and grandmother. From past experience, she knew that any evidence of Mrs. Asaki's nosiness was guaranteed to hold their attention. But the Japanese code of conduct deemed that children—even teenagers—should remain unsullied by any awareness of adult conflict, so Sarah made her remark with an air of bland innocence.

To her satisfaction, the women once again exchanged knowing glances.

"Granny Asaki has sharp eyes," said Mrs. Rexford dryly. Then, catching herself, she switched to a tone of bright geniality. "Not nearsighted, like the rest of us! Her health is remarkable, especially for someone her age . . . it must be the good family genes! *Ne,* Father?"

Mr. Kobayashi, who shared his elder sister's robust health, chuckled with pleased pride, and his wife murmured that good health was indeed a quality to be envied. The two women turned back to Sarah with expectant faces. Then, perceiving that this was the extent of the girl's contribution, they drifted off to another topic.

"That reminds me," said Mrs. Kobayashi several minutes later, "I think you and Sarah should go visit them first. They usually finish breakfast by eight thirty. So eat fast and run over there, quick, before they show up here."

"Why *shouldn't* they show up here?" Mrs. Rexford said. Relaxed and smiling, she made no attempt to eat faster. "I'm the older one. Masako should come to *me,* even if her husband's a little older than I am."

"No, no," said Mrs. Kobayashi. "Forget Masako's husband. Granny Asaki's the real head of that house. And she outranks *our* head . . ." She nodded toward her own husband, whose face was obscured by the lacquered bowl from which he was drinking.

"But, Mother, it's not Granny who's going to be coming

over. Everyone knows I'll pay her my formal respects during visiting hours. We're just talking about *my* generation."

"There is no such thing," said Mrs. Kobayashi, "as just *my* generation." She glanced surreptitiously at her husband. He was drinking a mixture of rice and tea with loud abandon, clearly uninterested in the conversation.

Mrs. Kobayashi leaned forward and silently mouthed the words *Be careful.* The women's expressions were no longer amused but grave.

Watching this, Sarah felt the first stirring of curiosity.

Mrs. Rexford looked up at the clock. Sarah followed her gaze. The clock was a shiny modern piece, incongruous with the aged wall post on which it hung. The wooden post dated back to a more traditional time, when aesthetically minded craftsmen used to leave small remnants of nature in their work. Each wall post in the room retained some individual quirk: a curious burl, or the serpentine tracks of beetle larvae just below the surface of the wood.

"A little more rice, Father-san?" Mrs. Kobayashi asked, holding out her hand in anticipation of her husband's empty bowl. They waited in silence while he drank down the last drop.

"*Aaa,*" he said, handing the bowl over. He then turned to Sarah. "Do people in America talk this much about manners?" he asked. "They just do whatever they feel like, right? Anytime they want?"

"*Soh,* pretty much." She giggled politely, and her grandfather chuckled with her. But there was more to this than etiquette. What it was she couldn't say, but there was definitely something more.

chapter 3

Someone was tapping on the frosted glass panels of the kitchen door. The women froze, chopsticks in midair, and looked up at the clock. It was far too early! Only a quarter after eight!

But it was just the two little girls from the Asaki house, ages eight and eleven. They had slipped away from their mother in their eagerness to come early. They stood bashfully outside the kitchen door, peering up at the breakfast scene. They had to look up, since the vestibule was a foot above ground level and the main tatami floor was another two feet above that.

Instantly the energy of the house altered; there were peals of excited laughter from the women, exclamations of "Come on up! Don't be shy!" and "Look, Sarah, you have visitors!" There was a flurry to fetch additional floor cushions, which were encased in summer cotton covers of white and blue to suggest the coolness of ice and water. Room was made at the breakfast table, a tin of chocolates brought down from the cabinet. Mr. Kobayashi, outnumbered by all the females, picked up his cup of green tea and wandered off to a quieter room. On his way out, he stooped down and affectionately ruffled the little girls' heads as they bent over to line up their sandals properly in the small cement vestibule. Grinning up at him, the barefooted girls clambered up the high wooden step onto the tatami mats.

There was no choice now but to stay and entertain them; this resolved the etiquette dilemma for both houses involved. Sarah wondered if the girls' mother, also unsure as to the best policy, had purposely turned a blind eye. If so, it had been a tactful move on her part.

"Look at you both, how big and fine you've grown!" Mrs. Rexford cried, grasping each girl's shoulder with a Western-style physicality that Sarah had never seen her use back home in America.

Clearly smitten, the two little girls beamed up at her.

"So healthy and brown!" Mrs. Rexford's face glowed with heightened emotion. It was years since she had laid eyes on real Japanese children. Yesterday at the airport, she had followed her fellow Japanese travelers with avid eyes, remarking wistfully that in her youth, she had never really appreciated the cuteness of Asian babies. Sarah, vaguely stung by this comment, had made a noncommittal grunt.

The two girls sat down, their eyes moving rapidly over the elaborate breakfast spread. They looked nothing like the chubby little girls of five years ago. They had the same slender build, doll-like bangs, and high Kobayashi cheekbones that Mrs. Rexford had in old photographs.

Mrs. Kobayashi, as if thinking along these same lines, sighed. "You know, Yo-chan," she said, "they remind me so much of you as a child." Sarah felt a stab of jealousy.

Little Yashiko, her tan accentuated by a white tank top, eyed Sarah's pale arms with timid curiosity. "Do children play outdoors in America?" she asked.

"Yes, of course," said Sarah. "But I have to be careful so I don't burn and peel." The girls looked mystified. Mrs. Kobayashi and Mrs. Rexford and even their own mother were every bit as white as Sarah, but in their youth they had all been brown. It was a rite of passage: Japanese girls stayed in the sun until adulthood, upon which they switched standards and adopted pale makeup and shielded their complexions with parasols.

Momoko, the elder girl, politely changed the subject. "Auntie Mama," she said, using the Western title as if it were a proper name. "Can Big Sister Sarah come with us to Morning Tai Chi Hour, Auntie Mama? We already got her a summer pass."

"What an excellent idea!" cried Mrs. Rexford and Mrs. Kobayashi at the same time, which made everyone laugh. Sarah and Momoko exchanged shy looks of friendship. They had been playmates before Sarah's move but now they were self-conscious, preferring to use the adults' easy conversation as their conduit.

"Do they still do tai chi at Umeya Shrine, like they used to?" Mrs. Rexford asked. Momoko nodded importantly. She replied using some advanced phrase with which Sarah wasn't familiar: something about public office, or maybe community organization. "Teacher Kagawa's in charge of it this year," she added.

"Kagawa?" Mrs. Rexford turned to her mother. "Any relation to that family near the park?"

"Yes, yes! That's the one," said Mrs. Kobayashi. "Remember Emiko had a little sister? She's teaching at Tendai Elementary now."

"Ah, really!" Mrs. Rexford turned back to Momoko. "When your teacher was little," she told the girl, "she used to come to me for tutoring." Her lips parted in a proud, careless smile, and Sarah suddenly realized that her mother was beautiful.

It was becoming increasingly clear that she had underestimated her mother. Ever since their arrival in Japan, Mrs. Rexford had exuded the same air of relaxed entitlement that Sarah had observed in popular girls back home. Sarah herself was not popular; it was unsettling to be reminded that her mother belonged in a higher social league than her own. She felt embarrassed now, remembering all the times she had taken advantage of her mother's ineptness in English. One fight in particular she wished she could forget. Her mother, struggling to articulate the proper comeback, had turned away too late to hide tears of frustration. Their argument had stopped instantly. Mother and child, both stricken, had tried to pretend nothing happened.

Yoko Rexford was twenty-five years old when she and her husband first moved to America. They had stayed there ever since, with the exception of a few years when they lived in the Kyoto hills. Yoko's social dominance did not survive this move, although the proud posture and intelligence were innately hers. Her college-level English was good, but it lacked the elegant execution with which she had been used to cutting down opponents or carving out poetry. Her stature in the community, which she had always democratically pooh-poohed, was suddenly gone.

Ever practical, young Mrs. Rexford had channeled her energies into more realistic pursuits: gardening, cooking, needlework, all of which she tackled with her old academic zeal. Each Saturday she visited the town's small, outdated library, borrowing cookbooks by James Beard and Julia Child (as a new bride, not knowing what American men ate for breakfast, she had prepared for her bemused husband an elaborately arranged tray of fruit and nuts). She punched down homemade bread dough with arms still sculpted from tennis, experimented with coq au vin and crepes suzette. She executed complex projects of lace tatting, crewel embroidery, traditional American quilt patterns. In time, she became an expert in all the skills that modern American women had long since abandoned.

Sometimes she remembered, with the same wistful wonder with which amputees remember running, how it had felt to have all the right skills at her disposal, to have powers commensurate with the force of her personality. She fervently admired the tennis star Martina Navratilova. "She never plays it safe by trying to be liked," she told her husband. "She just goes out on the court, with no one cheering for her, and still beats every last one of them. Oh, I *envy* her that feeling!"

If Sarah could have probed to the bottom of her fourteen-year-old heart, she would have found there a pity for her mother that was too deep, and too painful, to be faced directly.

Meanwhile, at the breakfast table, she struggled to follow the rapid-fire conversation all around her. She felt an unfamiliar clenching between her temples. It occurred to her that her mother must experience this same clenching back home, as a result of the permanently strained vigilance with which she braced herself for American speech. Mrs. Rexford's English, although heavily accented and occasionally halting, was always grammatically correct; never, at any time, did she allow herself to lapse into pidgin.

But judging from her mother's manner at the table, there was no such tension now. She was eating heartily, interrupting the chatter every so often with a dramatic moan of appreciation for her mother's cooking, as if she hadn't eaten a square meal in years.

"Mother, this is absolutely delicious," Mrs. Rexford said, using her chopsticks to herd together some scattered flakes of leftover mackerel. "It's exactly the way I remembered it." A floodgate of appetite seemed to have opened up within her. She couldn't stop eating. "Have some," she urged little Yashiko who was sitting beside her, still too shy to speak.

Then, looking over at Sarah's fish plate, she exclaimed, "*Ara!* You haven't touched the skin at all. You don't like it?"

"There's this thick layer of fat on the inside."

"But that's where the best flavor is!" Mrs. Rexford looked insulted.

"I'll eat it," piped up Yashiko.

"Good girl!" said Mrs. Rexford warmly. "We can't let this go to waste, now can we?"

"*Aaa,* that's how you can spot a true-blue Japanese," laughed Mrs. Kobayashi. "Even the prime minister himself, I bet, wouldn't say no to salt-broiled mackerel skin."

Reaching over with her chopsticks, Mrs. Rexford picked up the strip of skin, which was toasted to a bubbly brown crisp and frosted with salt, and transferred it from Sarah's rectangular fish plate to her own. Their eyes met, then looked away.

Something like pity flickered over Mrs. Rexford's face. "The child can't help it," she said quickly. "They don't even sell mackerel in the stores back home. Did you know that on the East Coast, where John grew up, oily fish was considered lower grade? They actually *preferred* the bland white types like sole or flounder."

"*Hehh?!*" cried Mrs. Kobayashi in amazed disbelief. She and Momoko darted a quick, curious glance at Sarah, as if the explanation for such a peculiar fact might somehow be detected in her American face. Little Yashiko, nestled against Mrs. Rexford, finished off the mackerel skin with quiet efficiency.

chapter 4

At 8:30 on the dot, Masako Nishimura arrived to apologize for her daughters' untimely intrusion.

Mrs. Nishimura and Mrs. Rexford gave off such different energies, it was hard to believe they were cousins. On closer scrutiny, however, one could see they shared the same high cheekbones from the Kobayashi side. Sarah had seen old school photographs in which they looked virtually identical with their bobbed hair, cat's-eye glasses, and young, unformed expressions. More than once, leafing through the Asaki album with her great-aunt looking over her shoulder, Sarah had gotten them mixed up. Mrs. Asaki would correct her patiently, murmuring, "It's a strong family likeness, *ne* . . ."

Over the years, the women's faces and even their bodies had evolved to reflect their different personalities. Mrs. Rexford's confident posture, and the hint of muscle in her arms and calves, were natural extensions of her personal strength. In contrast, Mrs. Nishimura was less substantial, almost ethereal. She had a physique more suited to traditional kimonos: narrow, sloping shoulders; a walk that was an unobtrusive glide, as opposed to her cousin's firm, decisive stride.

When it came to faces, Mrs. Nishimura wore one basic expression: one of pleasant, attentive cooperation. It was a classic "outside face." Every well-bred person used it at some point, usually on formal occasions or with strangers. Westerners, who were its most frequent recipients, assumed—understandably, if incorrectly—that this Japanese veneer of politeness was a permanent condition. And with Mrs. Nishimura, that may indeed have been the case. One always sensed in her a certain emotional reserve, even in the most casual situations.

Mrs. Rexford was the opposite. Among her Ueno neighbors, she frequently dropped her mask to show spontaneous reactions: affection, enthusiasm, gossipy fascination. In truth, these flashes of emotion were not always so spontaneous or genuine. But Mrs. Rexford, blessed with surer social instincts, understood the value of judicious lapses in etiquette. Since childhood, she had used this technique to downplay her achievements and make herself more approachable. Since this familiarity was used from a position of power, it gave the flattering illusion of inner-circle acceptance.

"I'm so sorry about the girls," Mrs. Nishimura now said in a voice as gentle as her face. Instead of standing squarely within the doorway, she peered around the sliding door in the pose of a hesitant intruder. "Bothering you, right in the middle of your breakfast . . ."

Mrs. Rexford laughed and waved away the apology. "*Anta,* don't be silly! Children will be children!" she cried, throwing an affectionate look at the girls. "Ma-chan, how have you *been?*"

Mrs. Nishimura decided to scold her daughters anyway. "*Kora,*" she admonished them softly. Momoko and Yashiko grinned with guilty embarrassment.

"Come up and have some tea!" said Mrs. Kobayashi, already pouring out an extra cup.

Mrs. Nishimura stepped up into the small vestibule. She still wore the short bob of her college photos, parted on one side and pinned with a barrette. There was a sheltered, almost virginal quality about her, emphasized by a pale pink blouse with a Peter Pan collar. As a child Sarah had subconsciously registered the shades and shapes that, like abstract art, made up her "auntie": the round bob above the round collar, the pastel clothing against the whitish cast of Japanese cosmetics. These combinations struck a deep chord of recognition within her, like the sound of the pigeons earlier that morning.

Once again, the currents in the house altered. Although it was relaxed and intimate, there was now a slightly guarded quality that hadn't been there before. It was as if two identical masks of kindness had dropped over Mrs. Kobayashi's and Mrs. Rexford's faces.

They all sat cozily around the low table, ignoring the uncleared breakfast dishes. Now the conversation no longer included the children but circled among the adults. Sensing this, Sarah and Momoko began talking to each other in low voices.

"Mama and I are coming over to your house later," Sarah said. "We'll probably bring French pastries, or maybe a cake."

"What kind? Do you know yet?"

"I'm not sure—we still have to go to the bakery."

"What are you doing later? Do you want to come up and play in our room?"

Little Yashiko, who had sidled over to sit beside her big sister, murmured that she had once tasted lemon custard cake, and she had liked it.

Having thus reestablished their friendship, the three girls were content to fall silent and eat chocolates out of the tin, all the while following the adults' conversation.

". . . a mere toddler! He was kicking that ball, running after it, kicking it, running after it, so *excited* . . ." Mrs. Kobayashi was reminiscing about one of their neighbors' sons, a young man who had recently moved to Berlin to study under the famous conductor Seiji Ozawa. "Laughing and drooling, with that soccer ball practically up to his knees . . ."

The children shrieked with laughter. Mrs. Nishimura rocked with mirth, demurely covering her open mouth with her hand.

"And he went right on going, out of sight!" Mrs. Rexford chimed in. "Just vanished over the horizon, like in some surrealist movie! You should have seen those little legs working, *choko-choko-choko* . . ." Mrs. Rexford and Mrs. Kobayashi worked well as a team. Their chemistry was so bright, it seemed to suck the air right out of the room.

They were all laughing so much that no one heard the footsteps on the gravel or the kitchen door rolling open. Suddenly Mrs. Asaki was standing in the doorway, smiling. "Good morning!" she chirped, in that singsong cadence of Kyoto old-timers.

There was a moment of surprised silence before Mrs. Kobayashi and Mrs. Rexford jumped up from their cushions. Even Sarah felt somehow caught in the act. "*Ara,* Granny-san!" Mrs. Rexford protested. "Sarah and I are supposed to visit *you*! We were waiting until ten o'clock!"

"We're so embarrassed!" added Mrs. Kobayashi, even though it was Mrs. Asaki who was clearly breaking the rules.

With both hands, Mrs. Asaki waved their words away. "*Maa maa,* everybody so formal!" She laughed. "What does it matter? We're all *family*!" Here the old woman cocked her head, like some coquettish bird, and appealed to Sarah—"*Ne?*"—as if the two of them were the only sane people in the room. Sarah, unable to keep from smiling in delight, agreed with a vigorous nod and an "*Nnn!*"

"Wait! Let me heat up some more tea," said Mrs. Kobayashi, rushing across the tatami and down the wooden step. The kitchen, which was an extension of the vestibule, stood on a lower level than the rest of the house. The architecture was a carryover from a bygone era when women had done their cooking away from the main house, in lean-tos or covered porches.

"No no, don't bother on my account." Mrs. Asaki climbed up onto the tatami and looked around at everything with her bright eyes.

Mrs. Rexford was waiting for her in an open space away from the others, seated with legs folded beneath her and fingertips pressed to the floor. "Sarah!" she hissed in her obey-me-now voice. Sarah scurried over and assumed the position next to her mother, self-conscious because everyone else was watching with interest.

Mrs. Rexford bowed first, barely giving Mrs. Asaki enough time to get down on her elderly knees. She had a finely trained bow that put the older lady's to shame, and she was fully conscious of this advantage. Mrs. Kobayashi, unlike her sister-in-law, had a background of rigorous training in formal etiquette associated with the high arts, and she had ensured that her daughter received this same training. Mrs. Rexford's skill was evident in the way she pulled back her shoulders and arched, catlike, to the floor.

"My mother, my daughter, and I," she said, shifting into a refined, inflectionless tea-ceremony voice, "live perpetually in your debt." She timed her bow so that its lowest point coincided with the end of her sentence. "With your gracious permission"— here she lifted her head from the floor and paused, then slowly began rising back up—"we remain indebted to your kind regard during this coming visit" . . . she straightened up to a sitting position for full effect, fingertips still poised on the floor . . . "and for many more years to come." She bowed once again, this time in silence. She knew it intimidated Mrs. Asaki to be faced with such a display of formality, and this knowledge somehow compensated for the fact that her flustered mother was down in the kitchen, scrambling to put together a pot of company-quality sencha tea.

Mrs. Asaki returned the bow with an appropriate response. Mrs. Rexford then looked pointedly at her daughter.

Now was the time for Sarah to bow correctly, as she had been taught. She counted silently to herself—one million one, one million two, one million three—timing her bow to end at the count of three. She could hear someone unwrapping a chocolate. Spine straight. Rear end down. It was a difficult, almost athletic feat. Her mother, trying to coach her a month before their visit, had said despairingly that a good bow just couldn't be faked, any more than a dancer's pirouette could. It took too long to train the right muscles. A bow was an acid test of one's daily habits.

Sarah returned to a full sitting position before she realized she had forgotten to utter a single word. She had learned a simple speech, something to the effect that she was happy to be back and grateful for Mrs. Asaki's kindness. But she couldn't remember a word of it.

"Well done, well done!" Mrs. Asaki sang out with her cheerful cackle, and clapped her age-spotted hands.

"Granny-san," said Mrs. Rexford, returning to a tone of affectionate familiarity that her daughter nonetheless suspected was an "outside" voice, "sit down here on my cushion. *Ne,* please." She smoothed the cotton fabric in a deferential gesture of invitation. Mrs. Asaki accepted, ducking her head in a pleased quarter-bow, and Mrs. Rexford went away to help her mother with the tea. "Sarah," she called back over her shoulder, switching once again to a disciplinary tone, "clear those dirty dishes off the table. Quickly!"

Sarah obeyed. Carrying the loaded clearing tray with both hands, she stepped down into the kitchen, feeling with her bare foot for the wooden step she couldn't see. She liked her grandmother's kitchen, with its vaguely primitive, backstage atmosphere that was so different from the rest of the house. It had a long narrow floor lined with wooden planks. Overhead were high exposed rafters blackened by years of smoke, from which a lanternlike fixture hung at the end of a long rope. Best of all, a miniature door opened right out onto the street so they could trade with vendors.

Here in the narrow kitchen, Mrs. Kobayashi and Mrs. Rexford were standing side by side. It was the only way they could both fit. Their backs were to Sarah, so they didn't notice her approach. A newly arranged tray of tea utensils lay at the edge of the counter, ready to be carried up to the guests. Mrs. Kobayashi was lining up individually wrapped tea cakes on another tray beside it. Mrs. Rexford poured hot water from the kettle into a teapot.

". . . like a hawk. Even now, she won't trust Masako and me together," Mrs. Kobayashi whispered.

"I still can't believe Granny came." Putting down the kettle, Mrs. Rexford wiped stray drops from the surface of the counter.

"Never let down your guard," whispered Mrs. Kobayashi. "She's aware of everything. Remember that."

Mrs. Rexford mulled this over. "It's so unlike Masako," she said finally. "Usually she's more careful. If she hadn't stayed this long, Granny would never have come over in the first place."

"It's awkward," agreed Mrs. Kobayashi.

Sarah, who all along had sensed some disturbing point outside her range of vision, felt a small thrill as it came into focus.

The girls' early arrival had been no accident. Mrs. Nishimura had *wanted* to come here; she had *wanted* to linger at this untidy breakfast table. Sarah recalled the guarded, apprehensive smiles of her grandmother and mother.

Now the two women fell silent.

"Hora . . ." Mrs. Kobayashi let out a sigh. "I had a *feeling* you should have gone there first. Didn't I tell you? After this many years, you develop a sixth sense about these things."

Noticing the girl's presence for the first time, the women immediately switched to an animated discussion about the freshness of the tea cakes.

chapter 5

There was no chance to ask questions until late that night, when Sarah and her mother finally lay down on their futons.

They were side by side in the parlor. The walls were plastered with a mixture of fawn-colored clay and chopped straw. Like all traditional parlors it had a tokonoma, a built-in alcove of polished wood. Within it hung a long summer scroll with flowing black script. The scroll was the only object of pure white in the room, and it leapt out at the eye from inside the shadowed recess. At the foot of the alcove, in a shallow glazed bowl, Mrs. Kobayashi had arranged a single yellow lily from the garden, deliberately angled across long clean lines of summer grass.

Back in America, Sarah hadn't remembered much about this room. But as soon as she arrived, everything had fitted seamlessly back into her memory, like the pigeon calls this morning. In fact when she first entered this room, she had immediately noticed that the stringed koto, which her mother had played in her youth and which stood in its original sheath of faded red silk, was now leaning against the tea cabinet wall instead of the tokonoma wall.

Sarah and her mother lay on their backs. Moonlight shone through a gap in the heavy drapes, which were slightly open to let in the breeze. For the first time that day, the house was utterly silent.

"When I was little," said Mrs. Rexford, "there used to be a snake living up in the attic."

"Ugh, a snake!" said Sarah. "Did you see it?"

"No. I just heard it at night, when I was lying in bed. The mouse would run—its nails went *k'cha k'cha*—then there was a quick dragging sound. After that, it got quiet again."

"Weren't you scared?" Sarah asked, even though she knew better. Her mother disapproved of timidity in any form.

"What for? Snakes bring good luck to households, remember? In the old days, farmers stored grain in the attic. Grain attracts mice, and mice attract snakes. So having a snake in your attic meant you were wealthy. During the occupation, I'd listen to that sound and feel safe, because the snake was protecting our black-market rice."

"Black-market rice? In this attic?" Sarah strained her eyes in the moonlight. She could make out the shadowed, roughly hewn rafters of the ceiling, curiously out of sync with the polished gleam of the alcove and wall posts. The attic was silent. Never in her lifetime had Sarah heard any sound. But these were modern times after all, when nothing exciting ever happened.

She shifted her body to look over at her mother, and the buckwheat-husk pillow gave a loud crunch. Mrs. Rexford lay with her hands clasped behind her head. In the moonlight her face looked unformed and unfamiliar, framed by a cloud of hair loosened from its French twist.

They had never slept together in the same room before.

"Mama?" Sarah spoke softly, aware that these rooms were

divided by nothing but paper panels. "How come things are awkward with Granny and Auntie?"

"Hmm?"

"I heard you talking in the kitchen."

Mrs. Rexford gave a sigh of reluctance. Sarah waited patiently. Usually her questions were met with a brisk, "You're still a child, it's none of your business." But this time—she felt sure—her mother would take her into her confidence as a form of damage control.

Sure enough, her mother whispered, "I suppose you're old enough." She switched to English. "But you're not to tell Momoko or Yashiko—they don't know yet. And don't bother your grandmother."

"Okay."

"Your auntie Masako was adopted as a baby. The Asakis weren't her real parents."

"Oh. Then who were?"

"She and I have the same parents," said Mrs. Rexford. "She's my full sister by birth."

"So *Grandma's* her real mother . . . ?" Sarah's mind raced back over that morning. The tightness between her temples intensified as her brain realigned itself.

"That means your auntie is your *true* aunt. And Momoko and Yashiko are your true cousins."

Sarah mulled this over. "Why did Grandma give her away?"

"She didn't just *give* her away. It was more complicated than that."

They were silent. Outside in the lane, a neighbor's bicycle crunched slowly over the gravel.

"Here's what you need to know. After your real grandfather died in the war, your grandmother was beholden to the Asakis. It was wartime and . . . things were complicated. She didn't want to give up her baby, but she felt she had to. That's it, basically."

"But why—"

"No more questions." Her mother switched back to Japanese. "We have to get some sleep." Resigned, Sarah rolled onto her back and pulled the light summer comforter up to her chin. "Good night," she said.

"Good night."

She closed her eyes. Despite her exhaustion, she couldn't shut down her brain. It was as if she'd been awake for so long, she had forgotten how. Inside her skull the echoes of Japanese voices chattered on and on, and would not stop.

After several minutes, her mother spoke again. "You mustn't judge your grandmother. It was a difficult time."

"I won't."

"In-family adoptions are actually an old tradition. In the villages, if you didn't have children there was no one to take care of you in old age. So extended relatives had to help each other out. But they always kept the child inside the family. Japanese people never give away their babies to strangers."

"Hmmm . . ."

"People still do it. Sometimes it's to maintain the family line. That's really important, you know, because family altar tablets have to be passed down from generation to generation. Or else rich families do it so they can pass down assets to a member of their clan."

"Is that why—"

"No. Go to sleep."

Mrs. Rexford soon drifted off. Sarah lay listening to her deep breathing.

If she had known of this adoption as a child, she probably would have thought nothing of it. Small children accepted everything as normal. After all, how was this any stranger than her grandmother marrying two brothers? Talk about keeping things within the family! Mrs. Kobayashi had married twice, the first Mr. Kobayashi for love and the second Mr. Kobayashi out of necessity. It had never occurred to the girl to find this curious. As a child, all she cared about was that her grandpa was related to her by blood, even though he wasn't technically her grandfather.

Her thoughts drifted to the attic, silent now, emptied of snakes and black-market rice and the energy of a turbulent past. She thought of the war that polite people never mentioned—the war that had brought illegal rations into this house, caused her grandmother's second marriage, and somehow contributed to her aunt's adoption. In the shadowy rafters, the brutality of those times seemed to still linger.

chapter 6

After the formal visits of the first day, the two houses kept mostly to themselves. They did, however, drop by almost daily to share freshly cut flowers from their gardens, or an extra eel fillet bought on sale, or half of a designer melon received from a visitor. On certain evenings, Mrs. Kobayashi had Sarah walk over a platter of tempura or pot stickers, hot and crisp from the frying oil. These were greeted with great enthusiasm because—as Mrs. Kobayashi explained privately—the cooking over there was not so good. The Asaki household followed the old Kyoto tradition, using seasonings so subtle they were practically flavorless. (Mrs. Kobayashi, the Kobe native, went on to say that Kyoto people were notorious for donning beautiful silks in public but making do with substandard cuisine in private.) Sometimes Mrs. Asaki, laden down with shopping bags and beaming—she loved going downtown, where all the action was—tapped on the Kobayashis' kitchen door on her way home and dropped off a French bakery bag filled with brioches and frankfurter pastries. But these exchanges lasted only a few minutes, and the women rarely took off their shoes and entered each other's houses.

"How come we never sit around and talk, like we did the first day?" Sarah asked. Deep down, she knew why. But a childish part of her was disappointed, even petulant; she had been hoping for a constant round of social activity.

"Goodness, child. Who has the time! A house doesn't just run itself," said Mrs. Kobayashi, laughing.

Mrs. Rexford shot Sarah a glance of warning. "People need boundaries," she said.

Luckily the children had no such restrictions. Sarah spent hours at the Asaki house. Within that household were two different worlds, one downstairs and one upstairs.

Downstairs was Mrs. Nishimura's domain—not just during the day but also at night, when she and her husband rolled out their futons in the television room. Unlike the sunny rooms upstairs, the ground floor was tinged with restful green light from the garden. Since the formal dining room was used only for guests, the children gravitated toward the informal eating area that directly adjoined the kitchen. Under the large low table, stacked in tin boxes, were snacks: rice crackers wrapped in seaweed, shrimp crackers, curry-flavored puffs.

In the pale underwater light, Mrs. Nishimura glided in and out of the kitchen bearing delicate glass dishes of flan pudding, or salted rice balls, or crustless sandwich triangles garnished with parsley. "*Hai,* this is to wipe your fingers," she told them, offering steaming-hot hand towels rolled into perfect tubes, just like the ones in restaurants. Her conversation was as soft and serene as the leaf-filtered light. "Do you like juice?" she would ask gently, as if Sarah were still seven or eight instead of fourteen. She made conversation by saying things like, "Yashiko's favorite spoons have Hello Kitty on them, don't they, Yashiko?"

Sarah sometimes wondered if her aunt switched personas as

soon as she was alone with her own children, dropping her outside face and talking in rapid, droll sentences like everyone else.
She watched carefully when her aunt was in the company of
other women. Although Mrs. Nishimura did switch to an adult-
level vocabulary, her demeanor remained as soft and ethereal as
with the children. She lacked the impulsive, gossipy spark that
the other women seemed to share in abundance. Once, in a private uncharitable moment, Mrs. Rexford sighed sharply to her
mother, "I swear! She's like a blancmange pudding."

Then Mrs. Rexford had immediately rectified her blunder
("Because blancmange pudding is pure and white, never sullied
by anything ugly") to ensure that there would be no true under-
standing on her daughter's part.

"It's okay, Mama, I know," said Sarah. "She's sort of like a
Christian Madonna, isn't she."

Mrs. Rexford's relieved eyes met hers. "Exactly," she said.

It wasn't as if the two sisters disliked each other. Mrs. Rexford was protective of Mrs. Nishimura, who in turn looked up
to her big sister with sincere admiration. But they weren't
everyday friends, the way Mrs. Rexford was with their mother.

When the girls tired of playing downstairs, they climbed up
to the second story, where the tatami mats were warm from the
sunlight flooding in through the glass wall panels. Sometimes
they slid shut the latticed shoji screens against the midday
glare. Then a soft, diffused light glowed through the rice paper
and created a lovely effect, as if they were living inside a giant
paper lantern.

The girls' room wasn't a true "room" in the Western sense,
since the entire second floor was one enormous room. In place of
solid dividing walls, there were *fusuma*: wall-to-wall partitions
of sliding doors that were left open during the day and slid shut
at night. These doors were covered on both sides with thick,

durable paper whose fibrous surface was interwoven with what looked like delicate strands of green seaweed.

Momoko and Yashiko's side looked out over the back garden. Much of the view was obscured by the leafy branches of a huge persimmon tree. But Mrs. Asaki's side, which faced the gravel lane, had a striking panoramic view. Sarah loved standing on her great-aunt's balcony and gazing out over the tiled triangular roofs: some slate gray, others gray-blue, all sprouting television antennae like feathery weeds. Every so often, this somber expanse was interrupted by the imposing black sweep of a temple roof or the bright vermilion of a tall shrine gate. In the distance, against the green backdrop of the Kyoto hills, a cluster of tall commercial buildings rose up through the summer haze.

From this vantage point she could also look down directly into her grandmother's garden, as Mrs. Asaki had done that first morning. It gave Sarah an uneasy thrill to realize how clearly visible everything was from here, right down to the pink comic book she had left outside on the veranda. Once Sarah saw her mother and grandmother outside in the garden, crouching side by side near the lilies and pointing excitedly at something in the dirt. She waved but they didn't see her.

This view reinforced her feeling that the Asaki house was somehow incomplete, in spite of its large size and pleasant rooms. Its soul seemed to look out toward the Kobayashi house instead of inward unto itself. Of course, that might have been her imagination. But Momoko and Yashiko seemed to feel it too. "Big Sister, can we go play at *your* house now?" one of them invariably asked. Sarah would have preferred to stay. She liked the novelty of an unfamiliar household, and her aunt served frequent snacks. But she yielded to her cousins, whose mute urgency was like that of dogs straining at a leash. She felt, in some strange way, that she owed it to them.

"Don't stay too long and become a bother," Mrs. Nishimura called gently from the doorway, waving after her children, who had already broken into a run. And Sarah, lingering behind to return her aunt's wave, felt once again that odd compunction.

There wasn't much to play with at the Kobayashi house. It had none of the Asaki house's amenities: no colored pencils or origami, no finches in hanging cages on the balcony, no ancient turtles floating in mossy stone vats. But when the girls stepped up into the kitchen vestibule and saw Mrs. Kobayashi and Mrs. Rexford doubled up with laughter over their tea or spiritedly gossiping in the kitchen as they chopped vegetables for the evening meal, they always felt they had arrived at the true center of things.

"They sure do love to come here," Sarah remarked one day after her cousins had gone home. She had spent the last half hour watching them dart between her mother and grandmother, tugging on the women's sleeves and crying, "Aunt Mama, Aunt Mama, guess what?" and "Look, Granny Kobayashi! Look what I got."

"Why do they need *your* attention?" she asked her grandmother irritably. "They see you all the time. They live right here."

"They're only allowed to come over when you're visiting," Mrs. Kobayashi said.

Sarah opened her mouth, but her mother silenced her with a look.

During these early days, the girl observed many things. She saw that her grandmother never approached the Asaki house, not even to drop off flowers or food (the exception was formal holidays such as New Year's or O-bon, when both families dined together). She saw that her grandmother never chatted for very long with Mrs. Nishimura unless Mrs. Asaki was also present.

Mrs. Kobayashi showed a similar, though lesser, restraint around Momoko and Yashiko, which disappeared if they were all in a group.

But everyone else interacted freely. Mrs. Asaki came visiting—alone, without her daughter—on the pretext of paying respects to her ancestors' family altar. She lingered afterward for a jolly gossip over tea and slices of red-bean jelly. And Mrs. Rexford had once stayed at the Asaki house for several hours, calling Mrs. Asaki "Auntie" and drinking beer with Mr. Nishimura, although she generally refrained from such visits out of loyalty to her mother.

Sarah wondered if Mrs. Kobayashi and Mrs. Asaki had set up these boundaries right from the start. Perhaps they had silently evolved over the decades. If that first morning was any indication, there must have been slip-ups. For how could such an arrangement not foster, on either side, countless small moments of sorrow and resentment?

chapter 7

There was an old saying: a well-bred woman thinks several steps ahead. "It's like playing chess, *ne,*" Mrs. Rexford explained to her daughter. "Before you make a move, you have to consider all possible consequences."

Usually the women's strategies were simple. If Mrs. Kobayashi or Mrs. Rexford realized they were laughing too loudly, one of them might utter "Shh . . ." and jerk her head in the direction of the Asaki house.

Or they might say to Sarah, "Let's not mention that we went out for sushi without them, *ne?* It's just easier."

"Why would they even care?" Sarah asked. "They do things without us, and *we* don't mind." Her elders merely looked at her with weary patience.

One day, to Sarah's delight, the women announced they were taking her downtown for an afternoon of shopping. It was then that she learned how complex forward-thinking could be.

"Should I run over right now and invite Momoko and Yashiko?" Mrs. Asaki always invited her along when she took her granddaughters shopping. They had ice cream on the sixteenth floor of the Takashimaya department store, and they were allowed one item each from the Hello Kitty shop.

"*Soh soh,* run along and invite them," urged her grandfather, who happened to be passing by on his way to the workroom. He carried a sheaf of sketches and his hair was rumpled. He was preparing for an upcoming jewelry exhibition.

Mrs. Kobayashi waited until he passed, then shook her head at Sarah. "Don't listen," she whispered. "He doesn't know what he's talking about." The two women exchanged wry smiles of exasperation.

"You mean they can't come?" Momoko and Yashiko adored the French pastry shops and the department stores that lined Marutamachi Boulevard.

"It would be best if you didn't mention it," her grandmother said.

Sarah pouted as she and her mother stood in the parlor, changing into their downtown clothes. "Grandma's stingy," she complained.

Mrs. Rexford laughed. When the three of them reconvened in the family room, she told her mother, "We need to educate this child. She thinks you're being stingy."

"*Ara maa.*" Mrs. Kobayashi smiled indulgently.

Mrs. Rexford took to her task right away. "Now use your chess brain," she told Sarah as the three of them put on their shoes in the vestibule. "What would happen if you invited the girls?"

"They'd be allowed to come. Granny and Auntie would say it was a lovely idea."

"You're absolutely right. They'd certainly *say* that."

Mother and daughter stepped out into the lane and watched as Mrs. Kobayashi drew the curtains behind the glass panels of the kitchen door. She then rolled the door shut and locked it, even though Mr. Kobayashi was still inside.

"Let's go this way," Mrs. Kobayashi said. They headed toward the paved street, avoiding the gravel lane that passed right under Mrs. Asaki's balcony. Their corner house was convenient for sleight-of-hand exits. The view from the Asaki house covered only the Kobayashis' formal guest entrance, not the kitchen entrance around the corner.

"So if they came with us, what would happen?" quizzed Mrs. Rexford.

Sarah had no idea. She had never been good at chess.

"Don't you think Granny Asaki would feel bad," her mother said, "sitting at home while her grandchildren were out having a good time with their real grandmother?"

Sarah darted a quick glance at her grandmother. So she knew that Sarah knew!

"*Would* Granny feel bad?" Sarah asked doubtfully.

"Of course! She's very insecure."

Before turning the corner onto the main street, they paused. Mrs. Rexford peeked around the wooden fence. Ahead of them was the neighborhood snack shop whose owner, chatty Mrs. Yagi, was usually outside gossiping with a customer. "She's not there. Quick," Mrs. Rexford said, and the three of them strode briskly past in their telltale clothes: Sarah in her good dress, the women in their heels.

They relaxed when they entered the long, tree-lined stretch of Ginnan Street, where the crosstown bus stop was.

"So if Granny feels insecure and frustrated"—Mrs. Rexford was slightly out of breath—"then what happens? She takes it out on—whom?"

"*Nnn* . . . Uncle?" Sarah knew something about the in-law situation; her parents had discussed it. Things were a bit strained because the mother-in-law, not the son-in-law, owned the deed to the house. In theory it made perfect sense to take in a son-in-law and his family—the house was too big for a widow living alone. But there *was* something emasculating about it. And apparently Mrs. Asaki was not above taking subtle advantage of the situation.

"Very good," said Mrs. Rexford. "Then what would happen?"

"There's *more?*"

"This is really not that hard," her mother said. "Use your brain. If the harmony of their house is disturbed, who has to act as go-between and calm everyone down?"

"That would be your auntie," said Mrs. Kobayashi. "And a thankless task it is," she added grimly.

"So then you'd have three adults upset and troubled, all because you didn't think ahead. Is that what you want?"

"No! I don't want that."

"Then as strange as it may seem," concluded her mother, "slipping out like this is actually the best solution."

"Very true," said Mrs. Kobayashi.

For Sarah, this was an unfamiliar way of thinking. It was exciting but also exhausting, like that playground game where balls came at you from every direction. Despite the good intentions, it struck her as vaguely distasteful. The Asaki household would be shocked and hurt if they knew how much strategy lay behind her grandmother's and mother's actions . . . or *would* they? Apparently large families were much more complex than Sarah had imagined. Those big, jolly families she read about in children's books, the kind that stood around the Christmas tree holding hands and singing, never seemed to face these kinds of issues.

"Are they really that sensitive?" she asked her grandmother later that day. "Do you really think we have to be this careful?"

She had waited to catch her grandmother alone, because she feared her mother would tell her to mind her own business.

"*Saa . . . ,*" Mrs. Kobayashi replied, "it's better to be safe than sorry, don't you think?"

"Are all Japanese families like this?"

"Probably not," her grandmother said.

chapter 8

Normally Sarah and her mother and grandmother walked to the open-air market together, but one morning Mrs. Kobayashi stayed behind. She was cooking a big pot of curry while the day was still cool.

"What I'll do is divide this into packets and put them in the freezer," she told Mrs. Rexford. "That way, we can heat them up anytime we're in a rush." She demonstrated by crouching down and pulling open the door of the icebox, which was barely half the size of the Rexfords' freezer back home. Women in the Ueno neighborhood didn't need much storage space, since they bought fresh fish and produce every day. "See?" Mrs. Kobayashi revealed a tiny freezer compartment crammed with small, shrink-wrapped lumps and squares. "Look, I even froze the potato croquettes. Plus that filet mignon Sarah didn't finish—actually we could chop that up today, don't you think, and use it in fried rice?"

Sarah and her mother now strolled through the narrow lanes toward the open-air market. Mornings in this part of the neighborhood were always heavy with silence, except for those brief periods when clusters of children tramped to Tai Chi Hour or summer school meetings. Dark wooden houses rose up on either side, somber and shrinelike. Up in the trees, cicadas shrilled and shimmered, their unrelieved drone intensifying the silence instead of lessening it. Walking through this noise was like walking through the very heart of summer.

For a while, neither said a word. They hadn't been alone together in the daytime since . . . probably since America.

They passed old-fashioned houses similar to the Kobayashis'. One had a charming trellis fence made of bamboo poles, whose deep golden hue contrasted nicely with the black twine knotting them together. Tall shrubbery from the garden poked out through the square openings, creating a nice textural effect while protecting the occupants' privacy. Many of these fences were deliberately rustic, homages to country dwellings of the past. Sarah's favorite was a fence that looked like a solid wall of dried twigs, cleverly held in place by slender crosspieces. But she also admired one of its neighbors that stood farther down the lane. It was a large property, with the slightly forbidding air of a *yashiki* manor. The fence consisted of a low foundation of boulders that was reminiscent of the stone bases of imperial castles. From these stones rose a solid, dun-colored wall of mud plaster, topped by a miniature rooftop of gray tiles. Above it, only the tops of the trees within were visible.

"I used to come and play here all the time," Mrs. Rexford said, trailing her fingers along the mud wall. And Sarah marveled that none of this held any mystery for her mother.

They reached Umeya Shrine and cut through its grounds toward Tenjin Boulevard. Umeya was a tiny neighborhood shrine, well below the radar of those official tour buses that rumbled in and out of the So-Zen Temple complex several blocks away. The grounds here were deserted, the white expanse of raked sand emphasizing the gravity of the dark, moss-stained structures lining its periphery.

This was where Sarah and her cousins came each morning, before breakfast, to do tai chi exercises. They were joined by other neighborhood children, as well as old people who no longer needed to go to work or prepare breakfast for their families. At first, the children had stared at Sarah. But by now they had grown used to her presence, although there were still some who sneaked glances when they thought she wasn't looking. Momoko and Yashiko didn't seem to mind being seen with her; they acted nonchalant, as if they hosted Western visitors all year round.

Today a young mother stood in the open space, tossing out bread crumbs to a half circle of pigeons and urging her toddler to do the same. The little boy clutched a fistful of his mother's skirt and gazed distrustfully at the bobbing, pecking birds. "*Hato po'po . . . ,*" the woman sang softly, trying to encourage him with an old-fashioned ditty about feeding pigeons in the temple.

"Do you remember that song?" asked Mrs. Rexford. "I used to sing it to you when you were little."

"I remember," Sarah said. It seemed a lifetime ago. It was unsettling to hear this strange young woman singing it. She remembered a time when her own mother's voice had held such unguarded tenderness, and sharp sorrow slipped through her belly.

They walked on, passing a stone statue of a fox deity, and entered the shade of a row of maple trees. "Granny Asaki says that starting in October, it'll be against the law to feed pigeons," Sarah said. "She says their droppings are ruining all the wood."

"Did she? Well, it was bound to happen," said Mrs. Rexford,

"with so many tourists nowadays. But it'll be strange, won't it, not having them around anymore."

Within these cloistered grounds, they sensed the busy, noisy world lying in wait just beyond. Somewhere behind one of the shrine buildings, someone hammered, paused, then began hammering again. At the other end of the grounds, in the gap framed by massive vermilion gateposts, cars and buses flashed by with a muted whizzing.

Mrs. Rexford halted in the shade of the maple trees. Lowering her parasol, she lifted her face toward the leaf-laden branches.

"Look, Sarah," she said, pointing up. "You see how the sunlight's coming down through these leaves?" She had a tendency to lecture when she felt deeply moved. "This is exactly the way it used to look when I was a child. The exact same way." She kept on pointing, as if determined to press these unremarkable trees onto her daughter's memory.

"Oh," said Sarah.

Mrs. Rexford raised her parasol, and they walked on.

Once Sarah had read a poem about "a lifetime caught in a fall of light," or perhaps it was "a century caught in a fall of light." She remembered nothing else about the poem, just that phrase, which rose up from nowhere to claim the moment.

She pictured her mother hunting for cicadas as a child, perhaps in these very trees: a tomboy with a bamboo pole, squinting up with determination through the knife-edged glints of light flashing through the leaves. She pictured her mother in later years, reading and sketching outdoors. There must have been moments when she paused in her work to look up at just such a canopy of tiny, star-shaped leaves, their green made translucent by the sun. She thought, too, of an anecdote her grandmother had told: when Sarah was a baby, her mother had held her up to a tree branch, then laughed and laughed with delight when her child reached out and curled her tiny fingers around a low-hanging leaf.

How did it feel to be her mother, to look up at a tree and be transported back to all those previous lives? Was it like hearing pigeons in the morning? *Caught . . . in a fall of light . . .* Something unfamiliar stirred in the girl: an inarticulate feeling, diffuse and layered like the groundswell of an orchestra. She knew it was an adult emotion, one caused by the passage of time.

They reached the vermilion gateposts and descended the shallow stone steps to the sidewalk, where floating dust motes vanished in the direct sunlight. As if in response to this abrupt change in atmosphere, Mrs. Rexford switched to English. "Okay, which route should we take?" she said briskly. "The weavers' alley? Or So-Zen Temple?"

The magic spell was broken. "The weavers' alley," Sarah replied, switching the conversation back to Japanese with a hint of her old asperity. It annoyed her when her mother used English for no good reason. Sarah had once asked her to speak nothing but Japanese while they were here, only to be told, "Sometimes English is more efficient." She was too embarrassed to insist, for it was true there were gaps in her Japanese. She certainly couldn't say, "I feel more loved when you use Japanese. Your voice becomes warmer . . ." Nor could she admit how much of an outsider it made her feel, having to use a different language from the others.

In her own youth, Yoko Kobayashi had taken quiet pride in standing out from the masses. She sported a sleek, traditionally cut bob while other young women were frazzling their hair with Western-style permanent waves. Having no shortage of male admirers, she considered herself exempt from girlish affectations such as covering her mouth when she laughed. As a badge of distinction, she liked to wear something unusual but not ostentatious—a man's muffler, or an outré piece of jewelry designed by her stepfather—catching in people's eyes that flash of respect. Years later in Fielder's Butte, she took a perverse pleasure in wielding her parasol with poise as she walked past the apartment pool where American women slathered in baby oil lay baking their bodies in halter tops and short jean cutoffs. Although these American eyes met hers with curiosity, condescension, or blank dismissal, there was a fleeting instant when they assessed her neckline and slender figure with the universal glint of female rivalry. She knew they noticed her skin, which was exceptionally smooth, with a porcelain sheen that had attracted attention all her life.

Where, then, did her daughter get her timidity?

Not from her husband. John Rexford was fifty-seven, his wife's senior by eighteen years. Formerly a physicist, he had taken early retirement in order to "read and think." He admitted this humbly, almost sheepishly. Mrs. Rexford admired his modesty. She bragged to Sarah on his behalf, explaining in detail all she knew of his professional accomplishments, of his wide range of knowledge and interests.

But the mere fact of her husband's modesty wasn't what held her interest. It was what she sensed behind it: a genuine lack of need for public approval. Mrs. Rexford, who secretly struggled to reconcile what she had been with what she was now, envied his strength of mind. Her husband, like her, had tossed away the crutch of social position. But unlike her, he didn't seem to feel its loss. It helped, of course, that he was living in his native country. But even when they were living in Japan, he had stayed remarkably, transcendently unchanged. "You're hardly human!" she had cried during one of their rare fights. She was constantly trying, and failing, to emulate her husband. Her devotion to him was fueled by this enormous respect.

And yet Mr. Rexford was charming to the townsfolk, full of dry wit and a seasoned grace of manner. (Mrs. Kobayashi had once remarked that he put her in mind of those gentlemen in Sherlock Holmes movies. Having grown up near the cosmopolitan port of Kobe, she had always been something of an Anglophile.) Mrs. Rexford was fascinated by this social side of him, this flashback from a former life that excluded her.

Fielder's Butte was a small logging town, hours away from any major city. It was an ideal place for living within the tight budget imposed by Mr. Rexford's early retirement. Mrs. Rexford enjoyed the creative challenge of making do within monetary limits. Sometimes, though, she felt a keen loss for their social identities, not just her own but her husband's too. But in its place was a life more free and elemental than any she had ever known. It was no coincidence they both loved Thoreau's *Walden.*

When Sarah was small and they still lived in the Kyoto hills, Mrs. Rexford had tried to instill in her child something of this mental strength. "Stand up tall," she said. "Lift up your chin . . . like I taught you, like this. Then the boys won't bully you." She had even cut her daughter's hair short, striving for a jaunty, nonvulnerable look. But it was all in vain. Even after they moved to America, Sarah said things like, "Mother, I can't wear those pants. They're not what the other girls are wearing." Or, "Why can't we eat dinner at Burger King? The other families are all doing it."

It wasn't that Mrs. Rexford couldn't sympathize. She, too, remembered the shame of not fitting in. Once in middle school, some girls in her class had made a snide remark about her wearing the same sweater year after year. It was true: each summer, Mrs. Kobayashi would unravel the yarn and reknit it, adding new stripes in different-colored yarn to accommodate her daughter's growing body. Hearing the girls' words, young Yoko had felt a deep stab of humiliation. She had resolved, on the spot, to demand a new sweater the minute she got home.

But when she remembered her mother knitting late into the night, sweating in the summer humidity, so lovingly and carefully holding the sweater up against Yoko's chest for measurements, a surge of pity and then fury had made her lift her eyes to those girls and say, with a careless smile, "*Saa*—what can I say? Some mothers go to a lot of trouble for their children. That's how you know if they really love you."

"I guess our mothers show love in different ways," sneered one girl.

"Yes, I've noticed that," said Yoko. "I've noticed who brings the fewest side dishes in her lunch box. I've noticed whose mother *isn't* at the Temple of Wisdom, praying for her child, the evening before an exam. So when certain people talk big, they're not fooling *me*." And her knowing smirk had brought a flicker of anxiety to the aggressor's eyes.

Why couldn't Sarah, just once, stand up for *her* like that?

Mrs. Rexford felt a keen, wretched misery. Her daughter did not love her the way she loved her own mother. Mrs. Rexford had doted on Sarah with the same passion and focus that her own mother had lavished on her, but the results, like everything else she tried in America, had come out slightly skewed. "Can't you think for yourself?" she would snap at her daughter. "Is everyone worth imitating except your own mother?" And that was how their fighting would begin.

chapter 9

The open-air market was at the height of activity. As usual on a Monday, housewives were out in full force. Parked bicycles cluttered the sidewalks, forcing the shoppers out into the street, where they wove in and out among the slow-moving cars. A small crowd was stooped over the fish market display. Now that the rainy season had passed, dispelling worries about food poisoning and mold, a large selection of raw fish had been set out on crushed ice. Thin wooden tablets, stuck upright into the ice, displayed prices written in black brushstrokes. On the pavement stood a row of blue plastic buckets, in which live fish moved in slow circles.

"Ladies!" called a middle-aged fishmonger from behind the counter, his eyes locked on the mackerel he was speedily filleting. "*Haai*—welcome! How about some nice chilled sashimi slices? Take a little home for lunch!" He cast his voice out over the street in controlled, far-reaching arcs of sound, as a fisherman flings out his nets. Its reverberation reminded Sarah of the So-Zen priests who came chanting each morning.

A young man working beside him, probably his son, chimed in. "Baby octopus! Cockles for clear soup! Everything fresh fresh

fresh!" His energetic bellowing made up in volume what it lacked of his father's practiced resonance. At the far end of the counter, a woman in a white frilled apron stood over an open grill of eel fillets, using two battered cardboard *uchiwa* to fan the fragrant smoke out toward prospective buyers. The provocative aroma of glazed soy sauce and sugar hung in the air and made Sarah's mouth water, even though she had just eaten breakfast.

The housewives succeeded each other with quick, efficient footsteps that were at odds with their peaceful expressions. Mrs. Rexford wove through the crowd with nimble expertise, not bothering to look back. Sarah lurched after her mother, clutching her wicker basket and string bag and trying to avoid the sharp points of the women's parasols.

The produce booths were crowded too. Sarah's mother and grandmother usually made her wait on the sidewalk while they darted in to make fast, efficient transactions. Huge bundles of freshly picked edamame boughs were piled high on tables, the hairy pods still attached to the branches. Small green yuzu, or citrons, were in season but expensive. All booths featured carrots that were bright red instead of orange, a variety native to the Kyoto area. There were seedless *kyuuri* cucumbers, delicious when sliced and dipped in a mixture of Worcestershire sauce and sweet Japanese mayonnaise. "Let's get some of those!" Sarah suggested.

"Do you hear that jingling?" asked Mrs. Rexford as they walked toward the pickle shop. "Isn't it pretty?" The sound of countless tiny bells pervaded the street. It came from the stall owners' money bags, which hung overhead from rubber cords. Working the abacus with one hand, a vendor would pull down the bag with his free hand when he wanted to withdraw or deposit loose change. *Omamori*—religious charms with little bells attached, sold at local temples and shrines—hung from each money bag. When the vendor released his bag after a transaction, it bounced up on its rubber cord, and the *omamori* bells—as well as the coins within—continued jingling for a minute or so until the bag stopped moving.

"It *is* pretty!" said Sarah.

"People call that the sound of prosperous commerce."

After the street bustle it was a relief to enter the cool, restful shade of the pickle store. The pickle store wasn't a stall like the others, but an extension of a private home. When the proprietor emerged from the back of the store to serve them, they caught a momentary glimpse of tatami mats and white floor cushions through the open sliding door. There was a timeless, prewar quality about this place, due to the blackened wall boards and the wooden shipping barrels stacked against them.

"Welcome back, miss," the proprietor greeted Sarah. He was an elderly man with a thin strip of white cotton tied around his head, the traditional sign of a man ready and eager to work. "Remember how you used to stick your hand in the pickles when you were a little girl, before your mother could stop you?" Sarah giggled, embarrassed but also pleased that he had remembered. To hide her sudden shyness, she leaned over to inspect the lacquered display boxes. They held a large array of pickled items: long fat daikon radishes, cucumbers, scallions, lotus roots, Japanese eggplant, gourds, greens, seaweed. They lay limply within various fermented pastes, whose pungent aroma stirred up in Sarah some memory from her early childhood that fell just short of definition.

"Pickles are Kyoto's most famous commodity," Mrs. Rexford informed her daughter, primarily for the shopkeeper's benefit. "They're a cultural treasure, you know, with all the subtleties of wine. Visitors from other cities always stock up on these to take home as gifts." Sarah had received similar "lessons" in the presence of other vendors, for her mother and grandmother were skilled in the subtle flattery that resulted in spontaneous mark-downs.

The proprietor beamed as he scooped up Mrs. Rexford's order: sweet red pickle relish to serve with the curry Mrs. Koba-yashi was making. "You both look very cosmopolitan today!" he said admiringly. "Simple elegance—now *that's* what I like!" He too was good at flattery. But it was true that Mrs. Rexford and her daughter made a striking pair.

Mrs. Rexford wore a new blouse of lipstick red. Few other women could have carried off such an intense color. Sarah wore a wide-brimmed straw hat with a big green ribbon tied off-center beneath her chin. The green of the ribbon brought out the green-gray tints of her eyes. Naturally, Mrs. Rexford had chosen it. The girl hadn't resisted. She had no clue as to what was acceptable in this country, and she trusted her mother's judgment here as she did not in America. Yielding to her mother had filled her with a surprising rush of happiness.

During the course of their shopping, they ran into several acquaintances.

"I see you all the time with your mother," one woman told Mrs. Rexford. "But I can never bring myself to intrude . . . . you always look so close and intimate . . ."

"You're far too polite!" scolded Mrs. Rexford.

"It's so touching," the woman continued wistfully, "to see the way you scrub each other's backs at the bathhouse."

Some women from the weaving class, whom Mrs. Kobayashi would have regarded with some social reserve, took this oppor-tunity to draw near and chat.

"Do you live in San-Fran City?" they asked admiringly, look-ing them both over. "Do you wear trousers?" "Your girl's grown so big . . . so pretty . . ."

With a wide American smile, Mrs. Rexford chatted back.

Sarah watched and listened in silence. Among American women back home, her mother would have been the picture of Oriental demureness. Her attitude was one of wide-eyed fascination: "How smart and funny you are!" Privately, Mrs. Rexford considered the Fielder's Butte women her intellectual inferiors, and had the playing field been level, she would have considered them her social inferiors as well. So her stories at home, while observant and witty, were not always kind. But some American women were flattered and charmed. Nurturing instincts aroused, they went out of their way to offer tutelage and protection. "Honey, your mama's a real *doll*!" they would tell Sarah, handing her recipes for potato chip casseroles and Jell-O molds. "Give this to your mama, I know she'll enjoy it. She's an absolute sweetheart, such an adorable little Chinese lady!"

Mrs. Rexford now stood in the crowded market, her red blouse like a flame attracting the pale, mothlike shades of the local women's dresses. This flamelike quality was also in her face. Watching her, Sarah felt that same deep joy as when her mother had picked out her hat.

Their final encounter was at the poultry stall. They approached two other customers who were standing under the red-and-white-striped awning, peering down at a straw-lined display of eggs in various sizes and colors. "Auntie Sasaki!" Mrs. Rexford called out to one of them, in the breezy voice that came so easily to her in this country. "What dish are you going to make with those eggs?" The elderly woman turned around to see who had spoken. Her face brightened with pleasure, and they fell immediately into conversation.

"Just look at you, Yo-chan," the woman said at one point, patting Mrs. Rexford's shoulder in the overfamiliar manner of the weaving class. "I bet you're the queen bee over in America too, aren't you? Just like you were here. Oh yes, I know you are—don't deny it! *Anta,* I'm very perceptive! I can tell, just from looking at your face."

"Oh, *please!*" Mrs. Rexford protested, laughing. She dismissed the compliment with a languid wave of her hand, as she had been doing all morning. But this woman's bluntness caused a frisson of awkwardness to pass between mother and daughter. For Sarah knew what no one, not even her grandmother, fully understood: the truth of how things were in America.

"Is it true you once beat up a bully?" asked the second customer, a vacant-looking young woman in her twenties.

"Oh yes!" said the old woman. "That's a *true story.* I know, because it was my very own boy that was being picked on."

"Once a success, always a success," chimed in the poultry vendor, who had come over with some fresh boxes from the back. "You've done us proud." The little group beamed at Mrs. Rexford, their eyes shiny with approval.

On that note, they headed home. They passed a small tea shop, the last outpost before the street turned residential. Inside the display window was an assortment of skewered summer dumplings arranged on lacquered trays.

Sarah glanced at her mother. There was a pleased flush on Mrs. Rexford's cheeks, a glint in her eye, as if she had just come away from a party held in her honor. She caught her daughter's eye, then looked away.

"I guess the shopping took a little longer than usual," she said. She said this with a sheepish kind of dignity, and Sarah felt a rush of pity. Or maybe it was guilt: she, with her petty teenage cruelties, had been responsible for many of her mother's difficulties in America.

"Did it?" Sarah said gently. "I didn't notice." They walked on in silence.

The last time she had felt this sort of pain for her mother—

the kind that made her stomach feel sick—had been almost a year ago. Mrs. Rexford had made German coleslaw for Sarah to bring to her school potluck: an authentic recipe with caraway seeds and vinegar. Hardly anyone at school had touched it, preferring the more familiar mayonnaise-covered potato salad. On her way home, Sarah had dumped the uneaten remains in the grass. Her mother, greeting her at the door, had seen the empty serving dish and cried, "Why, they ate it all!" and her happy expression had haunted Sarah for days.

What did it matter, she now asked herself fiercely, if her mother wasn't a queen bee on both continents? How many people were that lucky?

Sarah herself had never been a queen bee anywhere. But these days her status was rising. The neighbors' admiration and affection for her mother flowed over onto her with little distinction between them. Even in her own family, Sarah belonged— if only partially—to her grandmother's inner circle, for no other reason than lineage.

Even though she knew she was merely basking in her mother's glory, the effect was heady. It was like the time when she was a little girl and her grandfather had carried her on his feet while dancing a waltz. In that moment she had understood, for the first time, how it felt to move through space with elegance and authority. "*Soh soh,* that's right," her grandfather had chuckled. "*Soh soh,* see? Your body knows it."

Lately there were moments when Sarah found herself gliding through daily life with uncharacteristic confidence and entitlement, just like her mother. It was surprising how easy it was, how natural and right it felt. During such moments she felt a glimmer of hope that her true personality had been in hiding all these years, just as her mother's had been, and the whole world was opening up before her.

chapter 10

They were halfway home when they met Mrs. Nishimura coming from the opposite direction. She held a parasol of pale blue linen in one hand and a woven straw basket in the other. The three stopped in pleased recognition. "You both look so nice!" Mrs. Nishimura said.

"So do you, Auntie," said Sarah. Her aunt wore soft pink lipstick and a sundress of the same general shade as her parasol. Under the blue-tinted shade her face looked delicate, almost translucent.

"Ma-chan!" exclaimed Mrs. Rexford, her eyes still animated from the marketplace encounters. "Listen: go to Hachi-ya as soon as you get there. They're having a sale on prayer incense— the good kind. And it's going fast."

"Really? Good thing you told me. We're almost out."

As they stood chatting in the street, Sarah became aware of a problem. Inside her string bag, clearly visible if anyone glanced down, was a box of cream puffs. It had been laid right on top so as not to get squashed, and it was wrapped in the distinctive blue paper of Ushigome Confectionery.

The problem consisted of several parts. On a simple level,

Mrs. Rexford hadn't bought enough to share with the Asaki household. If her aunt knew about the cream puffs, she and the girls might expect to receive some that evening.

On a more complex level, Ushigome Confectionery was far more expensive than the store where they had bought the Nishimuras' cake on the first day. No expense was being spared for the Rexfords' visit—the best cuts of meat, the most expensive fish, gourmet-quality desserts. Mrs. Nishimura, who was Mrs. Kobayashi's daughter too, had never had any such fuss made over her. Of course there were logical reasons for this. But there was a fundamental inequality here, one that mustn't be flaunted. Imitating the sleight of hand she had observed in her elders, Sarah casually shifted the basket behind her back.

Her mother shot her a look of approval.

That glance, coming on the heels of Sarah's remorse for her mother, triggered in her a burst of happiness.

Later, she would look back on this moment as one of the turning points of the summer. For it was the first time she had actively colluded against her aunt. Even in her happiness she was aware of crossing an invisible line of allegiance, leaving her auntie on the other side.

The lane that passed through the weavers' neighborhood was narrower than the lanes at home and covered with asphalt instead of loose gravel. Although seemingly deserted, it resounded with the *gat-tan, gat-tan* of wooden looms from the houses on either side. These were the poorer dwellings, lacking the buffer of gateways or garden entrances. They were packed so closely together that they gave the impression of being one continuous building, broken up only by individual roofs.

When Sarah and her mother passed the open windows, many

of which were lightly barred with old-fashioned bamboo, the general clatter resolved itself into individual rhythms. In one house, it was slow and uneven. In the next house, the pace was fast and furious; someone was probably speeding through an unpatterned section. This lane was extremely narrow, almost claustrophobic with so much noise and so many miniature potted plants lined beside each door. The two of them, walking abreast, took up its entire width.

Then Sarah felt her mother's hand slip into hers.

She stared straight ahead, unable to look. Her mother's hand was warm and slightly calloused, and it held hers with the close, familiar grip she remembered from childhood. Sarah thought of the woman in the shrine, singing to her toddler in that tender voice. A strange burning started in her eyes, a slow treacherous swell in her throat. She widened her eyes so that no tears would spill.

They walked hand in hand through the cacophony of the looms. A straggle of wild grass, still lush from the rainy season, had pushed up through a crack in the asphalt. Its detail refracted sharp and clear through the moisture in her eyes.

"This little lane," said her mother, "is the best barometer of Japan's economy. I tell you, it's so accurate you don't even need a newspaper." She said this nonchalantly, as if nothing out of the ordinary was happening.

"*Ng,*" said Sarah.

"Think about it," Mrs. Rexford continued. "When women have extra spending money, what's the first thing they do? They show off to their neighbors. They attend expensive tea ceremonies. They send their daughters for lessons in koto or classical dance. And what do all these activities require? That's right, kimonos and sashes. And who weaves the silk? People like these."

"So this noise means Japan's really prosperous right now?" Sarah thought of the bells attached to the vendors' money bags: the sound of prosperous commerce.

"*Soh.* The stock market and the looms move together. Every time. Remember that."

Noon was approaching, and it was hotter than when they had first set out. Their clasped hands became damp with perspiration. Even Sarah's bare arms felt moist. But she preferred this wet heat to the dry desert air of Fielder's Butte, where the harsh, undiluted rays burned the skin. She felt loose and open to the world.

The heat had caused one of the houses to leave its sliding door slightly open, in hopes of catching a breeze. From within, mixed with the looms' clatter, came a television's tinny sounds of applause and merriment. Above the tiled roofs white clouds were shining, like explosions of giant popcorn. Happiness, like those clouds, hung just within their reach.

chapter 11

"**D**on't forget," announced Mrs. Kobayashi, descending into the kitchen. "Granny Asaki's coming over after lunch to pay her respects to the altar."

"I'll put some new flowers in the altar vase," said Mrs. Rexford. She stepped up into the dining room with a tray of freshly filled condiment bowls. "What do you think, Sarah-chan?" she said to her daughter, who was setting the low table for lunch. "Red camellias? Lilies are too tall. Or maybe a branch from the yuzu tree?"

Chan was an affectionate diminutive paired with children's names, a word with no real equivalent in English. Hearing this endearment on her mother's lips, after all the years of grammatically correct English, made Sarah absurdly happy. Suddenly shy, she avoided looking at her mother.

"Yuzu sounds nice," she replied nonchalantly. "The baby fruits are so cute."

"That's what we'll do then," said her mother, unloading the tiny bowls for Sarah to arrange.

It was two days since they had held hands. A certain awkwardness still hung over them, like that of sweethearts after a first kiss. More than once Sarah had caught her mother watching her with an eager, open look.

Today Mrs. Rexford was in a playful mood. "Mommy," she called down to Mrs. Kobayashi, "can't Sarah and I have a little snack before lunch? We're hungry. Please, pleeeze?"

Mrs. Kobayashi climbed up into the room with a shallow wooden vat of steaming rice. "*Kora,* what a lazy, spoiled child I've got!" she lamented. She shook her head with mock despair at the sight of her grown daughter lolling at the low table, sneaking a bite from one of the condiment bowls. "There's a plate of sticky-bean cakes in the cabinet," she said, relenting, "but you'll just have to wait!"

Mrs. Rexford then turned to her daughter, who was watching the adults' silliness with a look of wary uncertainty. "Let's you and I raid the cabinet," she whispered loudly, "when your grandma's not looking." Sarah's eyes took on the look of a dazzled schoolgirl. Unable to come up with a response, she merely giggled at her mother.

"You two are hopeless," Mrs. Kobayashi declared, descending the wooden step into the kitchen.

After lunch, Sarah carried the finished yuzu arrangement into the family room. The household altar stood atop a dresser. It was a black lacquered box, with two doors that opened out like a dollhouse. Inside, on shelves, were tablets that looked like miniature headstones, each bearing the name of a deceased member of the Kobayashi line. Some of these tablets were so old, no one knew anything about them. On the bottom shelf were a small white candle, a sand-filled ceramic bowl studded with green incense sticks, a set of prayer beads, and a miniature inverted gong resting on a silk cushion. There was a doll-sized cup for water and a doll-sized cup for rice. Each morning, when Mrs. Kobayashi cooked a fresh batch of rice, she saved the first scoop for the altar—or more precisely for her first husband. Sarah was often awakened by the *chinn* of the gong—surprisingly resonant for such a small piece of cast iron—and the muttered sounds of her grandmother praying.

She placed the vase beside the miniature gong, then returned to the kitchen. Her mother was squeezing out a dishcloth and hanging it over a bamboo rod sticking out from the wall.

"Would you mind taking these flowers over to your auntie?" Mrs. Rexford nodded toward a plastic bucket in the kitchen vestibule. It was filled with yellow lilies, picked earlier that day from the garden.

"Wait," said her grandmother, who was bending over the icebox. "Let me wrap them up first."

"No, I'll do that. Stay there." Mrs. Rexford bounded up the wooden step into the dining room. "I'll go find some newspaper."

Carrying the armful of lilies—its scent redolent of wet newsprint, freshly cut stems, and spicy blooms—Sarah headed toward the Asaki house.

The Asaki property was large enough to have several gardens. There was a formal one in the back and another one in the front, and two narrow utilitarian gardens on either side. Sarah took the left-hand path, which led to the kitchen entrance. The air was heavy with the scent of hot flagstones and the mingled smells of foliage opening their pores to the sun. She brushed past a wall of hydrangea bushes that exuded palpable moisture, making the surrounding air almost too thick to breathe.

Her aunt stood framed in the kitchen window, washing dishes. The kitchen entrance was flanked by neatly tended rows of mitsuba, shingiku, and komatsuna. Mrs. Nishimura plucked these tender greens each morning for her family's miso soup, and often she sent her girls to the Kobayashi house with extras.

"Good afternoon!" Sarah called out.

Her aunt looked up with a welcoming smile, then came to meet her at the door. The kitchen was laced with the sweet, meaty smell of shiitake mushrooms cooked in soy sauce, and the tang of vinegared rice. They must have had *chirashizushi* for lunch, Sarah thought. "How are you, Auntie," she said, presenting the newspaper cone with both hands. "They sent you these."

"*Maa,* how lovely!" Mrs. Nishimura reached for the flowers with hands still covered in wet rubber gloves. "How well they're growing this year!" She held the bouquet away from her at arm's length, as if planning an ikebana arrangement in her mind. Her face, alight with pleasure and gratitude, filled Sarah with sudden shame.

Ever since the cream puff incident had ensured her place in her mother and grandmother's inner circle, she was aware of taking her aunt's rightful place.

All through her childhood Sarah had believed adults were immune to certain types of pain, just as lobsters (according to her grandmother) were incapable of feeling boiling water. That was because adults had perspective. They understood why things had to happen; they didn't take it personally the way children did. This belief had consoled her when she fought with her mother. Regarding her aunt's adoption, she had assumed that a grown woman would be mature enough to understand the situation.

But recently she had begun to question this. She sometimes imagined herself as her aunt, living just a few houses away and watching her real mother dote on the daughter she had chosen to keep. How would she feel, living so close but unable to rummage for sticky-bean cakes in the Kobayashis' cupboard, or even drop by unannounced for a cup of tea? She didn't think she could bear it. It was a wonder that her aunt had, all these years.

It was a wonder that everyone involved could go about their daily lives with such equanimity.

All of this stirred within her as she watched her aunt's glowing face. "Tell them I said thank you!" Mrs. Nishimura was saying.

Sarah felt oddly like crying. "I have to go," she mumbled. It was a relief to turn away. As she hurried past the hydrangea bushes she remembered seeing her own mother rush off this way after delivering something to the Asaki house. For the first time, she understood the contrition behind the two women's painstaking complicity. For their happiness, like hers, had come at the cost of someone else.

chapter 12

"What a lovely yuzu arrangement!" praised Mrs. Asaki. She stood before the altar, ready to pray. Sarah sat at the low table and watched her.

Reaching into her clutch purse, the old woman drew out a set of mahogany prayer beads with purple tassels. She also drew out a formal monetary envelope, which she placed on the altar. Her envelopes always contained several crisp ten-thousand-yen bills.

Mrs. Asaki closed her eyes. Reciting rapidly under her breath, she manipulated the beads with deft fingers. Then, switching back instantly from the ethereal to the earthly, she smiled down at Sarah.

"A little shopping for you and your mama." She nodded toward the envelope with twinkling eyes.

Mrs. Kobayashi and Mrs. Rexford entered the room with trays of tea and refreshments. "Won't you stay, Granny?" they asked. Mrs. Asaki promptly took a seat at the low table.

Despite their private resentments toward the old woman, Mrs. Kobayashi and Mrs. Rexford seemed to genuinely enjoy these visits. There was, after all, a certain kinship in the women's extroverted personalities. With Mrs. Nishimura out of the picture, they could all relax and gossip under the guise of religious duty. In no time at all, they were shrieking with laughter.

At one point the talk turned to Mr. Kobayashi. Mrs. Asaki took mischievous delight in exposing her little brother's childhood trials.

"Some older boys across the creek called him over to play," she told them. "So he trudged over the bridge, and they boinked him on the head. He came running back, crying. But then they called out their apologies and invited him over again. 'Kenji, don't go!' I told him. But no, he trudged over that bridge yet again—" The old woman did such a good imitation of a little boy's eager expression that they all burst into laughter. "And he got boinked yet again!"

Sarah, who had just come back from seeing her aunt, was annoyed to see them all having such a good time. They had wronged Aunt Masako. They had no right to be laughing and having so much fun.

Still laughing, the women turned back to their plates. Today was so hot they were eating chilled tofu. "This sauce is divine!" said Mrs. Asaki. "What is it? I can taste the citron zest . . . and . . ."

"Miso, and rice wine, and ground-up sesame seeds," supplied Mrs. Rexford. "By the way, we picked some extra citrons for you to take home."

A reflective mood fell over them.

"That Kenji . . ." Mrs. Asaki shook her head indulgently. "All he ever did was play around and dabble in things, right up till he got drafted to Manchuria. We thought he'd never settle down."

"And then he turned out to be so good at art! Who would have thought?" said Mrs. Kobayashi.

"Now, his little brother," said Mrs. Asaki, "he was success-
ful from the start. Shoehei was the one people noticed." Her
voice was hushed; Shohei had been her favorite brother.

Mrs. Rexford looked pleased. Mrs. Kobayashi lowered her
gaze modestly. It was not her place to say such things, but she
was perfectly willing to hear it from her sister-in-law's lips.

"Shohei was so smart," Mrs. Asaki told Sarah, "so witty.
Always at the head of his class. They picked him for the executive training program when he was only—what? Twenty-five?"

Mrs. Kobayashi and Mrs. Rexford, both smiling, nodded.

Mrs. Asaki grew expansive in her generosity. "It was entirely
fitting," she said, "that the first hieroglyph in his name—*sho*—
stood for rectitude and integrity."

Sarah recalled old photographs she had seen. Shohei was tall
and handsome. Her step-grandfather, Kenji, was handsome too,
but much shorter.

A girlish sparkle appeared in Mrs. Asaki's eyes. "Your
grandpa," she told Sarah, gesturing vaguely toward the other
end of the house where Mr. Kobayashi was tap-tapping away in
his workshop, "had a secret crush on your grandma for years.
But she only had eyes for Shohei."

Sarah happened to know—she had overheard her parents—
that marrying the second Mr. Kobayashi had not been her
grandmother's wish. She had been pressured into it, quite force-
fully, by Mrs. Asaki herself.

Sarah had never seen the tough side of Granny; her great-aunt
was unfailingly cheerful and charming. But she did remember
that when Momoko and Yashiko were small, Mrs. Asaki used to
punish them by touching a lit stick of prayer incense to the offend-
ing part of their bodies: the hand, if hitting had been the offense;
the tongue, if one of them had talked back. It was the old-
fashioned method from the country. Momoko had claimed airily

that it didn't hurt at all. "You can't even see the mark," she said. But the very idea had made Sarah dizzy with terror.

That night at bedtime, she broached this confusion to her mother.

"You know about *uchi* versus *soto,* right?" Mrs. Rexford said.

Uchi versus *soto:* inner circle versus outer circle. Daytime television was full of family dramas based on this concept. *Uchi* meant the few allies in whom a woman could place absolute trust. *Soto* was everyone else—social acquaintances, in-laws, sometimes one's own children—around whom it was best to remain vigilant.

"Smart women know who's inside and who's outside," Mrs. Rexford said. "Wishy-washy women get confused and make poor decisions."

"Granny's outside, right?"

"Of course. And your grandma and I never forget it. But that doesn't mean we can't enjoy her company. Or feel compassion and affection, like civilized human beings. Just as long as those feelings don't interfere with our true loyalties."

"But that's hard," said Sarah.

"Well, you learn."

"It would be easier if people were enemies or friends, with nothing in between."

"That's a child's way of thinking," said her mother. "You're a young woman now."

chapter 13

S arah sat outdoors, trying to remember how it had felt to be a child.

She was perched on the shallow step leading up to the Kobayashis' visitor gate. The gate had slatted sliding doors, set upon grooved sills that were raised slightly off the ground. If she twisted around and pressed her face against the vertical wooden laths, she could peer in at the walkway of stepping stones and bamboos that led up to the main door. From this vantage point the garden looked bigger, more imposing, the way it used to when she was little.

She sat attuning herself to the afternoon silence. Closing her eyes, she breathed in the smells of the lane: the aged, musty undertones of wood, mellowed with moss and warmed by the sun; hot cotton hung out to air; banks of perspiring leaves in the carefully tended gardens; and floating in from somewhere (someone was cooking a late lunch), a faint bitter whiff of grilled sardines. Mixed in with it all was some complex, private scent inseparable from early childhood.

"Big Sister! Big Sister!"

Sarah looked down the lane toward Mrs. Asaki's upstairs balcony. Momoko and Yashiko were leaning over the railing, waving at her with all four arms. "How come you're sitting there all by yourself?" Momoko called. "We're coming right down!" The two girls vanished from the balcony.

Soon they were all squeezed together on the Kobayashis' stone step. Rolling their sandaled feet back and forth over the gravel, they discussed ways to amuse themselves. A wind chime tinged, sounding muffled in the humid air.

They decided to play American Emotions. They had invented this game shortly after Sarah's arrival, while they were playing at the Kobayashi house. Sarah, wanting to seem as Japanese as possible, had been parodying American movies. "I love you, son," she said in a deep voice. "You are very special to me." Momoko and Yashiko had been delighted; they recognized this kind of dialogue from Hollywood films that occasionally aired on Japanese television.

Encouraged by their laughter, Sarah had continued. "I care about you, son. I care very deeply." Even Mrs. Kobayashi and Mrs. Rexford broke into reluctant smiles.

Afterward Momoko said thoughtfully, "It's like American people use words that are stronger than what they feel. I mean . . . they yell and cry, but it's almost like it's on the outside . . ." She stopped, unsure how to express herself.

"Americans believe it's unhealthy to keep feelings inside," Mrs. Rexford had explained to her nieces. "So if they feel an emotion coming on, they try to get it out of their system before it affects them too much." Everyone listened respectfully; she was the resident expert on America. "They're afraid if they keep it in too long, it'll fester and cause damage."

"My father isn't like that," added Sarah quickly. "He's more like us, because he grew up on the East Coast."

Momoko was gazing at Mrs. Rexford, nodding slowly as if

cementing this new knowledge into her memory. "So that's why they're always talking about the way they feel," she said.

Sarah had another theory, which she kept to herself because her language skills weren't up to the task. Americans, she thought, were like people slightly hard of hearing. On an emotional level they didn't register subtle sounds; they needed loud voices and overly clear enunciation in order to prevent misunderstandings. She herself was perfectly comfortable with this. But ever since entering her grandmother's household she had noticed a change in her own emotional acuity, as if she had sprouted the ears of a rabbit that could prick forward, swivel, and sense underground vibrations.

"That's right," Mrs. Rexford told Momoko. "So their words have a certain thin quality, like you said. It's like grape juice compared to wine. People like us, we keep our feelings inside and let them ferment—till the happy and the sad and the good and bad get all mixed together so we can't tell them apart."

Ever since that day, the three girls had performed many variations of American Emotions. Now they rose up from the stone step, disturbing some pigeons pecking halfheartedly among the gravel. They took their stances in the middle of the lane. They had decided, on Sarah's suggestion, to do a mental therapy scene. Sarah had the role of therapist; as the tallest and eldest, she held the most authority. Momoko, second-eldest, was the patient. Yashiko stood eagerly by, awaiting the supporting role that would be created for her once the game got under way.

"I'm filled with rage," said Momoko. "I'm going to kill myself."

"More emotion, Momo-chan," Sarah prompted. She realized too late that she should have taken the role of patient instead. It required a certain flamboyance that Momoko seemed to lack.

"I'm *filled* with *rage!*" said Momoko loudly. Baring her teeth, she pulled at her hair. "I'm going to *kill* myself!"

Yashiko clapped with approval and anticipation.

"Excellent! Let it all out!" said Sarah. "Get all your feelings out of your system!"

Momoko stood at a loss, unsure how to improve on what she had already done.

Sarah came to her aid. "But first," she said, "you'll need love! Let me give you a hug." With both arms, she folded Momoko in a tight embrace. The daring physicality of this move drew little shrieks of nervous laughter. Now the game was really under way.

"Pretend you're chewing gum!" cried Yashiko, recalling one of their previous games. "With your mouth wide open!"

Amid their cries of laughter, Sarah became aware of an urgently hissed *"Kora! Kora!"* coming from the balcony. It was Mrs. Asaki. Sarah looked up, and for a fleeting instant she caught a look of revulsion in the old woman's eyes, a look that pierced her to the quick.

She understood instantly that their physical antics were in bad taste. It didn't matter that she had been *mocking* these foreign mannerisms in a spirit of Japanese solidarity; her great-aunt would only see that it was an unsavory influence on her cousins. Now Mrs. Asaki would probably talk to her granddaughters in private, explaining that Big Sister came from a "different world" and they mustn't imitate everything she did. Sarah had grown up listening to Granny Asaki's talks; she and her cousins had been constantly warned not to imitate the slang used by children from the weaving district, or the precocious mannerisms of child stars on television. "It's fine for *those* people," Mrs. Asaki would say, "but our family has different standards." All of this flashed through the girl's mind, and her face burned with humiliation.

By now, they had all stopped playing and were looking up at the balcony. Smiling benevolently, the old woman placed her forefinger to her lips as if noise had been her only concern. Then she gave a little wave and turned away.

Had Sarah imagined that steely look? No. It had been there.

For the first time, she felt the start of a slow-rising anger: against Mrs. Asaki, and against these children who had to be so carefully protected from her crass influence.

chapter 14

Still in shock, Sarah followed her cousins into the Kobaya-shi house. At the sound of the kitchen door rolling open, Mrs. Kobayashi and Mrs. Rexford looked up from the low dining table where they sat doing sums on scraps of paper. From their guilty expressions, Sarah guessed they had been making financial calculations. In this period of rising yen, the vacation money that Mrs. Rexford had recently converted was increasing in value. And Mrs. Kobayashi's stock investments, which she secretly funded with part of her household budget, were rising as well. These days, a good many Japanese housewives indulged in financial speculation for pocket money. But they were discreet about it, for such activities were not becoming to a lady.

"Girls! Why don't you go over to the snack shop and get yourselves some ice cream," said Mrs. Rexford. "We need a little privacy to discuss adult matters." She stood up, rummaged in a cupboard drawer, and gave them a handful of loose change.

"What's wrong, Big Sister?" Momoko asked as they walked over to Mrs. Yagi's snack shop.

"Nothing," Sarah replied shortly.

They ate their ice cream sitting outside in public, on a wooden bench set up next to the snack shop. They had purchased the new ice cream phenomenon, Jewelry Box, currently advertised on television. It was a single-serving container of vanilla ice cream, in which "jewels" were embedded: shards of colored ice in red and blue and yellow and green.

The afternoon street was deserted, with cicadas droning in full force. The girls scraped carefully with their wooden spoons. "Look," said Momoko. "I got a red diamond!"

"I got a green one!" said Yashiko.

As Sarah's shock wore off, her anger grew. She itched to strike back at Mrs. Asaki, who overprotected her grandchildren at the expense of another child's feelings. And those grandchildren weren't even hers!

Yashiko left the bench and wandered away to examine an anthill.

"She really likes bugs," Momoko remarked. "She says she's going to be a scientist when she grows up."

Sarah turned to face Momoko. The gathering force of her feelings flickered into a flame of intention.

"You know what?" she said. "I bet you didn't know that Granny Asaki isn't your real grandmother." After so many weeks of vigilance it was a relief, like poking at a house of cards.

Momoko listened, looking suitably awed. But she accepted the story much more readily than Sarah would have expected.

"I *thought* there was something funny," she said finally.

"You did? Really? Why?"

"Because Granny's so much older than all my friends' grandmothers."

"Oh." That simple logic had never occurred to Sarah.

They sat in silence. Sarah's anger, now drained, was replaced by dawning horror at what she had just done. If the grown-ups ever found out . . . ! Her mother's new tenderness, her place in the women's circle, everything would be ruined.

"You can never, never tell anyone you know," said Sarah desperately. "Do you promise? *Ne,* do you promise?"

"*Nnn,*" agreed Momoko in that bland, agreeable way of children. It did not inspire confidence.

Sarah thrust out her pinkie finger, and Momoko hooked it with her own. But Sarah felt doomed. An eleven-year-old child could not be trusted. She herself had already slipped up, and she'd known for less than a month.

"Sarah-chan, don't pick at your food," said Mrs. Rexford. "It's an insult to your grandmother's cooking."

In the two days since the incident with Momoko, Sarah had eaten hardly anything but rice and umeboshi. To the puzzlement of the adults, she had taken to watching television in the middle of the day until Mrs. Rexford firmly turned off the TV set. This afternoon Sarah had hidden away on the garden veranda and watched Mr. Kobayashi sketching designs for his upcoming show.

She now gave a short bow of apology toward her grandmother. She choked down a bite of breaded prawn. Her mother watched her with an inscrutable expression.

"Let's go for a stroll," said Mrs. Rexford after dinner. "I want to show you a special place."

Mother and daughter strolled through the lanes until they reached the main thoroughfare. It was pleasantly busy with evening traffic: people coasting by, straight backed, on bicycles; locals strolling to the bathhouse carrying plastic washbasins and towels.

With the sureness of a local, Mrs. Rexford slipped into a

small opening between a cigarette shop and a bus-token stand. Here, tucked away from the outside world, was a pocket-sized temple area. A roofed platform displayed a standing stone Buddha with an outstretched hand. At the foot of the statue lay homely offerings of flowers, in glass household jars washed clean of labels.

"I like this little place," said Mrs. Rexford. She headed for a bench and Sarah followed her. In the dim gray light of evening, this little clearing had a magical quality. They sat for a while in peaceful companionship.

After a while her mother turned to her and said, very gently, "What's wrong?"

Before this tenderness to which she was still unaccustomed, Sarah crumbled. As she blurted out her secret, she watched her mother's eyes change from puzzled concern to sharp comprehension. At this, she began to cry with dry, harsh sobs.

"I don't know why I did it," she sobbed. And it was true, for at this point her reasons seemed nothing short of insane.

She hadn't cried like this with her mother in years. Some detached part of her now savored this reversion to childhood, knowing it was probably the last time she would cry with such abandon.

As if from a great distance, she heard her mother saying, "Sarah-chan, Sarah-chan, it's not the end of the world. I'm not angry. There's no need to cry."

She lifted her eyes. The light had grown slightly grayer. In the silence between her hiccups, she could hear the peaceful pulsing of crickets.

"Momoko would have found out sometime," Mrs. Rexford said.

"She wasn't supposed . . . to know until . . ." Traditionally, adopted children weren't told of their status until they came of age. Neighbors and friends were trusted to keep a discreet silence.

"Oh, that doesn't matter with the second generation," said Mrs. Rexford. "A grandmother's hardly the same thing as a mother."

"But why . . . then . . . all the secrecy . . ."

"It's to protect Granny Asaki. She wants so much for those girls to think of her as their real grandmother. She'd be really hurt if they switched their affections to someone else. But as long as they pretend not to know about it, there's no harm done."

"But I'm afraid . . . Momo-chan will blab. I've been so worried."

"It'll be all right," said Mrs. Rexford confidently. "Sure, she might tell someone, but it'll be her mother, it won't be Granny. That girl knows her way around. This is how it is when you grow up in a complicated family. Your aunt and I were like that too. We were used to the pressure, so we never buckled."

Sarah felt utterly chastened.

"I'll go talk to your auntie tomorrow, just to make sure," Mrs. Rexford said. "But don't worry. It'll be all right."

"Will she be mad?" At the thought of her aunt's gentle face, Sarah almost began to cry again.

"To tell you the truth," her mother said, "I think she'd like her girls to know who their real grandma is." There was a knowing quality in her voice that made Sarah realize that the sisters, for all their differences, shared some deep, unspoken rapport.

"Slipups happen to the best of us," Mrs. Rexford continued. "Your auntie learned about her situation when she was about Momoko's age."

"Oh no . . ."

"She heard a rumor at school and came to me to ask if it was true. She was quiet, kind of shaken. She seemed so alone. I sat her down and told her that our mother never wanted to give her away, that she'd always regretted it. I think it helped. I *hope* it helped."

They sat quietly. The dusk had deepened, and the standing Buddha was now a flat, dark silhouette.

"Did she talk to Granny?"

"No. We kept that conversation a secret from the adults. To this very day, neither your grandma nor Granny has any idea she found out early."

Sarah lifted her face to look at her mother. Their eyes met in relief that they had been spared such a fate.

Never again was Sarah fully at ease around the Asaki household.

She was ashamed to meet her aunt Masako's eyes. And in Momoko she no longer saw a simple child, but an additional complication in the forward-thinking game. Now, if her grandmother bought her a new dress or a trinket, Sarah hid it from her cousins. She constantly searched Momoko's eyes, alert for any signs of jealousy.

If she could be so angry after just one look from Mrs. Asaki, then how could it not be different for her aunt and cousin? What resentments did they feel that they could not express?

Thus it came about that Sarah drew away from the Asaki house, choosing to adopt the social boundaries of her elders. As the years passed, the distance between the girls would grow to resemble that of the generation before them.

chapter 15

In the parlor, next to the tokonoma alcove, a narrow storage recess ran horizontally along the wall. It had miniature sliding doors made of the same durable paper as the *fusuma* room dividers. This space had been designed to store seasonal hanging scrolls, but the Kobayashis used it for their photograph albums.

Five years ago Sarah had preferred the newer vinyl albums, filled with pictures of herself as a baby and a toddler. But ever since the talk about black-market rice and snakes and adoptions, she had become curious about the older albums at the back of the shelf. Those books were of better quality, covered with aged fabric that had faded to shades of brown and indigo. Their silk tassels, now rust colored, still had centers of bright purple.

Today she was leafing hurriedly through the "war and occupation" album. There weren't many pictures from that period, barely enough to fill up the book. The photographs were tiny. Some were the size of playing cards and others even smaller, glued onto the black cardboard pages like stamps in a collection.

She was looking for a specific photograph, and here it was:

the only picture of Mr. Kobayashi's former wife. It had been taken in their garden in Manchuria, a year before she contracted typhoid fever and died. She had a round, blank face and rosebud lips, exactly like a *kokeshi* doll, and she was so petite she made young Mr. Kobayashi look tall in contrast. The baby boy bundled in her arms would also contract the fever, but survive. After the war, Mr. Kobayashi would bring his sickly baby back to Japan and marry Sarah's widowed grandmother. This baby was Sarah's uncle Teinosuke.

She was looking for this picture because her uncle was coming for lunch today, and she had overheard her grandmother saying in wry tones that Teinosuke took after his mother. To the girl's disappointment, the face on the page revealed no new clues to the woman's personality. She scrutinized the picture, remembering Mrs. Asaki's words at their last tea. She had always assumed this doll-like creature was a romantic lost love, a parallel to her grandmother's Shohei. But in fact she had been second choice . . . just as her husband was now.

Sarah's uncle lived almost two hours away in Osaka. He was the same age as Mrs. Nishimura, and he was a bachelor. More important, he was insignificant within the family. He was on the periphery of the women's "outside" circle.

But none of this was outwardly evident. When he arrived, a heaping platter of his favorite food was awaiting him on the low dining table: fried pot stickers stuffed with pork, ginger, and garlic. This was accompanied by individual dipping bowls of soy sauce, vinegar, and hot chili oil. "Chili oil makes you sweat," Mrs. Kobayashi had explained to Sarah as they set the table. "Sweating is very healthy in the summer."

Teinosuke Kobayashi was noticeably shorter than his stepmother and stepsister. Either the babyhood fever had stunted his growth, or else he had inherited his natural mother's petite frame. Young Teinosuke had been afflicted, all throughout grade school, with thin, flyaway hair ("sort of brownish, like a Caucasian baby, very strange," Mrs. Rexford said), which was surely a lingering effect of the fever. Perhaps the illness had also affected his ability to learn. His grades were poor, and he was the only child in their entire extended family who had not gone to college.

But now, in adulthood, he exuded good health. Peering up at the others from under a glossy shock of black hair, he tucked into the gyoza heartily, his Adam's apple working up and down. He talked unendingly about business—he worked with insurance of some kind—in a loud, knowing voice.

"*Aaa,*" replied his father, nodding and chuckling affably. "*Aaa . . . Aaa . . .* is that right." But eventually the elder Mr. Kobayashi excused himself from the table and returned to his workshop. Over the years, his son's academic and professional disappointments had cooled his interest. For Mr. Kobayashi, who had always lived in the shadow of his more accomplished brother, success was extremely important.

After Mr. Kobayashi's departure, there was an awkward silence.

"Tei-kun," said Mrs. Rexford. "Are you still playing pachinko as much as you used to?"

Her stepbrother replied, rather stiffly, that he was.

"Take me sometime," she teased. "Come on!"

"No!" he said, scandalized. "You know nice women don't go to pachinko parlors!"

"You could be my chaperone. It would be fun."

"No, no," he said, shaking his head grimly. "It wouldn't be proper." But exercising this masculine authority had revived his confidence; before long he was bragging again about business.

Long ago, Teinosuke Kobayashi had wielded great power

within the family. As a child he had been instinctively clever about leveraging his position as a sick, motherless boy. When his stepmother disciplined him he sought out his father and complained, knowing he would get full sympathy. For Mr. Kobayashi had finally realized that although his wife performed all her duties with conscientious effort, she was never going to love him. And he found little ways to punish her for it.

Teinosuke also had a champion in Mrs. Asaki. If he ran down the lane to tell on his stepmother, the older woman marched right over to the Kobayashi house to demand an explanation for the boy's tears. In those days, despite the boundaries protecting her own adopted daughter, Mrs. Asaki had no qualms about meddling and keeping her sister-in-law in her place.

Yoko, several years older than her stepbrother, had watched all this and seethed. Knowing better than to confront Mrs. Asaki or her stepfather, she did all she could to make life easier for her mother. Her grades were impeccable, as was her conduct at home. She kept a sharp eye on Teinosuke. She itched to punish him in private, but that would have created even more trouble for her mother.

Sarah had little sense of how hard those years had been for her grandmother. But she did understand that time had brought about a gradual power shift. She felt great sympathy for her uncle. Apparently her mother did too; her stepbrother's reduced position brought out a noblesse oblige that was so warm and natural, so heartfelt, that even Sarah fell under its spell. Of course Mrs. Rexford was capable of putting on an act. And yet—the girl was sure of it—there was genuine kindness there, a kindness that belied or at least balanced out her earlier disparaging remarks.

"Remember that time, Tei-kun," Mrs. Rexford was saying, "when you ate three bowls of noodle soup at one sitting? *Aaa,* those were the days, weren't they?"

"They were, Big Sister," he said. Sarah was moved by his childish honorific.

After a leisurely lunch, Teinosuke took his leave. He ruffled Sarah's hair before stepping down into the vestibule. He had always been a kind uncle.

Afterward, washing dishes in the kitchen, Mrs. Rexford gave a snort of laughter. "Good Lord!" she said. "Will he ever stop putting on airs." But she didn't seem bothered. In fact, she seemed quite cheerful.

"You know what?" she told her mother. "I think living in America has liberated me."

"*Soh?* How's that?"

"I didn't feel any anger today," Mrs. Rexford said. "Not even a twinge. It's all gone." She hummed a little tune as she rinsed a porcelain dipping bowl.

"You did seem to have a good time," agreed Mrs. Kobayashi. She took the wet bowl from her daughter's hand and wiped it with a dishcloth.

"That's because I have perspective," Mrs. Rexford boasted. "I can empathize with the little boy he used to be."

"I'm glad to hear it."

"This is so encouraging," said Mrs. Rexford happily. "If it can happen with someone like Teinosuke, just think how nice it's going to be when Tama comes to visit!"

chapter 16

Tama Kobayashi—now Mrs. Tama Izumi—was Mrs. Kobayashi's final child, the only offspring of the second marriage. She lived in Tokyo with her husband and little boy. In a few days, they would be riding out on the bullet train for an extended visit.

"It's good timing," Mrs. Rexford told Sarah. "You can relax around your aunt Tama. She's *real* family." They exchanged a knowing glance.

Sarah couldn't wait. Her aunt Tama had been pretty and fun-loving, with fashionable clothes and bright lipstick. The girl could remember a time when her aunt was still unmarried, when she used to live here at home. She was constantly going off on dates in her fiancé's sports car instead of taking the streetcar like everyone else. Little Sarah, intoxicated by this whiff of an exciting outside world, had trailed her everywhere. She had fantasized about having her for a big sister. She had fantasized about having her for a mother.

In preparation for the Izumis' visit, Mrs. Kobayashi and Mrs. Rexford began pulling down extra futons from the storage closet. They hung them out to air in the laundry area, which was a tiny cement courtyard with a covered drain in the middle. One accessed it through the family room, stepping down from an inner veranda onto a neat row of red plastic utility slippers. This roofless space was rigged with washing lines for light items such as clothing, and sturdy bamboo poles for the heavier items. The strong summer sun flooded down, and the air quickly became suffused with the scent of warm cotton.

"Little Jun and his father can sleep in the receiving room," panted Mrs. Kobayashi as the two women, working in unison, heaved a silk coverlet over a lowered bamboo pole. Its patterned side faced out. The red and blue carp were slightly faded from age and sun, but the silk had been protected from human skin by a wide rim of white cotton casing. "Tama can squeeze in with the two of you in the parlor."

"Banzai!" cried Sarah happily. She was perched on the ledge of the inner veranda, swinging her bare legs and watching her elders as she nibbled on a snack of dried whitebait and cheese.

"So as I was saying"—Mrs. Rexford was also panting—"I was always so harsh to her and now I feel bad about it."

"Don't be so hard on yourself," said Mrs. Kobayashi. "You were only children."

The women lifted the bamboo pole in unison. Raised arms trembling with effort, each fitted her end into the loop of twine hanging overhead. Then Mrs. Rexford said, "I have a confession to make. Remember that time Tama drank the entire bottle of rationed milk from the icebox?"

"I do. I had to lie and tell Father I'd mismanaged the household funds. *Aaa*, he was so angry . . ."

"Well," said Mrs. Rexford, "I cornered Tama afterward. I was so mad I slapped her, right across the face."

"Oh, Yo-chan! She was just a little girl!" Then after a pause, "What did she do?"

"She stood there and sniffled. I said, 'Look what you've done! My mother's getting yelled at, and it's all because of you!'

"She looked ashamed, but she stuck out her chin and said, 'She's *my* mother too.' I told her, 'Then act like it!'"

Having finished with the futons, the two women climbed up onto the veranda and into the shade of the family room. Sinking down gratefully onto the floor cushions, they picked up round paper *uchiwa* and fanned the moisture from their faces.

Sarah followed them inside. "What's for lunch?" she asked timidly. But the women were too engrossed to pay her any attention.

"But Tama never learned," continued Mrs. Rexford. "Time would pass, then she'd do something else just as thoughtless. *That* was the problem."

Mrs. Kobayashi nodded regretfully. They fanned themselves in silence.

Little Tama had grown up largely unaffected by family tensions. She had both of her natural parents and she knew nothing about her half sister's adoption, at least until she was older. In truth she was a little self-centered. Mrs. Kobayashi, typical of postwar mothers, had raised her with unusual leniency, as if to atone for those hardships that had forced her older children into premature adulthood. Or maybe the girl was just born that way; someone had once remarked that she was, after all, Kenji Kobayashi's daughter.

"But she was always a good girl at heart," said Mrs. Rexford, "never sneaky or mean-spirited like Teinosuke. When I think of her following me around, wanting my approval no matter how much I scolded her . . ." She stopped, overcome with emotion.

"There, there," soothed Mrs. Kobayashi. She reached over with the *uchiwa* and gently fanned her daughter's face. "Forget all that. You're both grown women, and this is your chance to develop a true womanly friendship. *Ne?*"

Mrs. Rexford nodded.

"I know how much you wanted that with Masako," said Mrs. Kobayashi.

Mrs. Rexford nodded again. It was a source of sorrow that Mrs. Nishimura, whom she romantically regarded as her "true" sister, never dropped her outside face in her presence—or in the presence of anyone else. "It's so hard to *talk* to her," Mrs. Rexford had lamented. "She won't even gossip."

"At least with Tama," said Mrs. Kobayashi, "you have a chance."

Real family, all staying in the same house! Even after her experience with the Asaki household, Sarah had romantic notions about large families. She liked the companionable lulls: she and her cousins often sat on the garden veranda, watching Mr. Kobayashi as he chain-smoked and stared off into space and sketched in hurried spurts. With the women's occasional laughter in the background, the girls sat contentedly within the aromatic haze of his cigarette smoke, sucking on popsicles from the snack shop. Being on the periphery of adult focus was a new experience for Sarah. She liked it. It felt like a sign of tacit approval.

Neighbors, too, were family. There was always someone nearby to whom she could bow a greeting: housewives in the narrow lane, buying greens from the vendor's cart; an old man wearing geta and watering the shrubs outside his slatted wooden gate. Even strangers, passing through on their way to somewhere else, seemed to know who Sarah was. Early on she had made the mistake of bowing to random people in the open-air market, assuming everyone knew her family. "Who were you bowing to just now?" her mother or grandmother would ask, puzzled.

Best of all were the titles of familiarity. Friends of the family, shop clerks, even strangers who happened to drop handkerchiefs in the street were addressed as Auntie, or Big Brother, or Granny. To Sarah's satisfaction, Momoko and Yashiko addressed her as Big Sister.

"Don't you miss living here?" she once asked her mother. "Don't you ever wish you'd married someone from Japan?"

"No," said Mrs. Rexford. "And if I had, you wouldn't be here right now."

"Yes, I would! And I'd be completely Japanese, instead of just half."

It wasn't that Sarah had anything against Fielder's Butte. She liked its austere beauty: miles of empty fields that, in summer, gave off an aroma like bran muffins; giant oak trees left over from Indian days; an industrial-sized sky of flat blue, blank except for the freewheeling hawk or the white trail of a plane. But thinking of it now gave her a forlorn feeling.

This, here, was the center of the world. The landscape confirmed it: hills of bright green rising up all around them, a lovely distraction to her unaccustomed eye. Sometimes in the evening, when she and her elders strolled home from the bathhouse in the gentle gray light of the narrow lanes, she looked up at the hills glowing in the last pink wash of sunset. In that light they loomed so close, so clear, she could make out individual trees packed tightly together like broccoli florets. "In ancient days," her mother explained, "those hills kept our city safe from invading warrior clans. That's why it was the perfect location for the royal court." As they headed home, Sarah felt those hills shielding them from the huge sky that, in Fielder's Butte, made the sunsets so lonely and stark.

chapter 17

T ama Izumi was the most beautiful of the three sisters.
She had full, perfectly formed lips like the Egyptian queen
Nefertiti. She exuded a womanly coquetry that Sarah, despite
her own lack of experience, instantly recognized as being attrac-
tive to the opposite sex. But unlike some beautiful women,
Mrs. Izumi extended her good-natured flirtation to women and
children alike, as if inviting everyone to share in her feminine
appeal.

"Oh, Sarah-chan, you've turned out so *pretty*!" she said, and
the girl fell in love with her all over again.

The women followed Mrs. Izumi into the parlor and kept
her company while she unpacked her suitcases. This took a long
time, for she kept stopping to chat.

"It seems like yesterday that your mother brought you home
from the hospital, in a little bundle," Mrs. Izumi told Sarah.

"Remember that time you babysat," Mrs. Rexford said, "and
you fed her mandarin oranges? I was so mad when I found those
seeds in her diaper."

"But, Big Sister, she wanted some!" Mrs. Izumi protested,
laughing. "I swear! She threw a tantrum every time I stopped!"

Little Jun trotted into the room and stood over the open suitcase. He was an active four-year-old whose small brown legs, clad in little boys' short pants, were constantly on the move. His mother drew out a stack of tiny shirts and placed them in an open bureau drawer. "Those are mine," he told the women.

"Jun-chan, what a nice baseball cap you've got!" said Mrs. Rexford. It was navy blue with a yellow tiger's head on it, for Hanshin Tigers. Mr. Kobayashi had given it to him when he arrived. "You're one of the menfolk now," he had told the boy, reaching down to tweak his visor. Over the next few days the boy would insist on wearing this cap everywhere, even to the bathhouse.

"I'm one of the menfolk," Jun now told them.

"You certainly are!" said his grandmother. "It's a lucky thing you're here to protect us!"

Mrs. Rexford and Mrs. Izumi were reminiscing about friends of their youth. Bored, the little boy wandered away to the other end of the house.

"Mother," said Mrs. Izumi, "whatever happened to Big Sister's old boyfriend? The one who was studying Middle Eastern history?"

"Sekizaki-kun," supplied Mrs. Rexford.

"*Soh,* Sekizaki-kun! I hear he goes around consulting for the big petroleum companies now," said Mrs. Kobayashi. "Who could have guessed, back then, what would happen with Arab oil?" She turned to Sarah. "He was an odd one," she explained. "For whatever reason, he was fascinated with that part of the world. Think: all that work to get into Kyoto University, then he defied his poor parents and studied the most impractical subject ever."

"He had bite, that one," said Mrs. Rexford.

"What's bite?" asked Sarah.

"It's a certain bravery," said her grandmother, "an original- ity of intellect. Your mother's boyfriends, they all had bite. Some of them are important men now."

"No fair, Big Sister!" cried Mrs. Izumi in mock distress. "How come none of *my* boyfriends went on to careers of intellect?"

They all giggled.

"That's because you dated bon-bons," her sister said. Bon- bons were handsome, dashing boys from wealthy families who focused on sports cars and skiing trips instead of their studies.

Mrs. Izumi responded with a sour look, and they all laughed again.

Mrs. Izumi had met her husband in college. He was good looking and extremely polite; Sarah considered him romantic. His father was chief of neurosurgery at Osaka Municipal Hos- pital, but Mr. Izumi himself worked as an office manager. "Our Jun's going to be a doctor. He's going to take after his grand- daddy," Mrs. Izumi told the women.

Right now Mr. Izumi was in the family room, watching baseball. Mr. Kobayashi had joined him there, abandoning his work in order to play host. The men seemed slightly off-kilter, like caged animals waiting for their next meal. But they shared a certain solidarity, perhaps because they had been bon-bons in their youth. Little Jun, torn between his desire for male com- panionship and his attraction to the merrier women with their direct access to food, wandered back and forth between the two camps.

"What's in this bag here?" asked Mrs. Rexford. She peeked inside. "What are all these books and magazines? *Watchtower?* What's that, Jehovah's Witness? Tama, are you into Christian- ity now?"

Her stepsister nodded sheepishly.

Tama Izumi's personality had always tended toward the dramatic. Several years ago she had discovered Confucianism, and she had announced this conversion by sending the Rexfords a hardbound religious text written in the original Chinese, which no one could possibly have known how to read. Before that, it had been some fundamentalist sect of Buddhism, and Sarah had received a child's comic book depicting in lurid, colorful detail all the intricate levels of hell.

"Hmm," said Mrs. Rexford, losing interest.

"Auntie, what was it like growing up with Mama?" Sarah asked.

"Well," said Mrs. Izumi, "everyone admired your mother very much. But"—she made a little pout with her lovely lips—"she could be very *mean* to her little sister!"

"That's because you were a pest," replied Mrs. Rexford with an affectionate bluntness she would never have used with Mrs. Nishimura. "You were always bothering me and stealing my things."

Mrs. Izumi pretended not to hear. "Sarah-chan," she continued, "are you aware that your grandmother used to make me tiptoe past your mother's room while she was studying for exams? And then Big Sister would complain I was breathing too loud, and *I'd* get scolded!" She was so droll, so childishly indignant, that everyone burst into infectious laughter.

As an only child, Sarah found this fascinating and vaguely unsettling. Sibling rivalry was perfectly normal, she knew. But after so many weeks of heightened tact, it was odd to hear her grandmother's favoritism acknowledged so blatantly. Perhaps over the years, other family tensions had drained her grandmother and mother of sensitivity toward the baby of the family. After all, Tama was the lucky one. She had grown up with her real mother and father, she had been spared the war years, and she was clearly vocal enough to stand up for herself.

"Did you notice," whispered Mrs. Rexford later that day in the kitchen, "how she steered completely clear of the altar?"

Mrs. Kobayashi reached into the icebox for a package of yakisoba noodles. "Well, you know," she said. "Our tablets are barbaric idols, according to the Bible."

Mrs. Rexford snorted with impatience.

Mrs. Kobayashi sighed. "I wouldn't mind so much if it was a quiet, dignified sort of religion," she said. "But those people insist on going around and ringing strangers' doorbells, like peddlers from the deep country."

"I know. We have Jehovah's Witnesses in America too."

This was why the Izumis were visiting now in the beginning of July, instead of waiting until the midmonth O-bon holiday when families traditionally came together. Their new religion forbade the celebration of holidays: not just Buddhist holidays like O-bon, but also Christian holidays such as Christmas and— even worse in Sarah's opinion—neutral holidays such as children's birthdays.

"I don't understand," Mrs. Rexford said, "why she can't spend *two minutes* making a gesture of respect to her forebears." No one in the house, with the possible exception of Mrs. Kobayashi, was religious in a theological sense. Praying at the altar was routine, like eating rice or bowing hello.

Mrs. Kobayashi dropped a handful of onions into the sizzling oil, and its aroma drifted up into the dining room. Sarah, setting the low table, sniffed appreciatively.

Mrs. Rexford popped her head around the shoji screen. "Where *is* everybody?" she asked the girl.

"They're all out in the garden."

Her mother's head withdrew.

Eventually Sarah heard her saying, "When you die, Mother, and your tablet goes on those shelves, what does she plan to do then?"

"It'll blow over before that. Don't worry so much. Just enjoy being sisters."

Mrs. Rexford said nothing.

chapter 18

 S arah woke in the dark. Beside her, lying on sun-aired futons, her mother and her aunt were whispering.

She couldn't quite follow what they were saying. She was groggy and the vocabulary was difficult. They seemed to be discussing philosophy.

She lay still, letting their voices drift through her mind. What time was it? The long drapes were shut, but above them a narrow rectangular window stretched from wall to wall. Through its wooden slats, the night sky glowed an eerie Prussian blue. The trees in the garden cast strange shadows on the walls.

She still had moments of dissonance when she felt like a Westerner. She was aware of the house's smell: an exotic combination of wood, tatami straw, prayer incense, rice. Sometimes when she brushed her teeth she noticed, wafting in through the open window, some baffling night scent she could only associate with melons.

"... and his heart is so vast," Mrs. Izumi was saying, "he feels identical love for each one of his children. Robber or saint, it makes no difference—we are all the same in his eyes."

"It seems kind of impersonal," Mrs. Rexford said, "to measure out the exact same love for everybody, like sugar in a rationing line."

But it might be preferable, Sarah thought, to knowing that someone else was getting more than you.

"But that's what makes it a miracle." Mrs. Izumi seemed anxious to make her sister understand. "It's exact and fair like a science, but it's also extremely personal at the same time."

Mrs. Izumi had a new Tokyo accent, not just because she lived in Tokyo but because she had purposely cultivated standardized speech. She used phrases like "namely" or "the truth of the matter." Sarah knew this annoyed her mother, who scorned verbal posturing and took great pride in her Kyoto accent.

". . . so you can see its significance," her aunt continued. She had been talking for what felt like a long time. Sarah wanted to change position on the futon, but she was afraid to move. She had never heard this tone in her aunt's voice before. The playfulness was gone; she was making a self-conscious effort to converse on the same level as her sister. Perhaps Mrs. Rexford sensed this too, for she murmured, *"Nnn hnn,"* without any more commentary or dissent.

It had never occurred to Sarah that grown people would want to change their identities. She'd thought identity was like height: it resolved itself by the early twenties, one accepted it and moved on.

In that moment, her longtime crush on her aunt Tama began to fade. It was a surprise, like ice cracking. She saw ahead to a time when her crush would be a faint, poignant memory, and she felt a pang of sorrow.

Outdoors, someone clapped two heavy wood blocks together. There was a long pause. Then the *kon . . . kon . . .* sound came again, closer and more piercing, leaving a high-pitched ringing in the ears. Heavy footsteps sounded in the lane, striding hurriedly over the gravel.

Mrs. Izumi paused in her monologue. *"Hi-no-yojin* duty," she murmured, suddenly sounding soft and wistful. This was the traditional neighborhood reminder to make sure all fires were extinguished before going to bed. Centuries ago, their ancestors had listened to this same sound as they rested their heads on wooden pillows.

"Nnn," murmured Mrs. Rexford. She yawned. "They're late tonight." So it was only ten or eleven o'clock, not the early hours of morning as Sarah had thought.

"Remember," said Mrs. Izumi, "when we used to go with Papa, and he'd let us clap the blocks?" A hint of Kyoto dialect had crept into her voice, giving it a singsong quality. For the first time since her arrival, she actually sounded like someone's little sister. For a surprising instant Sarah was transported back to a time before her own birth, to some long-lost ordinary night when these two sisters must have lain in bed as children. Then, as quickly as it had come, the moment vanished.

"Soh ne . . . ," agreed Mrs. Rexford, echoing her sister's nostalgia. "Tama-chan, can you believe how fast the time went?"

"I know, Big Sister . . . so fast . . ."

The footsteps faded, and the intermittent claps grew fainter. In their wake, night settled with finality over the houses.

Then Mrs. Rexford said, "It was interesting, what we talked about. I'll definitely think it over." Her voice held the same gentleness Sarah remembered from the lunch with her uncle Teinosuke. For a moment, the girl wondered if her mother was actually thinking of converting.

"I'll show you my books tomorrow," said Mrs. Izumi. Those brief moments of shared nostalgia must have eased something in her mind, for she didn't follow it up with any more big words. They lay silent as if in a spell, listening to the last faint echoes of the wooden blocks.

chapter 19

The next day, while the Izumis were away paying their respects at the Asaki house, Sarah saw her grandmother's private photograph album for the first time.

She had been asking questions—about the war, about her real grandfather. "You're becoming quite the historian," Mrs. Kobayashi laughed, and turned to Mrs. Rexford. "What do you think, Yo-chan?" she said. "Is she ready to see some pictures?"

This album wasn't kept in the storage recess like the others. Mrs. Kobayashi opened a bureau drawer and slid it out from between layers of seldom-worn kimonos.

"Let's not mention this to anyone," Mrs. Kobayashi said. She and Mrs. Rexford carefully turned the pages, with freshly washed hands smelling of soap.

"When your mother was young," Mrs. Kobayashi said, "I used to show this book to *her.*"

Mrs. Rexford had very few memories of her real father. She had been three when he went off to war. Mrs. Kobayashi had been twenty-seven and pregnant with Masako.

"Here he is in his judo gear . . . Here he is at a company gathering . . ."

Shohei Kobayashi was handsome, like an old-time movie star, with perfectly proportioned features and eyes like elegant brushstrokes. Sarah had never seen a man like this outside of a samurai film.

"Here he is, holding your mother." They all leaned in to scrutinize the black-and-white photograph.

"Every minute he had free, he was carrying your mother. Walking around, always holding her in one arm."

"I think I remember being held by him," Mrs. Rexford said.

"Your mother got carried around so much, with her arm curled around his neck or mine, that when she was set down she'd forget to move her left arm."

The two women laughed wistfully.

"He's really handsome," said Sarah.

"Oh, do you think so?" her grandmother asked.

"Mother," said Mrs. Rexford, "don't be coy."

They had met through work. Before her marriage, Mrs. Kobayashi had been a typist in the head office of a large Kobe corporation—not a *common* typist (as she always emphasized), but a foreign-language typist, using a machine equipped with English alphabet keys. In the 1930s English proficiency was a status symbol, proof of the higher education given to daughters from wealthy, academically liberal families. She had worn high heels to the office, and modish Western dresses with zippers and buttons and flounces. After work, she and a group of coworkers frequented the new dance halls, where waltzes and foxtrots were all the rage among the young well-to-do. Shohei was a young executive from the Kyoto branch who often visited the head office on business.

"Is this *you*, Grandma? You look so glamorous." Sarah stared at a picture of a young woman with bobbed hair, lipstick, and a mischievous expression. "These pictures are so different from the others! It's like a whole different world."

"Granny Asaki was always jealous," remarked Mrs. Rexford, "because your grandma came from a cosmopolitan background and she didn't."

"Look at this one," Mrs. Kobayashi said quickly. "It's our wedding reception."

The photograph had been taken at night. A large party boat blazed with prewar exuberance: red paper lanterns hanging above the deck, serving women in dark kimonos balancing lacquered trays of sushi above their heads as they wove sinuously among the tightly packed guests. Sarah could almost hear the gay twanging of the stringed shamisen and the guests clapping time, their reserve loosened by cups of sake.

Mrs. Kobayashi gave a little smile. "I've often looked back on that boat," she said, "from the distance of time." Sarah wondered how she pictured it. Closing her own eyes, she imagined a small oasis of light and laughter, bobbing on the water's dark expanse and spilling an occasional "To your future!" that faded into the night above the quiet lapping of the bay.

It was strange how both women, in different ways, had ended up falling from their youthful heights. Sarah wasn't sure how to account for this. She could only sense vaguely that life was like a maze, and sometimes, through no fault of your own, a perfectly good path could veer off in an unexpected direction.

Over the next few days, Mrs. Izumi launched into her campaign of religious conversion. The women were patient and accommodating as she interrupted their conversations with clumsy segues into "love" or "the Lord." But Sarah saw in her mother the restless eye movements, the flared nostrils through which she breathed rather more loudly than usual. She was worried for her aunt; couldn't she see she was alienating the very people whose circle she wanted to enter?

One afternoon Sarah and the three women were sitting down to tea in the family room. The men were out playing tennis with some of Mr. Kobayashi's friends. Little Jun had gone downtown with Mrs. Asaki and the girls.

"Here, you do the honors," Mrs. Kobayashi told Mrs. Rexford, gesturing toward the teapot. She knew her daughter wanted to practice her tea skills as much as possible; she often complained that living in America had made her rusty.

Mrs. Izumi turned to Sarah and said with mock sadness, "You see? I never get to pour."

Sarah played along. "Because you're the youngest?"

"That's right." Actually Mrs. Izumi had little interest in the tea ceremony. Both daughters had been formally trained in tea and koto, but only for Mrs. Rexford were they important as the last remnants of their old Kobe lineage. In those difficult early years, mother and daughter had bonded by honing the social skills that elevated them above the Asakis.

Mrs. Rexford lifted the teapot, giving it a gentle swirl before pouring the tea into thin porcelain cups. To Sarah's relief, the tea service was casual. The formal teas, which she usually avoided, took place in the parlor. They involved heavy glazed bowls with deceptively rustic "flaws," a cast-iron teapot, and a wooden whisk for frothing the matcha tea, which tasted bitter to the girl's untrained tongue. Even the formal sweets were disappointing. Since the bitterness of the tea required a correspondingly strong sweetness, her grandmother served tiny artistic confections that, while beautiful to look at, tasted like pure sugar. "It's the blend of opposites that makes it pleasurable," she had explained.

Today's tea was a mild sencha. Sarah would have preferred

cold barley tea, but such a watered-down drink, she knew, was too lowly even for an informal tea: one gave it to small children or else drank it from a thermos in place of water. At least her snack of *ohagi,* a sticky rice ball covered with sweet bean paste, was something she could really sink her teeth into.

As each woman accepted her tea with a slight bow of thanks, a polite silence fell over the table. The first sip was followed by formal murmurs of appreciation. Then, since it was a casual tea, Mrs. Izumi resumed the thread of her earlier conversation.

Sarah took an absentminded pleasure in watching the women's fluid movements. It was like ballet above the waist; their precise alignment came from a lifetime of practice. Sarah envied their lack of concentration. She herself was always stiff and self-conscious when she took tea. She had sensed this same self-consciousness in Mrs. Asaki and Mrs. Nishimura. They made the right movements but they came from the brain, not from muscle memory. Sarah, remembering her recent grievance against Mrs. Asaki, felt a smug flash of pride in these women sitting beside her.

"So that big religious conference my friend went to, it was in the southern part of the country. I wanted to go too," Mrs. Izumi said. "But my husband put his foot down."

"People down in those southern areas eat a lot of pork," Mrs. Kobayashi said. "They boil enormous chunks of it in iron kettles, along with cabbage and all kinds of strange things."

"It wasn't in Okinawa, Mother," Mrs. Izumi corrected her. "It was a normal suburb of Kagoshima." With the snobbery of mainland dwellers, the women regarded Okinawans as not quite Japanese, existing in the same category as Ainu aborigines from Hokkaido.

"Kagoshima has its own regional cuisine, doesn't it?" said Mrs. Rexford. "When I went there on my school trip . . ."

Doggedly, Mrs. Izumi tried to steer the topic back to religion. Finally she pulled out a thin book from the pile next to her floor cushion. Turning to Sarah, she said, "Anyway, my friend brought me back some books. This one's for you."

Sarah was pleased, for her aunt usually ignored her when she discussed religion. "Wait, what does that word mean?" Sarah always demanded at crucial moments, knowing her mother and grandmother wouldn't mind the intrusion. "Wait, wait! What does it *mean?*"

"Thank you, Auntie," she said now, accepting the book with both hands and examining the cover. Some of the Chinese characters were unfamiliar—she recognized only the ideograms for *thousand, love,* and *ultimate*—but the illustration was clear enough. There was a grassy park with children of various nationalities laughing and playing in the foreground. Behind them, smiling parents strolled two by two beneath colorful fruit trees, past a lion and a lamb lying together in the shade.

The two women paused in their discussion of boiled pork. With wary expressions, they leaned forward—straight-backed, still in proper tea posture—to peer at the cover.

"Very nice," said Mrs. Kobayashi faintly.

"Would you be interested," Mrs. Izumi asked Sarah, "in meeting some people your age from the local branch?"

"*A, a!* Don't even think about it," said Mrs. Rexford. "The children are off limits."

"Fine." Mrs. Izumi sighed with comical resignation. She sipped her tea and took a bite of her *ohagi.* Then she looked up at the two women, this time with a flash of defiance. "You two don't take me seriously," she said. "I'm like a lapdog to you. Cute. Silly. A nuisance."

The women looked up from their teacups.

"What if it turned out I wasn't so stupid after all? What if it turned out I had the key to something that could completely change your lives?"

Mrs. Rexford thought for a moment. "I don't think you're stupid," she said finally. "And maybe you *do* have the key. But right now I don't want to change my life. I just want to talk with you like a real person, Tama-chan. I can't seem to find you underneath all this religion."

"But Big Sister, this *is* me."

"It's not the sister I used to know."

"Well, of course not! I've grown up. I can't live in your shadow forever. And now I have something important to share. I can *teach* you something. So why won't you let me?" Mrs. Izumi was dead earnest now; she seemed to have forgotten Sarah's presence. "Why can't you both, for once, follow *me*?"

The women were silent.

Mrs. Kobayashi cleared her throat. "It's a lovely idea, Tama-chan," she said. "But—" She gestured up at the family altar, and they all knew she was referring to the late Shohei. "It would mean abandoning *him*. Who'd be left to say sutras for him every morning?"

But he's dead, Sarah thought, and she's alive. But even as she thought this, she knew it didn't matter.

"And when Mother dies," Mrs. Rexford chimed in, "I'll be there to say sutras for her. That's the way it has to be. You can't just throw away history, Tama."

There was silence as everyone pictured the chain of favoritism stretching forward into the afterlife.

"But don't you think God understands? He can make provisions. The magnitude of his love . . . it transcends genealogy."

"Maybe," said Mrs. Rexford. "But here on earth it doesn't

work that way. History creates commitments. That means certain people take priority over others. I can't see any way
around it."

Mrs. Izumi made a moue as if thoughtfully considering this
theory, but Sarah saw that her eyes were watery.

chapter 20

Shortly afterward, Mrs. Izumi went away to pay a call on someone she had met through church.

Mrs. Rexford was irritable and restless. "I think I'll go out," she told her mother.

"*Soh soh*, that's a good idea," said Mrs. Kobayashi soothingly. "Take a stroll through one of your old haunts." Mrs. Kobayashi herself did not go in for aimless walks; she left that to the young people.

"I think I'll go out for an ice. Come on," Mrs. Rexford told Sarah.

"Are we going to the snack shop?" Sarah asked.

"No. I'm taking you to an old-fashioned teahouse, the kind we used to go to before they came up with those dreadful convenience stores. Can you believe it, Mother? That a child of mine has never eaten shaved ice at Kinjin-ya in the middle of summer?"

"It's downright un-Japanese," said Mrs. Kobayashi. "You should fix that right away. Run along, then. Go enjoy yourselves."

They strolled through the lanes, becoming absorbed in the larger outdoor world of cicadas and trees and wind chimes and bicycle bells. Sarah felt her mother's agitation fade. Smugly, she thought how silly her aunt Tama was to ruin a perfectly nice visit with all that religion.

Her own position, in contrast, felt sweet. How things had changed since America! It seemed ages ago that she had whined because her mother insisted on trimming her sandwich crusts or drawing little sketches on her brown paper lunch bags. Sarah pushed those memories away, ashamed of herself.

And yet—would the changes last? She remembered a science experiment at school, where she had dropped an egg into various liquids. In some, the egg floated to the surface; in others it sank like a stone. What if Japan was the only alchemy in which she could float?

The Kinjin-ya teahouse was small and unpretentious. Sarah had passed it many times on the way to the open-air market but had never gone inside. Its atmosphere was quite different from the modern tea shops downtown. It reminded Sarah of the pickle shop, with its aged wooden walls from when Japan had been a poor country. On one side hung a row of rectangular wooden tablets, one for each item on the menu, bearing the name and price in old-fashioned black brushstrokes. At this time of day the tables were empty; the only other customers were a little boy about Jun's age and his mother. The boy was spooning his way through a plate of om-rice—an omelette stuffed with ketchup-flavored rice—a children's favorite since the postwar years.

Mrs. Rexford and Sarah ordered shaved ice topped with a mound of sweetened azuki beans. It came in fluted glass dishes with long-handled spoons. "My generation grew up on this," Mrs. Rexford said. "*Maa,* it really takes me back!"

They were silent, savoring the crushed ice and the creamy sweetness of the beans.

"Remember this, remember the way it tastes," Mrs. Rexford told Sarah. And Sarah did, decades later. Many random experiences would be cemented in her mind by her mother's phrase "remember this."

Mrs. Rexford leaned back in her chair, gazing about her with a pleased expression. The seasonal cloth flaps over the open doorway cast a bluish tint on the room. Every so often, a breeze broke apart the heavy flaps and let in a flash of sunlight.

Taking advantage of this peaceful moment, Sarah ventured, "It's weird now, isn't it, with Auntie being Christian."

"Well," her mother said, "she never had top priority growing up. But it couldn't be helped—you know how complicated things were back then."

Sarah nodded.

"It's an issue in every family, though. Remember that day we had snacks at the Asaki house?"

"Oh right, the bottle of Fanta."

There had been one large bottle of orange Fanta to share among the three children. Dividing it was quite a project: first the empty glasses were lined up side by side, then each one was filled with the same number of ice cubes, and finally Mrs. Nishimura had poured the Fanta, little by little, until the levels were precisely equal. Momoko and Yashiko seemed familiar with the routine. They had crouched down on their hands and knees so as to be eye-level with the glasses, making sure that neither sibling got a milliliter more than the other.

"You and I are lucky," said Mrs. Rexford. "Some people never get to come first." Sarah thought of her aunt Tama making a moue to hide her tears. She thought of her aunt Masako waving from her shadowed gateway as the Kobayashi household strolled past, laughing and chatting, on their way to the bathhouse.

But now for the first time her sympathy was tinged with

something hard, an unwillingness to give up her advantage. Her grandmother's favoritism might not be working in her aunts' favor, but it was working in hers. For the first time in her life she was blooming. This was the luck of the draw, and she was tired of feeling guilty. In some dim recess of her mind she had begun to feel she deserved it, that fate had recognized her worth and was finally rewarding her.

"I guess there's no way around it," Sarah said, echoing her mother's words from earlier that day.

"I guess not," said Mrs. Rexford. They were silent, spooning up the last of the azuki beans.

"When you come first in someone's heart," Mrs. Rexford said, "it changes you. It literally, chemically changes you. And that stays with you, even after the person's gone. Remember that."

Sarah nodded. The idea of chemical change resonated with her, and once again she thought of the eggs floating.

She let out a little sigh of well-being. So this was how it felt to eat shaved ice at Kinjin-ya in the middle of summer. It was pleasant to sit in the path of the old-fashioned fan and feel the air flow over her moist arms and legs, exactly as it must have done when her mother was a girl. She felt curiously relaxed, all her pores open to the world. For the first time she noticed that some defensive part of herself—her habitual readiness to shrink and harden at a moment's notice—had melted away, leaving a sense of implicit trust in the world. This, she thought, is how it must feel to be a queen bee.

They left the teahouse in excellent spirits.

"That was yummy." Sarah used the childish word on purpose.

"It was, *ne*," agreed Mrs. Rexford.

They walked slowly, in no rush to get home. They took a roundabout route through a neighborhood Sarah had never seen.

Some of the houses had old-fashioned thatched roofs instead of the usual gray tile.

"They look like the houses in those history books Grandma sent me," said Sarah.

"This lane hasn't changed in generations," Mrs. Rexford said. "It's never going to change, I'm sure."

They passed under the shade of a large ginkgo tree that leaned out over an adobe wall into the lane. The fan-shaped leaves, dangling from thin stems, fluttered and trembled. The *meee* of cicadas was directly overhead now, sharpened from a mass drone into the loud rings of specific creatures, each with a different pitch, a different location among the branches. Mrs. Rexford paused and lowered her parasol to see if she could spot one. Not finding anything, she lifted her parasol and resumed walking.

"Mama?"

"Hmm?"

"Were you always Grandma's favorite?"

"Mmm-hmm."

"Even before she knew what kind of person you'd turn out to be?"

"*Soh,* even then. Because I was part of her old life before the war, back when she was happy and in love."

The lane narrowed and they fell into single file. The dappled shadows danced on the back of Mrs. Rexford's parasol.

Sarah pictured Shohei's handsome, unfamiliar face. It was odd to imagine anyone other than her mother holding such power over her grandmother's heart. That it was a man seemed especially strange. Sarah had grasped early on that while the men in this family were flattered, catered to, and fed extremely well, they were not that important in the scheme of things.

"When your grandfather died," said Mrs. Rexford, "all her love for him had to go somewhere. So it came to me, all of it.

Maybe I turned out the way I did because of that early love. It's hard to say."

"So it's like you piggybacked off of what they had," Sarah said.

"That's right. And now you're piggybacking off of what she and I have. That's why you're the favorite grandchild, you see?"

Sarah pondered this. She had always thought love began and ended with the actual person involved. She remembered her mother telling Momoko about emotions fermenting over time and getting blurred together till you couldn't tell them apart. It seemed that love, too, was blurry when it came to recipients. The remainder of one love could go on to feed the next, like those sourdough starters that American pioneer families had handed down for generations.

"It's not on your own merits," said Mrs. Rexford. "Not yet. You reach her through me. Remember that."

"Okay," Sarah agreed.

They strolled through the shifting tree shadows of late afternoon. The *k'sha k'sha* of gravel was loud beneath their feet. The buzz of traffic floated over from some larger street several blocks down. Trailing her fingers along a low wall, Sarah felt its braille of pebbles and straw; she breathed in the scent of sun-warmed adobe. She felt perfectly happy.

They approached two young boys standing under a tree with a plastic insect cage at their feet, staring up at a horned beetle just above their reach. They turned toward Sarah with that look of avid curiosity she knew so well. But they seemed mollified to see her mother was Japanese; she wasn't, then, a complete outsider.

"Where are your nets, boys?" Mrs. Rexford called out in the friendly tone of a fellow enthusiast. "Do you need me to get that for you?"

The boys gazed with tongue-tied gratitude as she pulled the horned beetle from the bark and transferred it to their plastic cage. "Look at the size of these antlers," she said. "It's a real beauty." Too shy to speak, the boys broke into big foolish grins. Sarah, who had always felt uneasy around small Japanese boys, marveled at how harmless they could be, how sweet.

As they resumed walking abreast Sarah remarked, "Little kids don't stare as much when I'm with you." It was the first time she had openly referred to her shame.

"Let them stare," her mother said breezily.

"Soh ne," agreed Sarah with her new queen-bee expansiveness. What had she been so afraid of?

Mrs. Rexford gave her daughter an approving glance but said nothing.

Years later Sarah would remember this afternoon for its intensity of color: the gleaming lacquer of the beetle against the bark, the hills rising all around them in a crescendo of green. The parasol cast a rose-colored glow over her mother's face, drawing Sarah's eyes to its unfamiliar beauty. Even the air had color, a whitish glow like light refracted through a shoji screen. When she grew older and began falling in love with men, she would experience this same sense of heightened color—although in a weaker form—and see this for what it had been: her first and most powerful romance.

chapter 21

O-bon was almost upon them. It was a three-day festival of reunion, when spirits of dead relatives returned to visit the living. Families were walking en masse to bus stops and train stations that would take them to ancestral gravesites out in the country. This was the time for graveyard maintenance. The fathers carried garden tools; the mothers carried delicate food offerings for the dead (and, if they were old-fashioned, a hearty picnic lunch for the living) discreetly wrapped in silk *furoshiki;* the children trudged behind with flowers.

As the Kobayashi household ate breakfast, they could hear the crunching of gravel as chattering families passed directly outside, taking shortcuts through the narrow lane. A woman's voice cried, "*A!* We forgot the thermos!" It was the last weekend before the holiday. Everyone, it seemed, was heading out to the country.

"They're getting ready for O-bon," said little Jun in a sullen voice. Everyone else was silent, chewing.

"I'm afraid we've held you back in your preparations," Mr. Izumi said. He was referring to the housecleaning, for family altars were just as important as graves. "It was thoughtless of us," he said. Sarah's heart went out to him. His fine long eyes, slanted ever so slightly downward, gave his face a mournful air.

"Not in the least, Izumi-san!" Mrs. Kobayashi batted the air dismissively, as if to swat away his concern. "The O-bon dinner will be over there"—she gestured toward the Asaki house—"so there's really nothing for me to do."

They all knew this was a lie. Housewives cleaned obsessively before a priest's yearly visit. The priests from So-Zen Temple had already begun their neighborhood rounds, chanting long incantations before each family altar to guide the spirits on their return journey. This was a grueling time for priests, who made back-to-back calls from morning till evening. It was for such occasions, as well as for funerals, that they practiced year round. No priest from So-Zen Temple had yet marred a ceremony with coughing or hoarseness.

"This house is spotless all the time, anyway," said Mrs. Izumi.

"Mommy," said Jun, "can't we stay for O-bon night dancing?"

"No—I already told you. We're going home tomorrow."

Another set of footsteps crunched by on the gravel. They heard a small child's excited voice saying, ". . . great big rice balls, sprinkled with sesame salt!"

"I don't envy those people," said Mr. Kobayashi with well-meaning heartiness. "It's going to get really hot today."

"You're absolutely right, Father-san," Mrs. Kobayashi replied. "Maybe we should have grilled eel for lunch. It's good for heat fatigue. Would everyone like that?"

"O-bon, O-bon, it's almost O-bon," Jun droned tunelessly.

"Jun-chan, stop that," said his mother. "No singing at the breakfast table."

Sarah felt bad for her aunt. In the excitement of the upcoming holiday, the Izumis' departure would create hardly a ripple.

Afterward, washing dishes at the sink, Mrs. Rexford said, "I can't believe she went out to pay calls *again*. On her last day. Who's she visiting, us or the Jehovah people?"

"It's all right," said Mrs. Kobayashi. "It doesn't matter."

"Mother, it's *not* all right."

Having finished the dishes, Mrs. Rexford began wiping the sides of the sink. Mrs. Kobayashi continued to dry, passing the dishes up to Sarah, who was kneeling on the tatami floor of the dining room. The girl stacked each item on the shelves of the floor-level cabinet. Every time she reached into its depths, she breathed in a faint, familiar aroma from her childhood: the wooden damp of freshly washed chopsticks, soy sauce within its cut-glass cruet, condiments such as seven-spice and sesame seeds.

"She won't even help around the house." Mrs. Rexford wrung out the dishtowel with an angry twist. "You know what? She hasn't changed at all. She says long prayers at the table but doesn't care if our food gets cold while we wait. She sips tea and talks about charity, and meanwhile her aging mother's slaving away down in the kitchen."

"*Nnn!*" protested Mrs. Kobayashi. " 'Aging mother'?!"

Mrs. Rexford refused to be sidetracked. "That kind of hypocrisy earns no respect from me," she said. "*None!*" Sarah was fascinated, even excited, to see her mother angry at someone other than Sarah herself.

"Don't," said Mrs. Kobayashi quietly. "You know how guilty I feel about her."

There was a long pause. "I'm sorry," Mrs. Rexford said.

Afterward Sarah and her mother went to a graveyard in the city to see the O-bon decorations. The somber headstones were transformed by *sasaki* grass, fruit and flower offerings, and branches of umbrella pine; the crumbling baby Buddhas were resplendent in new red bibs. White threads of incense wavered up by the dozen, hovering in the humid air like ghostly forms bending over their own headstones.

"We'll visit our own graveyard after your aunt and uncle leave," Mrs. Rexford told Sarah. "It won't be as crowded as this one, because it's out in the country. But it'll be lovely too in a different way."

Lately, with Mrs. Izumi away so much, Sarah and her mother had been going out alone. Sometimes they visited a little-known restaurant whose only item on the menu was dumplings from a secret family recipe handed down since the Momoyama era. Once they visited the Gion district to look at geishas. But mostly they wandered through out-of-the-way haunts from Mrs. Rexford's youth. They strolled past the tennis courts of her old high school or lingered in a neglected children's park on the bank of the Kamo River. Mrs. Rexford told stories of her youth, and Sarah listened with an attentiveness she had never shown back home.

When they arrived home, Mrs. Izumi's and Jun's shoes were already lined up in the vestibule. "Welcome home!" called Jun's treble voice from the family room. He was sitting at the table with his hands curled around a cold glass of sweet, tangy rice Calpis. "Mommy's changing her clothes," he said.

Sarah pulled down some blue-and-white floor cushions from the stack in the corner. The electric fan on the floor whirred gently, swiveling back and forth like a spectator at a tennis game.

Mrs. Rexford soon entered, followed by Mrs. Kobayashi bearing a tray with a large Calpis bottle and glasses. "The men went across the lane to see Uncle," she said. The Asaki house had already finished its gravesite duties.

When everyone except Mrs. Izumi was settled, Mrs. Koba-yashi said, "So did you have fun today, Jun-chan? Did you meet some nice people?"

Jun nodded, taking a noisy gulp of his drink.

"What did you all talk about?" Sarah asked curiously.

"Heaven."

"Oh! That sounds nice."

Jun nodded again, pleased to be the center of attention. "We're all going there," he said, as if discussing an upcoming vacation. Then, remembering something important, he turned to his grandmother with an anxious look. "Grandma," he said, "Mommy says you don't want to go to heaven with us."

"It's not that I don't want to, Jun-chan. But there are other reasons, you see."

"Grandma, they told me I should ask you to come." He widened his eyes, the whites so babyishly clear they had a bluish cast. "Because I don't want you to go to hell, Grandma."

"I'll be just fine, dear. There's no need for you to worry."

"No, Grandma. Listen!" Jun's brow puckered with the effort of trying to make her understand. "Listen! Hell is a really, really scary place. You won't like it there. I don't want you to go there, Grandma."

Mrs. Kobayashi said nothing. She looked distressed; the lines around her mouth deepened until they looked like parentheses. She reached out helplessly and stroked her grandson's crew cut.

Jun seemed baffled by his grandmother's lack of sense. "How come you don't want to go with us?" he persisted.

By this time Mrs. Izumi had returned and was standing in the doorway, watching her mother's predicament with a smug expression on her face.

Mrs. Rexford looked over at her sister, and her lips compressed. A mighty force seemed to rise up in her, charging the room like air before a storm. Sarah had never seen this brutal, avenging side of her mother; back home, she hadn't defended anyone but herself. Sarah remembered the stories of her mother as a child, protecting the weak on the playground.

"Raise your child any way you want," Mrs. Rexford said. Her voice, though quiet, had such intensity and force that Sarah wondered for one crazy moment if her mother would stand up and hit her sister the way she had when they were children. "Raise him any way you want, but don't you *dare* use him to hurt my mother."

The sisters stared at each other for several minutes.

Then, surprisingly, Mrs. Rexford's face contorted. "Mother," she said, and suddenly she was crying.

Sarah and her aunt exchanged a glance of surprise and concern.

Mrs. Kobayashi got up and went over to kneel beside her daughter, running her hand up and down her back. "There, there," she consoled, her face twisting in sympathy. "Shhh, now."

Sarah felt a terrible sickness in her stomach. This was how her mother must have felt as a child.

Mrs. Rexford turned her face away from them, tensing her shoulders in an effort to stop her sobs.

At this point, Sarah and her aunt both remembered little Jun, who was sitting rapt, his mouth open with curiosity.

"I'll take him," Sarah whispered to her aunt. She stood up and held out her hand to the boy. "Come on, Jun-chan."

"Big Sister, how come Aunt Mama's crying?"

"I'll tell you later. Let's go, now."

As she led him out of the room, she heard her aunt saying in a small, stunned voice, "Big Sister, I'm sorry."

"It's all right, both of you," said Mrs. Kobayashi's voice. "It's all right, now."

As Sarah passed through the dining room to the opposite

end of the house, she came face-to-face with her grandfather. He must have come home early in order to get some work done. Like Sarah, he was heading for the opposite end of the house, with a sketch pad in one hand and a cup of cold tea in the other. He must have heard part of the women's conversation, but it was hard to tell his reaction.

"Can we come watch you work, Grandpa?" she asked.

"Sure, sure," he said, smiling.

Still holding Jun's hand, Sarah followed her grandfather down the hallway to his accustomed spot on the garden veranda. Even in her agitation, she was aware of the pleasant coolness of varnished wood under her bare feet. The garden side of the house had an austere quality—perhaps it was the earthen walls or the formality of the dark wood—that required a certain mental adjustment, like entering a museum from a busy street.

Jun, active as always, immediately clambered down onto a pair of gardening sandals and trotted into the garden. Squatting down, he picked up an empty cicada shell. "Look, Big Sister! Come look what I found!" he cried, already forgetting about his Aunt Mama in the other room. Sarah found another pair of gardening sandals and climbed down after him.

They crouched together, searching for more cicada shells. Eventually Mrs. Izumi came out and joined her father on the veranda.

The two adults sat for a while in silence. Mr. Kobayashi lit a cigarette, and its scent wafted out into the afternoon air like a rich, comforting incense.

He cleared his throat and said, "It's no use trying to change them, you know." He spoke gruffly, for he knew he was intruding into women's territory.

"I know," Mrs. Izumi replied, a bit shortly. Again they were silent.

Sarah knew her aunt Tama had been his favorite as a child. The family albums were full of photographs of little Tama beaming at the camera, her gap-toothed smile playing up to her father behind the lens. Being his favorite should have been enough for her. But Sarah understood why it wasn't; nothing else compared with the brightness that was her grandmother and mother.

"It runs too deep," Mr. Kobayashi said, and an echo of private remembrance gave his words a strange resonance.

"I know," Mrs. Izumi said again.

Sarah glanced over at her aunt. There was an uncharacteristic stillness about her, as if her coquettish energy had finally run out.

chapter 22

In the lull of late afternoon, Sarah knelt before the vanity mirror and practiced pressing her lips together the way her mother had done. *Don't you dare use him to hurt my mother.* She felt a little thrill as her face, with its pointy Caucasian features, became transformed with authority and passion.

She was alone in the house, with nothing to do. The men had taken Jun to a baseball game. Her grandmother had gone to the open-air market at this uncharacteristically late hour to pick up something for dinner. "You mind the house," she had told Sarah, "in case any of them come back."

Mrs. Rexford and Mrs. Izumi had gone somewhere together. Wherever they were, Sarah knew, her mother would be treating her little sister with utmost tenderness. She knew this from experience; after a fight, her mother always channeled her heightened emotions into intimate revelations or optimistic lectures. Sarah never admitted it, but those winding-down sessions made her feel cleansed and very close to her mother.

She fiddled with the brushes on the vanity. Kneeling on the tatami floor, she slid open the drawer and rummaged halfheartedly through its contents: Shiseido cosmetics, bathhouse tokens, an old-fashioned wooden ear cleaner.

For the first time she missed Momoko and Yashiko. She hadn't seen much of them since the Izumis arrived. They were being kept at home, out of everyone's way, for traditional women all understood the strain of hosting an in-law.

As matriarch of the Kobayashi clan, it was in Mrs. Asaki's interest to support her sister-in-law. So the Asaki house was always open for company, as a sort of second home where the adults could go (although Mrs. Kobayashi never did) for a conversational change of pace. The children were encouraged to play there, and Jun visited often—he was fond of the snack tins under Mrs. Nishimura's table.

Sarah thought back to those innocent hours she had spent playing at the Asaki house, safe from adult issues that didn't concern her. Ever since she joined the ranks of her mother and grandmother, she had left behind that world of glowing shoji screens and warm tatami mats, the leaf-filtered light in the kitchen and crackers in tin boxes. And she couldn't go back. She realized this with a twinge of sadness; it was like that magic land in Peter Pan, out of reach to children who had grown up. Not that anything was keeping her from going. But at this point it was too much trouble: thinking ahead to keep Momoko from being jealous, seeing her aunt Masako's gentle face.

She thought of the times she had run freely to her aunt Tama as a child. "Where are you going?" she would say. "Take me with you." She couldn't imagine doing that now. It wouldn't be right somehow, after the strolls she had taken with her mother—it would feel like a betrayal.

She glanced out through the open partitions at the laundry area, with its empty poles and lines. For the first time she noticed that summer had passed its peak; the sunlight had changed from hazy white to deep gold, almost amber. The late afternoon sun angled down in dust-moted shafts, reminding Sarah of stained glass. Accustomed to California sun, she was strangely affected by this aged, regretful light of a foreign longitude.

The kitchen door rolled open. Mrs. Kobayashi called out, "*Tadaima!* I'm home!"

"Welcome back!" Sarah called. She could hear the icebox door opening and closing in the kitchen. This was comforting after the strange, sad light outside.

By the time Sarah descended into the kitchen, her grandmother was standing at the counter and unwrapping newspaper from an enormous bundle of garlic shoots. A plate of thinly sliced raw beef lay nearby, its dark red an appealing contrast to the green of the shoots. As always, her spirits lifted at the sight of food.

"Can I help, Oba-chan?" she asked. Helping with the cooking was normally her mother's job, not hers. Since only two people could work comfortably in the kitchen at one time, the women took advantage of this legitimate excuse to hold hushed, private conversations. "Put on your apron, Yo-chan," Sarah occasionally heard her grandmother say, as if her daughter were still a child. "Yo-chan, are you holding your knife right?" Both women seemed to enjoy this.

"*Maa,* that's very kind," Mrs. Kobayashi now said. "Why don't you get me the *konnyaku* and the *fu* out of the icebox. But put on an apron first."

Sarah took down one of the aprons hanging from a nail on the wooden post. She tied the strings behind her with quick, efficient jerks the way her mother always did. It was like stepping into her mother's body, and suddenly she felt shy.

Sarah's relationship with her grandmother wasn't as personal as her relationship with her mother. Since the two adults were so close, she was rarely alone with her grandmother. The girl loved her wholeheartedly but in the uncomplicated way of a child.

Emptying the gelatinous strands of *konnyaku* into a colander, she asked, "Did Mama used to cry like that when she was a girl?"

"No. Not at all. She was quiet . . . but you always sensed how protective she was, how strongly she felt things. I'm still surprised I gave birth to someone like that. Do you know the story of Benkei?"

Sarah nodded. Her mother had read her the story out of one of the books her grandmother had sent her. Benkei was a legendary vassal warrior, greatly feared for his brute strength and sword skills. He had earned a place in history for his remarkable allegiance to his lord, Yoshitsune. This allegiance had lasted right up to their deaths, when the two of them were cornered by enemies. Yoshitsune had died first, taking his own life. Benkei, mortally wounded from an arrow, stuck his sword into the ground and expired on it. From a distance his propped-up corpse seemed to be in a stance of readiness, so their foes were afraid to come any closer. "Even in death," her mother had told her, "he protected his master. Nothing's more admirable than that kind of loyalty."

"There must have been a lot of Benkei in Mama," said Sarah.

"Yes," said Mrs. Kobayashi, "and it meant the world to me." They paused while Sarah rinsed the *konnyaku* under the faucet and her grandmother chopped the chives with loud thuds of the knife against the cutting board.

"It was a hard time," Mrs. Kobayashi finally said. "I'd lost my husband. I'd lost my newborn child. It felt like everyone was against me."

"Except for Mama."

"Except for your mama. Sometimes I used to go to the park where she was playing. And I'd beckon her over and slip a little something in her pocket. Like a bit of sweet potato, or a tiny rice ball with a pinch of umeboshi in the middle. The food was still rationed back then. Things were really tight." She paused in her work, remembering.

"There just wasn't enough," she said, "for the other children."

Perhaps to atone for today's unpleasantness, or perhaps to distract the family from this evening's O-bon foot traffic, Mrs. Kobayashi served sukiyaki for dinner. It was an odd choice. Sukiyaki was a winter dish, suggestive of old-world country folk huddled around a common pot. Setting it up required some effort. A gas hose had to be retrieved from storage. One end was attached to a wall outlet, the other end to a range built into the dining table (modern Japanese tables came equipped with such accessories). On this range, a shallow pan was kept simmering throughout the meal. They dropped in raw ingredients from a nearby platter, leaning over the steam to monitor for doneness before lifting it out into their private bowls.

"It's kind of festive, cooking right at the table!" Sarah said.

"That's why people eat sukiyaki at celebrations," replied her mother.

"Let's not worry about what's seasonal," Mrs. Kobayashi said to everyone at the dinner table. "With all of you living so far away, who knows when you'll have another chance to taste your grandma's sukiyaki?" Her husband gave a comical groan, fanning himself exaggeratedly. But he was quick to tuck in. The two men cracked one egg after another into their private dipping bowls. Little Jun, energized from his outing, recounted the baseball game in loud, happy detail.

"And then he hit a home run!" he said. *"Pow!"* He was wearing a new red baseball cap jammed on top of his old blue one. The men, too, seemed stimulated by their outing. They actually carried the conversation at the dinner table for a change, pausing every so often to wipe sweat from their faces with cotton handkerchiefs. Mrs. Kobayashi refilled their glasses with cold Kirin beer.

All of this, enhanced by the spectacle of sukiyaki bubbling on the table in the middle of summer, made for an unusually merry evening. Seven pairs of chopsticks dipped in and out of the pan like birds' beaks, pulling out meat, onions, garlic shoots, tofu, *konnyaku*—all gleaming with fat and sugared soy sauce. Christianity was never mentioned. No one noticed the neighbors returning from graveyard duty, their footsteps slow and heavy on the gravel. By some magic force everyone's tension had lifted, and the entire table seemed to float on a cloud of well-being.

As they ate, Sarah surreptitiously watched her mother and aunt. But they looked relaxed, even happy. They said little, laughing appreciatively at the men, who were joking about getting heatstroke at the dinner table. Mrs. Kobayashi pretended to be insulted, and the men grinned at her with their lean, handsome faces.

Mrs. Izumi lifted the teapot and refilled her big sister's cup in an intimate gesture, accidentally spilling some drops in the process. Mrs. Rexford wiped them away with an ill-mannered swipe of her finger, glancing furtively at her mother as she did so. Mrs. Kobayashi didn't notice. Both sisters giggled under their breath like naughty children.

Sarah felt sorry for her cousins, who were missing this dinner. Thinking of them reminded her of that strange regret she had felt this afternoon, when she knew she could never rejoin their world. She wondered if her mother had also known this feeling.

It was a fleeting thought in an otherwise golden hour. But in years to come, it would sadden her to remember two grown sisters giggling behind their mother's back like the partners in crime they had never been.

Part 2

chapter 23

It was a sunny afternoon well into spring. Cherry petals, criss-crossed with bicycle tracks, littered the Ueno lanes like old snow.

Mrs. Asaki had come home from shopping downtown, dragging her tired feet through the dirty petals. She tapped on the Kobayashis' kitchen door in order to drop off a package of seasonal grass dumplings. There was no answer. Gingerly, she slid open the door—the short curtain wasn't drawn, so someone had to be home—and heard a strange keening coming from the family room. Slipping off her shoes, she stepped up onto the tatami floor.

Mrs. Kobayashi, seated at the low table, looked up with blood-shot eyes.

"Yoko's dead . . . ," she said.

"*Hehh?*" Mrs. Asaki's shopping bags, all five of them, hit the floor with a thud. She sank down beside her sister-in-law. "Yo-chan? *Dead?!?*"

"Sarah just telephoned." Sarah was eighteen and in her first year of college. "Yo-chan and her husband were driving some-where together, and . . ." Mrs. Kobayashi winced, as if talking hurt her.

"Was it an accident?"

"It was instantaneous . . . both of them."

They continued to sit, at a loss for words.

It felt eerily similar to when Shohei had died in the war. Then, too, the news had come from afar. Like his daughter he had died in a strange land, suddenly and in his prime. Mrs. Asaki remembered young Mrs. Kobayashi saying, "I just got a telegram . . . ," with that same odd catch in her voice.

Mrs. Asaki's grief for Shohei had been intense, for the siblings were close. After their mother died, she had cared for him like her own son.

Now she said helplessly, "It's a terrible thing. A terrible thing."

Mrs. Kobayashi nodded.

If only she would cry, thought Mrs. Asaki. In the old days, her sister-in-law had trusted her enough to cry in her presence. Together they had sobbed over Shohei's death. It was the first time Mrs. Asaki had felt close to her. Until then, she had secretly resented this young woman who had captured her brother's heart so easily and completely. She wasn't proud of her feelings, and luckily Mrs. Kobayashi never suspected.

Mrs. Asaki's dislike went deeper than just Shohei; she had felt it in her gut the first time they met. Her sister-to-be had worn a Western dress of sky blue, with a purple sash and a small bunch of violets pinned dashingly at the base of her V-neckline. She had an air—not arrogance so much as a kind of bright self-satisfaction, typical of girls who had been sheltered all their lives.

"What a fashionable dress," Mrs. Asaki had said.

"Oh, it's just cheap fabric . . . I'm embarrassed, seeing the beautiful kimonos here in Kyoto." It was a perfectly correct response, but her expression belied the words.

Mrs. Asaki, confined to the Kyoto area all her life, had never had met anyone like her. She had never visited a dance hall. She had never worked outside the home. Every morning she followed her husband out into the lane, where she sent him off to work with a deep formal bow. Every Monday, he discreetly slipped her an envelope containing the household allowance for the week.

For the first time, the older woman had a dim sense of what she had missed: an unfettered, independent youth in which she might have tried out her own powers. Her envy was like physical pain. This would have surprised her Ueno neighbors if they had known, for in their eyes Mrs. Asaki's beauty surpassed anything the newcomer had to offer. Locals compared her to the popular actress Sono Fujimoto, for they both had a doe-eyed beauty and drooping distinction. She was admired by men and women for her graceful way of sashaying in a kimono that made her look liquid, almost boneless.

That was a long time ago.

"I think I'll lie down for a bit," Mrs. Kobayashi said.

"*Soh. Soh,* of course. Would you like me to pull down some coverlets for you?"

"That's very kind, but there's really no need."

Reluctantly, Mrs. Asaki took her leave. She hurried home to break the news to her daughter, the shopping bags banging against her legs.

Only then did she wonder what this might do to the carefully calibrated balance between the two houses.

In the Ueno neighborhood it was often said that Mrs. Asaki and her daughter made a picture-perfect pair. "Never a cross word between them, *ne . . . ,*" they said with wistful sighs. "So respectful of each other—a pleasure to see." One housewife had remarked, "They're so polite. You'd almost think they were in-laws." Only a careful observer would have noticed a certain thinness of flavor in their relationship, not unlike their cooking.

No one was more conscious of this than Mrs. Asaki herself.

How it started, she could not have said. She was better at acting than at reflecting. At any rate the process had been so gradual as to be invisible, like the growth of a child.

There was a time, decades ago, when Masako had been like any other child, with eyes only for her mother. Those early years still glowed in Mrs. Asaki's memory for their simplicity, for their lack of the emotional ambivalence that would haunt her in later years. One of her favorite memories was the day she had taken little Masako to Umeya Shrine for her traditional Seven-Five-Three Blessing. She could still see it: a crowd of children aged seven, five, and three, dressed up in their best kimonos and tottering about in their shiny new slippers like bewildered little dolls. And among them was her precious Masako, the only girl to wear a tiny white fur wrapped around her neck over her pink silk kimono. Mrs. Asaki had sewn the entire outfit herself, sacrificing the last of her prewar finery.

And it had been worth it. "Look, Mama, I'm *pretty,*" little Masako had breathed, eyes shining as she reached up to pet the unaccustomed fur with the clumsy, reverent fingers of a five-year-old. And Mrs. Asaki had known a moment of keen joy.

That night at the Asaki house, dinner was subdued. Cooking was out of the question, so Mrs. Asaki phoned in a sushi order for both houses. The delivery boy had just come by on his bicycle, balancing on one hand a precariously high stack of lacquered wooden boxes. As usual, only the women and children sat at the low table. Mr. Nishimura didn't come home until almost 9:00 P.M., a typical hour for a salaryman in middle management.

"I doubt if she'll have any appetite," said Mrs. Asaki. "But the sushi from Hideko is her favorite. If she can swallow even one or two bites, that'll be better than nothing."

There was a murmur of sympathetic agreement around the table. With guilty expressions, Momoko and Yashiko tried to eat more languidly. But it was hard, for sushi from Hideko was a rare and delectable treat.

"Probably Grandpa Kobayashi will make sure she eats," said Momoko.

Mrs. Nishimura wasn't eating much—just three pieces of sushi on a condiment plate—but that was normal. As a proper traditional wife, she ate just enough to tide her over until it was time to eat with her husband.

"I'll go over first thing tomorrow," Mrs. Nishimura said. Her eyelids were puffy. "She needs help in the kitchen, and the parlor has to be set up with the white cloth and everything, for when Sarah-chan brings home the ashes."

She said this dispassionately but Mrs. Asaki, her antennae sharpened over the years, caught the hint of eagerness that still brought a bitter taste to her mouth. Their history was made up of such moments: her daughter irreproachable in her behavior, she jealous and wounded but unable to find fault. It was frustrating because on some deep, fundamental level, she knew she was being wronged.

"*Soh,* that's a good idea." What else could she say? With a tragedy like this, boundaries went out the window. She wished she could help Mrs. Kobayashi herself, but this was a job for a young, able-bodied woman.

"She could use the help," Mrs. Asaki continued. "At least until her real family gets here." As a subtle reminder, she put the faintest of emphasis on the word *real.*

Mrs. Nishimura busied herself realigning the condiment

cruets in the center of the table: soy sauce, chili oil, Worcestershire sauce, vinegar, sesame salt. After some time had passed she
picked up the teapot—"Some more tea, Mother?"—and refilled
her cup with a filial gesture. Something about the patient droop
of her neck gave Mrs. Asaki a pang of remorse. She knew her
daughter felt guilty, had always felt guilty, for not cleaving to
her the way she should. To compensate, she treated her adopted
mother with such kindness and politeness that it alienated them
even more. There was nothing to be done for it. The heart wants
what it wants. If circumstances were different, Mrs. Asaki
would have sympathized with her dilemma.

She drank her tea. She was grateful, shudderingly grateful,
that her own Masako was safe and alive. Even now she could
hardly wrap her mind around this awful news. What irony: her
own child was alive and Mrs. Kobayashi's wasn't. There was a
story she had heard around the neighborhood: a man had
donated a kidney to his sick brother, then died of complications
while the sick brother went·on to thrive with the kidney that
wasn't his.

Should the sick brother have given the kidney back?

No, she thought, biting into a slice of red tuna. It was rich
and fatty on the tongue, the freshly ground wasabi warming her
sinuses.

"Poor Sarah-chan, *ne* . . . ," Yashiko remarked to the table at
large.

"*Soh,* poor Sarah-chan," agreed her grandmother. "Think
how lucky you are, both of you, that your mother's right here
beside you. It's a sad thing indeed when a daughter takes her
own mother for granted."

chapter 24

There is something bracing, almost exhilarating, about a catastrophe. Like a typhoon, it sweeps away the small constraints of daily existence. It opens up the landscape to bold moves and rearrangements that would be unthinkable in normal times.

It was in such an atmosphere that they buried Shohei. The war was escalating. Shortly afterward, American bombs fell on Kobe, Mrs. Kobayashi's birth city. Vast areas of the city burned down in the fires.

Mrs. Kobayashi's family, the Sosetsus, barely escaped with their lives. Hitching a ride on a farmer's oxcart, they made their way inland to Kyoto with nothing but the clothes on their backs. "We ran through the city with our coats over our heads," Mrs. Kobayashi's mother told them. She was freshly bathed, dressed in one of her daughter's kimonos. Her air was so refined that it was hard for Mrs. Asaki to imagine her running at all. "Look," she said, "where the embers burned through." Everyone stared in awe at the scorch marks on the Sosetsus' padded silk coats.

"What about your ships . . . ?" asked Mrs. Asaki. The Sosetsus' import business was the mainstay of their wealth.

"Gone," said one of the sons bitterly. "All except two that were out at sea. Our entire fleet was in that harbor."

Mrs. Asaki was enthralled in spite of herself. An entire fleet, destroyed! Her in-laws had sunk from wealth to poverty in the blink of an eye.

"I can't get over it," she said later that night to her husband. "What a change of fortune!"

"It could have been *us,*" he said in dazed wonder.

"Yes, it could have been *us* . . ." They were silent, pondering the upheaval the war had brought. The Asakis were doing better than their neighbors, even in this time of food rationing. Mr. Asaki was a high school superintendent. His public office gave him access to black-market channels in the prefectural bribery system. And Mrs. Asaki had farming relatives out in the country, a fact that had once embarrassed her.

"They can't possibly squeeze into that little house," Mr. Asaki said.

"Of course not!" There were six of them: Mrs. Kobayashi, her mother, three siblings ranging in age from thirteen to twenty, and four-year-old Yoko. When Mrs. Kobayashi delivered her baby, there would be seven in all. "She and Yo-chan should move in with us," she said, "till that family gets back on their feet."

She ran her eyes over the too-large house—the wide expanse of tatami matting, the long empty halls. She and her husband had always hoped for children. But now, on the brink of forty, she knew it was never going to happen.

"It'll be nice," she said, "having small children here."

The months passed. Japan surrendered in 1945. Mrs. Kobayashi gave birth to a baby girl called Masako.

One day Mrs. Sosetsu paid the Asakis a formal call and

announced they were moving back to Kobe. "We have a hard road ahead," she said, "but Kobe is our home." Her bows were deep and controlled, but the emotion in her face was real. "We can never repay you for what you've done," she said. "We'll never forget your kindness."

"Not at all, not at all," said Mr. Asaki. He and his wife bowed back in unison. "We wish you all the best."

"We wish you all the best," echoed Mrs. Asaki. This house was going to be lonely without little Yoko and the baby.

That night at dinner she asked, "Will you be moving back to Kobe as well?" Her eyes shifted from her sister-in-law to the baby strapped on her back. Masako was fast asleep; her cheek, round and soft as a dumpling, lay against her mother's shoulder.

"I'd like to," said Mrs. Kobayashi wistfully. "But there aren't any jobs in Kobe for someone like me. My children and I would just be a burden." She paused. "No no, Yo-chan," she told the little girl, who was reaching across the table with her chopsticks. "If you want more radishes, say, 'Please pass the radishes.'"

"Please pass the radishes," said Yoko obediently.

"When this rationing is over," said Mr. Asaki jovially, "we'll have meat again! And fresh fish from the coast! What do you think about that!"

The child looked at him blankly, then turned her attention to the boiled radishes.

"I'll move back across the street and get an office job," said Mrs. Kobayashi.

"Yes," said Mrs. Asaki, "and I can look after the children."

Mr. Asaki, who came from a traditional Kyoto family, looked up sharply from his rice bowl. "Times may be bad," he said, "but not so bad that a woman under my care has to go out in the workplace to be ordered about by strangers. What you need to do is get remarried."

Mrs. Kobayashi looked young and trapped. Mrs. Asaki's heart went out to her. Ever since Shohei died, the two women had become close. But Mrs. Asaki's sympathy was still tinged with a smug sort of pleasure in knowing that her sister-in-law's charmed days were now behind her.

Her husband, as if thinking along these same lines, continued. "You're not a privileged young girl anymore, working for pocket money." Then, more gently, "I know something of this world. I know it isn't kind or respectful to women over a certain age who work for their food. And you'd barely support your children on what you'd make."

"He's right, dear," said Mrs. Asaki. "Servitude in some office isn't the answer."

They were silent. Baby Masako flung out an arm in sleep. Little Yoko hunched over her bowl, picking out one grain of rice at a time with her chopsticks.

"Besides," said Mr. Asaki, "how many multinational companies are there in Kyoto anyway?" He leaned back and took a swallow of tea.

"Let's think on it, *ne,* dear?" said Mrs. Asaki soothingly. "We'll put our heads together and come up with a really good plan."

It was then that the wheels in her mind began to turn.

chapter 25

The morning after Yoko's death, Mrs. Nishimura headed down the lane with a bulky bundle—food and various supplies—wrapped in a purple silk *furoshiki* cloth. Mrs. Asaki stood on the upstairs balcony, hanging up socks and handkerchiefs to dry, and watched her go. Her daughter looked up and waved with her free hand. She waved back.

Later that day Mrs. Nishimura came home with a wealth of information. She recounted it all in painstaking detail, as if to ease her mother's mind by being as transparent as possible.

There would be no funeral, she said. Since Yoko had married into the Rexford family, it was technically not the Kobayashis' place to give her one.

"I'm sure the funeral in America will be very nice," Mrs. Asaki said.

Momoko looked doubtful. "I heard they don't even have cremation ceremonies in America," she said.

"That doesn't matter. At least they *do* cremations."

By all rights Mrs. Rexford's ashes should have stayed overseas as the property of her husband's family. "But it's not as if there's a Rexford cemetery," Mrs. Nishimura explained, "or even a Rexford family." Apparently Mr. Rexford had always planned to have his ashes scattered over the ocean. While that option was fitting and right for her father, Sarah had thought it wrong, somehow, for her mother. Although Mrs. Rexford had never actually stated her burial preference, other than to say she wanted cremation, Sarah felt sure she would have wanted to be buried in her homeland.

"Well, naturally!" said Mrs. Asaki.

Over the next few days, Mrs. Nishimura took charge of the wake preparations. While Mr. and Mrs. Kobayashi dealt with the voluminous paperwork for the temple's genealogical records (they were complex and highly accurate, going back for centuries), Mrs. Nishimura transformed the parlor. She set up a long low table, covered with a ceremonial white cloth, in front of the tokonoma alcove. She sifted through family photographs to find the most recent picture of Mrs. Rexford, which she framed and decorated with a black funerary band. This would stand on the low table, along with the cremated remains when they arrived. She bought incense sticks and small prayer candles for visitors to light when they came to pay their respects. Since incense had to be burned round the clock until the burial, she stocked up on special twelve-hour sticks that would burn through the night. She placed an order to have a personalized tablet made; this would be placed in the family altar after the burial.

More news followed. Mrs. Kobayashi had made private arrangements with the temple authorities to have her daughter's ashes laid to rest in the Kobayashi family plot.

"How did she manage *that?*" cried Mrs. Asaki in astonishment. "Yo-chan married out of the family line!"

"No one knows," said Mrs. Nishimura in her soft voice. "But a bereaved and determined mother can do surprising things."

Mrs. Asaki laughed and clapped her hands. "Well, that's Yoko for you," she said. She had always been fond of her plucky niece, and she felt extraordinarily pleased that Mrs. Kobayashi had managed to pull this off. "Even in death, she doesn't follow the same rules as everyone else!"

The burial, at least, would be traditional. It would take place thirty-five days after death, following a formal sutra ceremony. In the meantime, the Kobayashis were holding a monthlong wake in their home. Sarah would arrive in two weeks and stay until the burial.

Mrs. Asaki dropped by the Kobayashi house every so often, prayer beads tucked into her clutch purse, to offer up a prayer and discreetly check on the situation. She brought little gifts: flowers for the funerary table, a monetary envelope to help pay for So-Zen Temple's sutra services during the wake, a plate of altar-worthy fruit. It wasn't that she expected to catch them at anything. After this many years, it was unlikely that anything would happen. Even if it did, they would be far too careful to risk being caught. So it was a masochistic exercise, really. But the old woman had always believed in the power of prevention.

Today she approached the Kobayashi house with an armful of peach blossoms. The air in the lane had a caressing, restless quality peculiar to spring, as if it had just floated in from distant, sun-warmed fields. She sniffed with appreciation but also a little sadness, for this year she didn't feel part of it. A new physical weariness had been dragging at her lately. The changing of seasons was always hard on the body, but this tiredness was different. In the last few weeks, she had increasingly felt the full weight of her eighty-three years.

Mr. Kobayashi was standing outside the kitchen entrance, smoking a cigarette.

"*Aaa,*" he said in greeting, bobbing his head with a friendly nod. He lifted his face and exhaled a mouthful of white smoke that floated up into the low-hanging cherry branches overhead, blending in with the white blossoms.

"Is it mist, or is it cloud," she quipped, quoting a line from the classic cherry blossom song.

Her brother chuckled and nodded his head again. They always treated each other affably, although they weren't particularly close. There was no animosity; they simply didn't have much to say to each other. Even in childhood she had been closer to Shohei, who was small enough to cling to her after their mother's death. Kenji, the middle child, was an independent boy who moved in his own orbit. It was odd, she thought, how two people so biologically close could end up being practically strangers.

"Such a thing, *ne* . . . ," Mrs. Asaki said now, referring to the death. She wondered what he was feeling. He had a soft spot for his stepdaughter, she knew. Over the years, as he gradually lost interest in his own son, he had come to admire the child his brother had left behind. He had admired Yoko's intelligence and her accomplishments, which brought him honor over the years, and he had also admired her fierce and loyal spirit, though he himself had never been on its receiving end. It reminded Mrs. Asaki of his unrequited feelings for his wife. She felt a rush of pity for her brother.

"*Aaa, aaa,*" Mr. Kobayashi agreed. He took another drag of his cigarette. Then, the conversation being over, he rolled open the kitchen door to accommodate her flower-laden hands.

Stepping inside, she smelled fish stock simmering on the stove. Mrs. Kobayashi and Mrs. Nishimura were seated together at the low dining table, sharing a quiet moment over tea. They didn't look up as the door rolled open; they must have thought it was Mr. Kobayashi. In the brief instant before they realized her presence, Mrs. Asaki had a clear view of the soft, contented look on her daughter's face.

She felt that old twist of jealous misery. She had often felt it when her daughter was in her teens, but that rarely happened now, with her daughter fully grown and the boundaries so fixed between the two houses. So this moment, coming on top of her fatigue, surprised her with its impact. She was no longer a match—she realized it now—for the sheer tenacity, the sheer life force, that was her daughter's longing. It was like a stubborn mold spore that refused to die, biding its time for years and years.

Now the two women noticed her. After a brief, awkward moment, they invited her, "Come on up! Have a seat!" with expansive, welcoming gestures.

"No, no," she laughed, stepping slowly up onto the tatami matting. "I can't stay. I'm just here to say a quick prayer for Yo-chan . . ."

"Are those peach blossoms?" said Mrs. Kobayashi. Even in her grief, she was staunchly lipsticked, powdered, and pompadoured. "*Maa,* how lovely. Are they from the Morinaga vendor?"

"*Soh,*" affirmed Mrs. Asaki. "They're nicer than cherry, I thought." As if to make sure, she held out the long branches, with their reddish-pink blooms, at arm's length. "Not quite as common."

Mrs. Nishimura got up from her floor cushion and relieved her mother of the flowers. "Thank you, let me go arrange them," she said, as if this was her home now and Mrs. Asaki was a guest.

Mrs. Asaki shuffled slowly down the hallway toward the other end of the house. She no longer had the energy to keep wrestling for her daughter's heart. It was an indulgence, and she would have to give it up. At least her daughter would be there for her in old age. She would be taken care of, no matter what.

In the parlor, the glass panels had been opened to let in the spring air. The clear light, not yet tinged by the green foliage of summer, shone through the white gauze curtains and illuminated the currents of incense circulating in the room. She knelt before the funerary table, took out her prayer beads, and lit another incense stick. Before striking the miniature gong she glanced briefly at the framed photograph, taken four years ago during the O-bon festival. Mrs. Rexford looked relaxed and maternal in a summer cotton *yukata*. It touched Mrs. Asaki to see the womanly warmth that had replaced her niece's expression of wary attention.

She was an old woman and had prayed at many wakes. The first had been her mother's, when she was still a young girl in the country. "Pray with all your might," her elders had told her. They explained how, during those thirty-five days, her mother would labor up a mountain wearing a white funerary robe and carrying a wooden staff, her forehead adorned with a small white triangle of cloth. "Dead spirits are reluctant to leave this world," they had explained. "They're afraid of the unknown so they keep looking back, they keep stalling. It's our job to help them along. Each prayer we say is like a strong hand at her back, pushing her up that mountain. So encourage her. Tell her, 'Keep going! Keep climbing, Mother! You're almost there!'"

In this spirit Mrs. Asaki now prayed for her niece, physically leaning her torso into the words of the sutra. She remembered her athletic physique, her powerful tennis backhand, and she hoped those qualities would help to ease the difficulty of the climb. This one, she thought, will pass into the next world with a minimum of fuss. She'll go bravely, in order to spare her mother.

As she prayed she felt as if she, too, was laboring up a mountain. For the first time in her healthy life, she felt unequal to the climb before her.

Mrs. Nishimura entered the parlor just as Mrs. Asaki was putting away her prayer beads. She set down a celadon bowl from which the plum branches, their bases secured on short iron spikes, rose up at random angles like the live branches of a tree.

"Well done!" said Mrs. Asaki, admiring this simple arrangement with maternal pride. Ikebana was her special talent, one she had successfully passed down to her daughter.

As if to make up for having lingered over tea earlier, Mrs. Nishimura now removed a clean cloth from her apron pocket and began polishing the varnished wood of the tokonoma. "The priest's coming in a few hours," she remarked. "And then the Izumis are coming tomorrow." She ran her cloth over the surface with the sure movements of a woman who had grown accustomed to her surroundings. Mrs. Asaki knew what a thrill it must have been for her daughter to spend time here, inhabiting the Kobayashis' intimate space for the first time since those long-ago days when she had played with the Kobayashi children.

"What time are they coming?" she asked, referring to the Izumis.

"Late afternoon, I think she said." Mrs. Nishimura sounded wistful, for this meant her time here was drawing to its end.

Mrs. Asaki now rose to her feet, and an involuntary sigh of exertion escaped her.

"Are you still feeling tired, Mother?" Mrs. Nishimura sounded concerned. "I'll bring home some of that fish broth." She was making it from scratch to build up Mrs. Kobayashi's strength, using kelp for its iodine and red snapper heads for the therapeutic benefits of their glands and cartilage. This had once been a common household practice, but in the last decade or so, Ueno housewives had switched over to dehydrated fish powder.

"No, no," protested Mrs. Asaki. "She needs every drop of

that broth. We both know she isn't well." Mrs. Kobayashi had suffered from episodes of weakened eyesight where everything skittered into flashing lights. Once, on her way home from the bathhouse, her knees had turned to jelly for no reason and she had collapsed onto the pavement.

"But you don't seem well either," Mrs. Nishimura said doubtfully.

"No, no," Mrs. Asaki insisted, "I'm perfectly fine."

"Well then, if you're absolutely sure . . ."

"I'm sure."

If only her daughter was more like Yoko, with that willful protectiveness that warmed the heart. "Nonsense, Mother," she would have insisted. "There's plenty in the pot. I'm bringing some home, and I'm going to make you drink it!"

chapter 26

But maybe Masako was born that way, thought Mrs. Asaki as she shuffled down the lane. Having grown up in the country, she knew firsthand how gestational environment affected the personalities of young animals. During her first pregnancy Mrs. Kobayashi had been happy; she had been in love. She was constantly nibbling on some newfangled treat Shohei had brought home: imported bananas, buttered popcorn, Chinese pork buns. But her second pregnancy was filled with worry and grief. She had scraped by—as they all had—on a substandard diet.

This very lane, now covered over with gravel, had once been their only source of greens. The neighbors had farmed it until it was nothing but a narrow dirt path cutting through rows of radishes and chrysanthemum shoots and spinach. In between their black-market trips to the country, the Asakis, too, had coaxed vegetables out of the meager city soil, which they fertilized with human excrement carried out discreetly in covered buckets.

The things that shape us, she thought.

Take her own life. What if she had adopted a child like

Yoko? What if she had given birth to her own children? What kind of person would she have turned out to be?

And most important: what if she had allowed her only chance for a child to slip through her fingers?

War had created an opportunity. And Mrs. Asaki had grabbed it, with a cunning aggression that surprised even herself.

Heart pounding, she had broached the first part of her plan to her sister-in-law. "Why not marry Kenji?" she said. "He's coming home from Manchuria soon. And he's always been sweet on you." It was the perfect solution. They both needed spouses; the children needed a mother and father. All their family problems could be solved at once.

This time, when she saw the trapped look on her sister-in-law's face, she felt only a faint irritation.

Mrs. Kobayashi's lips worked silently as she searched for a polite excuse. "But—his child is the same age as Masako!" she said finally. It was a good point. Second marriages, especially those with children from both sides, were best forgotten by the public. But how was this possible, with two siblings so close in age? It would be obvious they came from different parents.

"I have a solution," said Mrs. Asaki. She was starting to sweat under her kimono. She shrank with distaste from what she was about to do.

"We've always wanted a child of our own," she began. She steeled herself to meet Mrs. Kobayashi's startled eyes. The words poured out: they could adopt little Masako. The neighbors could be trusted to keep quiet. All the children could still grow up together, right on the same lane. No one would have to miss out on anything.

"After all," she concluded, "these kinds of arrangements have been going on for centuries."

The amazement in Mrs. Kobayashi's eyes changed to gradually dawning awareness. For a brief unguarded instant, her eyes narrowed with hate.

Mrs. Asaki's own shame twisted into an answering flash of anger. This young woman had an inflated sense of what life owed her. How quickly she had forgotten the staggering debt her family owed. Where was her gratitude now?

"It seems to me you're forgetting how society works," Mrs. Asaki told her coldly. "Families survive by helping one another. We were there for you and your family in your worst hour of need. Who'll be there for us, when we're old and helpless with no children to look after us?"

Mrs. Kobayashi hung her head and said nothing.

"You already have children," Mrs. Asaki said. "You're young and healthy." She was stung by the unfairness of it. "You can still have many more."

Years later, when Mrs. Asaki broke the news to Masako about her adoption, she related these events in a far more benign light. In her version, both parties came to a mutual decision in the spirit of what was best for the family. Which, if one really thought about it, was exactly what had happened.

She told her daughter on her twentieth birthday, when she turned legally of age. She took her into the parlor to formally deliver the news.

"What a pity your father's not here," she said. Mr. Asaki had died two years earlier from lung complications. "He wanted so much to see you grow up."

Masako listened carefully as her mother told the story. But she didn't seem shocked. She asked no questions. Did she already know? That possibility had never occurred to Mrs. Asaki.

Masako finally asked one question. "Was she sad," she asked, "the day she gave me up?" She said this calmly, almost conversationally. But the nakedness in her eyes gave her away.

"Why yes, of course she was!" cried Mrs. Asaki. Then she paused. Part of her wanted to keep going, because it was what her daughter needed to hear. But the other part of her was reluctant.

So she compromised. "She shed a tear, and she stroked your head one last time before she handed you over to me," she said. "Then she bowed, and I bowed, and she thanked me for agreeing to raise you as my own."

In reality there had been no tears. Mrs. Kobayashi had seemed vacant, almost distracted; her complexion had a yellowish cast and there were dark circles under her eyes. And there was no ceremonial handing over of the child. When Mrs. Kobayashi took formal leave of the Asaki house, baby Masako had been sound asleep upstairs. While the two women exchanged formal bows and polite phrases in the outer guest vestibule, little Yoko stood quietly by, her shoes on and ready to go. She made no fuss, she did not ask after her little sister, she did not clutch on to the hanging sleeve of her mother's kimono. She seemed to sense that her mother was no longer strong enough to deal with childish demands. When Mrs. Kobayashi finally ushered her down the garden path toward the outer gate, the little girl had looked back with an expression of such gravity, such adult sentience, that Mrs. Asaki had shivered.

chapter 27

Back in her own house, Mrs. Asaki padded down the long hall toward the kitchen. It was time to make advance preparations for dinner.

She hadn't cooked in years. She had given it up when her daughter became the lady of the house. It was good to be back in charge again while her daughter was away.

But *ara,* what was this unwelcome intrusion? Mr. Nishimura was vacuuming the tatami floor of the informal dining area, wearing a thin undershirt and jogging pants. He did this every Sunday on his day off—Mrs. Asaki always heard the vacuum cleaner from the other side of the house—but she'd never realized how much he spread himself around in the process. The low table, pushed off to the side, was piled with his Sunday newspapers. Two empty bottles of beer stood among them. His jogging jacket lay flung into a corner of the room, and the radio had been switched to some unfamiliar station playing *enka,* those heartfelt torch songs heard in traditional drinking houses.

At his mother-in-law's entrance, Mr. Nishimura's expansive air shrank. This was *her* house, after all.

"*Maa maa,* so busy at work! Much obliged," laughed Mrs. Asaki as she passed through the dining area into the kitchen. She cast a pointed glance at all the clutter on the low table.

Mr. Nishimura grinned at her, but as soon as he was done vacuuming he gathered up his newspapers and beer bottles and jacket, then slipped off to another part of the house.

He was a good man. Mrs. Asaki had picked him out herself, with the help of a matchmaker. She had chosen astutely and well. He was a good companion for her daughter, and in all these years he had not disappointed. But she was still vigilant— on warm nights she left the upstairs glass panels slightly open, so she could hear his footsteps on the gravel and check them against the clock beside her futon.

He wasn't the kind of man she would have chosen for herself. Years ago, his coworkers had gone on strike because management had been grossly unfair. Mr. Nishimura, afraid of losing his job, hadn't joined them. When his coworkers were fired, he received a promotion for his loyalty. Mrs. Asaki had been filled with quiet contempt. Her own husband would have never been so cowardly. But as a mother, she was glad that Masako and the girls would be safe.

The Kobayashi daughters had not chosen arranged marriages. This was hardly surprising, given their mother's history. Take Yoko and her American husband—but there was no point in comparing Yoko to anyone; she was always the exception. Tama, on the other hand, had been coaxed by her father into some introductory meetings.

Back around that time, Mrs. Asaki had visited the Kobayashi house and found Tama alone, looking over some résumés that a matchmaker had dropped off. Little Sarah was hovering over her aunt's shoulder, even though she was too young to read.

"You're breathing on my neck," Tama said irritably. She was in a bad mood. Her college sweetheart, Masahiro Izumi, had not yet proposed.

She eventually relented, allowing the little girl to hold two photographs that had come with the résumé. It was a running joke that parents always reached for the résumé first—which listed a candidate's education, current employment, parents' affiliations, and hobbies—whereas young people reached for the photographs.

"*Maa,* pictures! What fun! Let's see!" Mrs. Asaki dropped onto her knees beside the child, who obligingly held out the photographs so they could both share. In one photo, an earnest-looking young man stood in a formal suit; in another, he stood on a riverbank and grinned as he held up a fish on a line. Wordlessly, Tama handed over the accompanying résumé. Mrs. Asaki scrutinized it.

"He seems like a fine candidate," she told her niece. "Well educated, hardworking, with a good future."

"Yes," said Tama brightly. "And in his free time, he enjoys fishing!" Her voice held such amused contempt that the little girl glanced up with interest.

Mrs. Asaki felt the sharp sting of insult. Her own daughter had married a man like this—Mr. Nishimura's résumé was almost interchangeable with the one she held in her hands. But she could secretly relate to her niece; she would have felt the same way in her position. For Mrs. Asaki, too, knew what it was to possess beauty and charm, to have the arrogance that came from having options.

Introductory meetings had been arranged—the tense, stilted kind with both sets of parents present. A few weeks later, Mrs. Rexford dropped by with an update.

"She sabotaged it," she said, eyes dancing. "What a show!

She talked nonstop about herself, she kept interrupting . . ." She gave a ringing laugh of approval. "I told her, 'Tama-chan, it's not such a stretch from your usual behavior!'"

"*Ara!*" said Mrs. Asaki.

"Our father's giving up out of sheer embarrassment."

"That's a shameful way to act," said Mrs. Asaki. "Wasting everybody's time."

"Well, the whole business is downright medieval," Mrs. Rexford retorted. "Marriage isn't a job opening. It's pathetic, having to get interviewed like some kind of applicant."

Mrs. Asaki felt an echo of her long-ago dislike for Mrs. Kobayashi and her port-city airs.

Luckily, Masako hadn't rebelled like her cousins. But then her situation was different. She had attended an all-girls' college; it was what her father wanted. And college aside, she lacked that certain wayward sparkle with which her cousins had drawn young men their way.

No, Masako had never caused her parents the least bit of trouble, even as a child. For this Mrs. Asaki was grateful, even smug. But she had felt a dim sort of worry when she saw how the neighborhood children, especially Yoko, shielded her from the full brunt of their rough games.

As the years passed, Mrs. Asaki had taken a special interest in Sarah's upbringing, for she, too, was an only child. On the surface her grand-niece seemed quiet and well mannered, just as Masako had been. But in Sarah's eyes there was nothing shuttered; Mrs. Asaki suspected she could transition quickly into anger or grief. And why not? There would be no consequences if she did. The Rexfords were self-contained, living far away from family or anyone who cared. Mrs. Asaki yearned for their simple life.

Sometimes she dared to wonder if Masako's docility came from being adopted. They had tried so hard to give her a carefree childhood. But if there had been a leak . . . if her daughter had carried that burden all those years and never come to her . . . But no, that possibility didn't bear thinking about.

chapter 28

Across the lane at the Kobayashi house, Mrs. Nishimura was leaving for the day.

She stepped down from the tatami floor into the kitchen vestibule. Mrs. Kobayashi followed her down to see her out. Standing close together on the small square of cement, they slid their feet into comfortable household flats.

The older woman reached out and, in a spontaneous gesture of warmth, gripped her daughter's hands in both of her own. "Thank you, Ma-chan," she said. "Thank you for everything. I don't know what I would have done without you."

Pleased and shy, Mrs. Nishimura squeezed silently back.

She had a sudden memory of standing in this very same spot with her sister Yoko. She was thirteen years old. There had been a birthday party for little Tama, and the children had feasted on fried chicken. This unusual dish, resurrected from Mrs. Kobayashi's Kobe days, had excited the young guests. Frilled drumsticks clutched in bare hands, they laughed and joked with boisterous abandon.

Masako, crowded around the low table with the others, felt something within her loosen and spread out in this easy warmth.

It had been several months since she last visited this house. Now that the children were older, they were busy with their own friends, their own activities at school. And since learning of her own adoption—she had known for almost a year—Masako had become self-conscious about visiting. Today, sandwiched in between Yoko and Teinosuke, she basked in this cozy intimacy that could have been hers. She pretended she was one of them— she pretended so hard she could almost feel herself changing into the bright, carefree sort of girl she might have been if she lived here with her real family.

She had gazed at Mrs. Kobayashi presiding at the table, smiling and ladling hot rice into the children's bowls with soft, youthful hands that were so different from the veined, aging hands of her adopted mother. She felt a great yearning to touch one of those hands, to say the word *mother*. What the result of such an action would be, the girl couldn't imagine. She thought it would be like puncturing the sac of an egg yolk, releasing something slow and rich and golden and momentous that would flow over her the same way it flowed over Yoko. But she didn't yet feel entitled to this or resentful about its loss. She just felt a vague, primal shame about being given away.

After the neighborhood children had left through the formal guest entrance, Masako put on her shoes in the kitchen vestibule. Yoko did too; she had changed into her tennis clothes and was going out to practice. The two girls stood together on the small square of cement, leaning over to pull up the backs of their sneakers.

Masako wasn't ready to return to her big, quiet house. There was a hollowness in her that threatened to widen out into terrible infinity. In a sort of controlled panic she turned to Yoko.

"I want to call her Mother," she said. "Just once." It was the first time she had mentioned it since their talk a year ago.

Her big sister looked at her with such sympathy and under-standing that something in Masako loosened even further, and she felt herself on the verge of tears.

"Just wait a little longer, *ne?*" Yoko said. "For everyone's sake. You have to be strong. Hold on, just a little bit longer."

Now, decades later, Mrs. Nishimura gripped her mother's hands and felt that old childhood desire. But it was no longer the terrifying thing it had once been. The years had rendered it down to something poignant and small, worn thin by day-to-day life.

For the first time, she decided to make an overture. And here was a rare chance, as perfect and fragile and unexpected as a glis-tening soap bubble—a chance that, deep down, she had always hoped would come. She felt her heart starting to pound. It would do no harm . . . just one small, intimate remark that would be answered in kind, creating a lovely moment that would resonate afterward. Their lives would not change. She knew this. They were grown women with a firm grip on reality and duty.

But the moment of opportunity had passed. Mrs. Kobayashi withdrew her hands and turned away to open the kitchen door. Mrs. Nishimura felt a sag of relief, followed by disappointment. Such a chance might never come again.

"You and I," she said quickly to her mother's back, "we're the only ones left . . ." It was a reference to the original family unit consisting of Shohei, her mother, Yoko, and herself.

The kitchen door, rattling noisily in its groove, drowned out her soft voice. Mrs. Kobayashi caught something about being left behind, but she assumed Mrs. Nishimura meant the fish broth cooling on the stove. So she stepped outside onto the stone step and exclaimed, "*Maa*, how warm it's gotten lately! If this keeps up, it's going to be fine weather for Yo-chan's burial."

She stood on the gravel and saw her daughter off, waving a fond good-bye as she turned the corner.

If the timing had only been right, she would have responded with genuine emotion. It had always saddened her that her daughter never mentioned the adoption. "But my hands are tied," she had lamented to Mrs. Rexford. "If she came to me, I'd jump at the chance. But she never has."

"Maybe she's waiting for *you*," Mrs. Rexford suggested.

"Don't be silly. She knows it's not my place. No, she's just closed off to me. All I get is that outside face. Sometimes I wonder if deep down, she hates me."

Mrs. Rexford had shaken her head, baffled. No one had much insight into Mrs. Nishimura's inner life.

Mrs. Asaki was upstairs, sitting on a floor cushion and folding laundry, when she heard her daughter come home. There was a faint clatter down in the kitchen and soon Mrs. Nishimura came upstairs with the usual tray of tea and rice crackers to tide her over until dinnertime.

"These dried so fast today," Mrs. Asaki remarked, gesturing to the small pile on the tatami mat that she had just unpinned from the balcony clothesline.

"*Soh ne,*" Mrs. Nishimura agreed, setting down the tray on the low table. Her tone held an unaccustomed sharpness that alerted Mrs. Asaki to her next words. "Mother," she said, "you forgot to turn off the gas on the stovetop. Again."

Ara! Had she? Mrs. Asaki, who prided herself on her sharp, youthful mind, felt a stab of fear, then shame. It was immediately followed by anger that her daughter had felt the need to point it out. What difference did it make? This was her last day in the kitchen anyway.

"Well," she replied in a humble tone that didn't quite hide her petulance, "it's probably best for an old woman like me to stay out of the way."

Mrs. Nishimura said nothing. She moved across the room and passed beyond the open glass panels to the balcony. She stood there, resting her forearms on the wooden rail and gazing out onto the view.

Mrs. Asaki went back to folding the laundry, but her eyes stayed on her daughter. She was leaning her weight onto her forearms, hunching forward like a child so her shoulder blades jutted out under the thin cardigan. From behind, her slight figure could almost pass for that of the teenager she had once been. In years past, Mrs. Asaki had watched her leaning against the railing in this same forlorn pose.

It was early evening now, and somewhere out in the lanes a tofu vendor was making pre-dinner rounds. His horn made a plaintive, mournful tune—*toooofuuu . . . tofu-tofuuu*—that signaled the day's end. But it was still light, for the days were growing longer. The air still had that burgeoning quality Mrs. Asaki had noticed earlier, that sense of currents floating in from distant, sun-warmed places. It seemed to release yearnings all across the narrow lanes until they rose up, hovering like kites, ready to swell at the slightest lift of the breeze. The pet finches, in their bamboo cages hung from the balcony eaves, sensed this too and were restless, ruffling their feathers and hopping from perch to perch.

Whatever was going on with Masako, it was probably to be expected. All that time spent at the Kobayashi house, her daily routine turned completely on its head; who knew what feelings had been stirred up as a result? And now it was over, for the Izumis were arriving tomorrow and then Sarah would come, along with all sorts of visitors paying condolence calls. The Kobayashi house would become busy and insular, the Asaki household would once again recede to the fringes, and life would go back to normal.

Mrs. Asaki felt sorry for her daughter. She understood—better than anyone—how it felt to be near someone day in and day out, knowing that person was missing someone else. How ironic that they had this in common.

But another part of her, the part that was a woman and not a mother, was unmoved. *What about me?* she thought. *It's no more than what's happened to me.* And all because of her daughter's misguided fantasies. Adoption or no adoption, Mrs. Kobayashi would never have had eyes for anyone but her firstborn. Look at Tama and Teinosuke: they were raised in the Kobayashi house, but what good did it do them? They were nothing more than second-best. Masako, on the other hand, had a mother all to herself. She was the center of attention; she had wanted for nothing. If not for her stubbornness, the two of them might have had what Mrs. Kobayashi and Yoko had.

Mrs. Asaki rose to her feet. She carried the pile of folded laundry over to the black lacquered *tansu* chest, which had been part of her wedding trousseau. She pulled open the drawers, the round iron handles clanking against the wood. From her standing position, she looked past her daughter to the view beyond. In this transient light the tiled roofs had solidified to dark, one-dimensional squares; the television antennae and the power lines had melted away until it was once again the neighborhood of prewar days, with cherry blossoms glowing dimly in the dusk and wisteria draping the wooden fences.

It's no more than what's happened to me, she repeated to herself. She felt an angry kind of sorrow—not so much at her daughter, but at the vagaries of a life that had molded her into someone so possessive, so dependent on this one child. When Mrs. Asaki was young she had never chased anyone. People had sought *her.*

She had some special quality, but what it consisted of, she could not have said. Maybe it wasn't the sort of thing that translated well into old age. At any rate, the last of it had run out several years ago, as her granddaughters outgrew their granny and turned into teens with better things to do. But she still remembered, deep in her viscera, how it had felt to be that person: all these years had not dulled the loss of the woman she had been.

Padding back to the low table, she sat down to her tea. She reached out for the long string hanging from the ceiling lamp. It hung down almost to the floor—a convenient length for small children and for those seated on floor cushions. Grasping the red silk tassel, she tugged. The room filled with a cozy, rice-papered glow, and she felt a sudden desire to reach out to her daughter, for out on the balcony it was growing dark. "I know how it feels," she wanted to say. She longed to convey some great tenderness with those words, some solidarity that only a fellow survivor could give. For a moment, infected by the spring breeze, her heart rose with the possibility.

But then sanity returned, and with it the long memory of quiet hurts that now came crowding up into her chest. How much rejection could one allow? She was old. She was tired.

So Mrs. Asaki did nothing.

She wondered if she would have felt differently if Masako was her biological child.

When feelings run out, when relationships die, it's often a long time coming. The end comes in quiet lulls and falls away, like a leaf from a branch. Mrs. Nishimura would never know what had changed in her mother's heart, for their gentle interactions would go on unaffected for years.

Standing at the balcony rail, lost in her own thoughts, Mrs. Nishimura was hardly aware of the electric light switching on behind her.

chapter 29

A few days later, Mrs. Izumi came visiting alone. "Auntie!" she greeted Mrs. Asaki, who was out in the front garden, feeding the turtles in the mossy stone vats. "I've come for a girls' chat." She held out a package of roasted miso dumplings, still hot from a local tearoom and smelling of wood smoke.

"What a treat!" said Mrs. Asaki. "Go right on up. Ma-chan'll make us some tea."

The Izumis were here for only a few days. They would not be coming back for the burial. For one thing, it was a non-Christian ceremony; for another, the Izumis lived too far away to make a second trip. They had left Tokyo several years ago, abandoning the main island altogether and relocating to the southernmost tip of the country. Mrs. Asaki knew very little about that region, only that it was tropical and people there had extremely brown skin.

She followed Mrs. Izumi into the informal dining area. After four years, it still offended her that her niece wouldn't stop at the parlor to pay respects to Mr. Asaki in the family altar. It just wasn't right. Her late husband had been especially kind to the Kobayashi children. When they were small, he would take them to a special restaurant on Christmas Eve for American hotcakes and syrup. Didn't Tama remember? If Mrs. Asaki were younger she would have made some acidic remark. But in her old age, she was increasingly careful to ingratiate herself with her family. So she merely sang out, like the agreeable granny that she was, "*Maa!* Those dumplings smell wonderful!"

With the kettle on the stove, the three women sat down at the low table.

Mrs. Nishimura emptied the contents of the package onto a large plate. "Tama-chan, you've brought so much!" she said. "We can't possibly eat this all. I'll save some for the children." She transferred a couple of skewers onto a smaller plate and slipped away behind her sister's back—not to the kitchen, but out into the hall. Mrs. Asaki knew she was headed for the family altar, where she would deftly, discreetly offer the dumplings on her sister's behalf. She felt a warm rush of gratitude.

She felt sorry for Mrs. Kobayashi, whose daughter refused to pray at her own sister's funerary table. The Izumis had their own brand of prayer, which was invisible to others as it required neither chanting nor kneeling nor going anywhere near the funerary table.

But as the tea progressed, Mrs. Izumi didn't mention religion at all. Her new, quiet maturity was more disturbing than her earlier fervor. Back then, in her childlike way, she had needed their attention. Now this gracious "outside" face reminded Mrs. Asaki of her own daughter.

"You know, after I heard the news," Mrs. Izumi said, "that very same night, a snake appeared in my dream."

"*Maa,* how auspicious!" said Mrs. Asaki with warm approval. "Snakes bring good luck." Her late husband had carried a snakeskin wallet for many years, as a traditional way of attracting wealth and good fortune.

"Big Sister was born in the year of the snake," added Mrs. Nishimura.

Mrs. Izumi nodded. "It's surely a sign," she said, "that she's doing well on the other side."

The women fell silent, nodding at the truth of this statement.

Mrs. Izumi and Mrs. Nishimura were not particularly close. Even as children, they were too far apart in age, in temperament, in social interests. All they had in common was their big sister.

Under their placid expressions Mrs. Asaki sensed deep emotional currents, revealing themselves in a twist of the mouth or a look in the eye. Their relationships with their big sister had been complex and personal—perhaps even painful?—and they would hold it close to their chests.

She steered the conversation toward happier ground. "When Yo-chan was young, she simply refused to wear ribbons," she told them. "She was a stubborn one. Quiet, but stubborn." The women laughed indulgently as she trotted out reminiscences from Mrs. Rexford's childhood.

"It was a simpler time," said Mrs. Izumi.

Mrs. Asaki remembered those days as anything but simple. But each generation, she knew, viewed its childhood with blind nostalgia.

The last of their laughter faded into the midday stillness of the house. They sipped their tea.

"How's life in your new place?" Mrs. Nishimura asked.

"It's nice out in the country. There's a big community of church members. It's so cheap to live there, we can work part-time."

"How nice. We're envious."

"There are orchards too. Last year, I pickled my own umeboshi."

"You?! Pickling?!" cried Mrs. Asaki in astonishment.

"Did you do it from scratch?" Mrs. Nishimura wanted to know.

"Yes, I did," said her sister proudly. Then her expression turned sheepish. "But I messed up the vinegar or something," she confessed, and giggled. "They turned out so hard and bitter, nobody would eat them."

Now *that's* the Tama we used to know, thought Mrs. Asaki. It saddened her that these flashes would appear less and less often, then one day fade out altogether.

On the morning after Sarah's arrival, Mrs. Asaki and her daughter visited the Kobayashi house to pay respects to Mrs. Rexford's ashes. The house was crowded and noisy, for the Izumis were still there. Stepping up onto the tatami floor, Mrs. Asaki felt rather festive.

"The girls will be coming by after school," she announced. "And their father, after work."

"Granny!" cried Sarah. "Auntie Masako!" She was eighteen now. Her body reminded Mrs. Asaki of Mrs. Kobayashi's when she had been young. It was in the slope of the shoulders, the straight set of her neck . . . When Sarah walked away to fetch some extra floor cushions, the old woman recognized the outline of her sister-in-law's long waist.

"She's grown!" she whispered to Mrs. Kobayashi.

"Yes. But she's still the same little girl she always was," Mrs. Kobayashi whispered back.

"She seems to be doing well." The loss did not show on Sarah's face as starkly as it did on her grandmother's. Young people were resilient. But in the days to come, Mrs. Asaki would notice that sometimes, when the girl thought no one was looking, her eyes would take on the same unfocused glaze that Mrs. Kobayashi's did.

"She has good restraint," she added. She expected nothing less from a member of her own family, but one never knew with Americans.

It was time to move to the parlor. "Let's welcome your mother home," said Mrs. Asaki. She and Mrs. Kobayashi, fellow matriarchs, led the way into the incense-clouded parlor. The others trooped in after them, filling up the small room.

Mrs. Asaki was taken aback by the urn on the funerary table. She was expecting the usual: a ceramic container small enough to cup in the palm of her hand. But this was a wooden box of some sort—varnished, lacquered, handsome enough in its own way, but big enough to hold a potted plant.

"Americans don't pick out the symbolic bones," Sarah explained. "They keep all the ashes. That's why it's so big."

"*Ara maa,*" Mrs. Nishimura said weakly.

"Granny, look! Auntie, look!" Eight-year-old Jun pointed to a red Japanese passport lying on the table among the flowers and fruits. "Big Sister had this taped right on the side of the box! Just like they pin notes on little kids in kindergarten." He was clearly tickled by this comparison.

"I thought there'd be trouble getting her through customs," Sarah said. "But the man at the airport was really, really nice about it."

Everyone stood staring at the sturdy, outsized box.

"That's a lot of ashes!" said Mr. Kobayashi from the back of the room.

Mrs. Nishimura turned to Mrs. Kobayashi. "Would you prefer to have the bones picked out properly? And placed in a more . . . ehh, *fitting* receptacle?"

"No, no." Mrs. Kobayashi reached out and touched the box,

as if to reassure her daughter within. "I don't want her disturbed any further."

"Maybe the Americans are right," Mrs. Nishimura said softly. "The more we have of her, the better."

Mrs. Asaki kept staring at the box, packed full of ashes by the gram. It was a stark reminder of the physicality of death. Her own time was drawing near.

"It's somehow fitting, don't you think?" said Mrs. Izumi. "It's just like Big Sister."

"*Soh,*" said Mrs. Nishimura. "She had such a presence, bigger and bolder than anyone else . . ." She laughed, her voice catching a little as she did so, and everyone laughed along with her. But the break in her voice had caught them unawares, and Mr. Kobayashi was heard to clear his throat.

chapter 30

M̲rs. Rexford's burial was a quiet affair, attended by only the two households.

"Let's not bother telling anyone," Mrs. Kobayashi said. "I simply haven't the strength to deal with them all." Normally such an attitude would have been self-indulgent and improper, but the circumstances were so unorthodox that it felt natural— and quite freeing—to make up rules as they went along. "Yo-chan wasn't one for convention anyway," she added.

"Proximity," quoted Mrs. Asaki, "is the truest intimacy of all."

They caught the JR—the Japan Railways train—at Nijo Station, next to Nijo Castle. It was the second stop on the route, so the platform was crowded. Mrs. Asaki and Mrs. Kobayashi, veterans of public transportation, scurried to the "silver seats" reserved for the elderly. The rest of the party, including Mr. Kobayashi, who was too proud to take advantage of his age, fended for themselves. They were soon lost to view in the crush of bodies swaying from overhead hand straps.

As the train wound its leisurely way through the city, dis-charging smartly dressed professionals along the way, the seats emptied and everyone could sit down. The stops grew increasingly obscure as the city limit gave way to open fields, bright yellow with rape flowers. The passengers changed as well: plainly dressed folk on errands, students in navy uniforms commuting to school. The atmosphere in the train was peaceful now, almost timeless, like the wartime trains they used to take out to the country for black-market rations.

Now, as then, Mrs. Asaki sat by the window. She gazed out at the open fields and rice paddies, at the encroaching foothills. The decades had left their mark. There were more roads now, more houses dotting the landscape—newer, smaller tract houses such as one saw in certain parts of the city. Every so often they passed an old-style farmhouse, the kind she remembered from her childhood: ponderous structures with steeply pitched, top-heavy roofs in the tradition of temple architecture.

"Have you noticed," said Mrs. Kobayashi, "that Sarah's hand—the place where her thumb attaches—is the spitting image of her mother's?"

"Is that so?" said Mrs. Asaki sympathetically.

"Take a look when you get a chance. It's uncanny."

Mrs. Asaki was reminded of the years after Shohei's death, when her sister-in-law would point out such traits in little Yoko: a certain crook of the arm, the curve of a brow. She hoped this meant Sarah would be replacing her mother in Mrs. Kobayashi's heart. She was the natural choice, the one least disruptive to the status quo. But the girl lived so far away, and she was of the wrong generation. Who knew what unpredictable turns a mother's heart might take?

They took two separate taxis to the temple. Mrs. Asaki sat by the window, her fatigue temporarily forgotten, clutching the sill with both hands and glancing about with eager eyes. She hadn't been here in decades, not since the black-market days. There were no relatives left; they had died or scattered into oblivion.

"*That* wasn't there before!" she exclaimed as they passed a snack shop on the corner. Her fellow passengers did not respond. Mrs. Nishimura was unfamiliar with the area, having grown up tending the Asaki gravesite in the city. Momoko and Yashiko were too young to care.

They rode on in silence. "I wonder if Sato-san's place is still there . . . ," she said. Mr. Sato was the farmer who had bartered rice in exchange for their silks and family jewelry. After the transactions were completed, he always invited the Asakis to stay for lunch. His wife served sushi made with freshly killed raw chicken from their farm, for ocean fish was scarce in wartime. Squeamish at first, they eventually warmed to it and, in later years, even referred to it fondly.

Mrs. Asaki wished she had ridden in the same taxi as the Kobayashis. She and Mrs. Kobayashi could have reminisced together. *We're the only ones left,* she thought.

"This place has completely changed!" she mourned.

"What did you expect, Grandma?" said Momoko. "This is the twentieth century."

"Momoko," admonished her mother in a low voice.

Mrs. Asaki's excitement deflated before the girl's withering tone. Over the last few years, a subtle change had come over Momoko. Her insolence had an underground quality; it never rose cleanly to the surface but would insinuate itself into some innocent remark. Her own Masako had never been this way, even in adolescence. Was it a modern thing? Sometimes Mrs. Asaki suspected it was indeed personal, that it stemmed from some deep-seated resentment she was at a loss to account for. She was baffled. In traditional families it was usually the parent who bore the brunt of such behavior.

The sting of it stayed with her while they greeted the priest and seated themselves for the formal ceremony.

Eventually, calmed by the priest's sonorous drone, she turned her attention to her surroundings. A wall of shoji doors, drawn shut against the morning sun, glowed with a fierce yellow light that lit up the wide room, with its empty expanse of tatami matting meant for funerary parties larger than their own. A mahogany altar, decked out in ornate gold-and-brown brocade, held an assortment of bronze lotus blossoms rising up toward the ceiling on tall stems. Shielded from the sun's glare, the bronze glowed softly as if radiating light from within.

In the row directly ahead, Sarah and her grandparents sat quietly on black floor cushions. Mrs. Asaki noted the odd way Sarah sat: on folded legs so her backside rested directly on her heels, placing pressure on the tops of her feet. This was no way to sit for extended periods. Mrs. Asaki sat pigeon-footed so that the outsides of her feet, not the tops, bore directly on the mats. She had faint calluses on the sides of her feet from decades of contact with the floor. Modern children—those raised in Western-style houses—could no longer sit for hours as their predecessors had. But that was in the newer districts; in the Ueno neighborhood, Sarah was still the only exception. Mrs. Asaki remembered watching with surprise and disapproval as the little girl hauled herself away from the table after an unusually long sitting session, dragging her paralyzed legs behind her like a seal and gasping, "Pins and needles . . . ," between bursts of uncontrollable laughter. She hoped there would be none of that today.

Her worries were unfounded. Partway through the ceremony, when it was time for each person to rise, approach the altar, and transfer a pinch of incense from a small bowl to a large smoldering urn, Sarah acquitted herself well. She bowed nicely, with an elegance of line unexpected in a foreigner. That's Yo-chan's doing, Mrs. Asaki thought, and she felt a surge of affection for this girl who would stand between Masako and her biological mother.

Finally the priest brought out an antiquated brush-writing set and began grinding ink and water on the stone. With a flourish of calligraphy, he wrote Mrs. Rexford's name on a long wooden tablet. Bowing deeply, he presented it with both hands to Mr. Kobayashi, who bowed back and received it with both hands.

"Are you sure," the priest asked afterward, "that you wouldn't like a cup of tea before you go?"

No, no, they laughed, bowing copiously and talking all at once, thank you so much, but we couldn't possibly rest till this is done! They left the temple and headed down a short road toward the gravesite, with Mr. Kobayashi carrying the long, narrow tablet before him like an upright spear.

The road skirted the edge of a rice paddy. The day was growing warm. A faint mist rose up from the young green shoots, and with it a long-lost smell from Mrs. Asaki's childhood, that brackish tang of paddy water. It brought back the past so strongly that her breath caught in her throat. She turned to her brother, wanting to share this moment, but she realized it was nothing new for him; he came here every year to tend these graves.

A small boy was crouching on the embankment of the paddy with a plastic pail at his side, peering into the murky water in search of frog eggs. Or would it be tadpoles at this stage in the season? Mrs. Asaki couldn't remember.

"Remember when you used to do that?" she asked, turning to her brother. "I can see it so clear in my mind—you and

Shohei coming home at sunset, with ropes of frog eggs slung over your shoulders."

Mr. Kobayashi's handsome face creased into a warm grin. "That's right," he said. "What fun that was!"

"When we lived in the Kyoto hills," said Sarah, "Mama would show me how to find them."

"We kept ours in that big stone vat," said Yashiko, "before we got the turtle. Remember, Big Sister?"

Momoko nodded. "When the tadpoles grew legs, they all hopped out."

They slowed their steps, gazing nostalgically at this tableau of Japanese childhood. Unnerved by their scrutiny, the little boy rose to his feet and slunk away, clutching his plastic pail.

The Kobayashi plot lay on a small rise, low enough for everyone to climb without too much trouble. It tired Mrs. Asaki a great deal, but she squared her shoulders and said nothing. She wondered if Mr. and Mrs. Kobayashi were feeling the physical strain as well. Single file, they climbed several meters up the short dirt trail. Lush foliage—vines and grasses and edible ferns—fringed their path in wild profusion, catching at their legs with damp, soft tendrils.

There were roughly fifteen Kobayashi gravestones, rising up haphazardly from the sea of vegetation. The oldest markers—small and moss-stained and porous—stood farther up the hill, their engravings long since rained away. They were so old the wooden tablets in the metal braces had rotted away and no one knew who the individuals had been. Nonetheless, they were family. Mrs. Nishimura, the most able-bodied adult, climbed up toward them, picking her way carefully among the damp foliage. She had brought a bag of bean cakes in her purse, and she placed one at each gravestone. Soon the faint smell of incense came drifting down to the others.

"Is this one of ours?" Mrs. Nishimura occasionally called down to Mrs. Kobayashi, for these family plots had no clear dividing lines.

When she came down to join the others, Mr. Kobayashi was kneeling down before the biggest and newest of the gravestones. Gripping a small garden trowel in one hand, he struggled to wedge it under the flat stone slab lying in front of the gravestone.

"Can you do it, Father-san?" said Mrs. Kobayashi worriedly. "Is it safe for your back?"

"May I help, sir?" asked Mr. Nishimura, starting to step forward.

"I'm fine," the old man replied, a little brusque at these affronts to his masculinity.

"Of course he's fine," Mrs. Asaki told the others. "Let the man do his work."

He lifted one end of the stone slab. With both hands, he dragged it to the side. And there it was—a small, granite-lined space that had lain undisturbed these fifty years. Lined up in one corner were three small porcelain urns bearing old-fashioned designs of their time. Mrs. Asaki's mother was on the far left, then her father, then her brother Shohei.

Everyone was silent: the children, for whom burial was a new experience; Mrs. Nishimura, beholding her biological father's urn for the first time; the older generation, whose memories stretched far back in time.

Mrs. Asaki was transported to when she had first stood here as a child, peering down into this small space. It was as if nothing of consequence had changed in the interim; she had come back full circle to this green-filtered light, this same sharp *pyoo-pyoo* of woodland birds. It was like blinking once, then finding three urns instead of one.

"*Hai,*" said Mr. Kobayashi, still in kneeling position, and reached out his hand for the box. His wife gripped it one last time, then handed it over.

It stuck in the opening. Mr. Kobayashi turned the box sideways, but it stuck again. No one spoke, no one breathed—but after a firm push it went in, no worse for wear except for a long scratch down the side.

Mrs. Kobayashi gave an audible gasp of relief. Everyone else, just as relieved, began laughing weakly.

"It sure was big," Sarah said after the stone slab was back in place.

"It took up the space of ten people," Yashiko said wonderingly.

Momoko wanted to know if they would need a new gravestone after this.

"I shouldn't think so. There's space for one more, at least," said Mrs. Kobayashi.

"Well," cackled Mrs. Asaki happily, "if that wasn't just like Yo-chan, all the way to the end!"

On this note, the burial was over.

They ate their lunch a few meters from the gravestone, on blankets spread under a cherry tree. They were famished. Mrs. Nishimura had brought a simple snack of rice balls to tide them over until they reached a restaurant in the city. A modern woman in her own way, she had bought them at a convenience store. They were huge, containing as much rice as four normal rice balls, and triangular in the Tokyo style. They were individually wrapped in an ingenious system of plastic wrapping. One tab broke apart the outer wrapping; another tab removed an inner plastic sheet that separated the crisp, dry sheet of seaweed from the moist rice.

"Which filling would you all like?" Mrs. Nishimura said. "Umeboshi? Or salmon with mayonnaise?"

"It's amazing," said Mrs. Kobayashi, "what they can do nowadays!" She still molded her husband's rice balls by hand when he went off with his friends for a morning of golf.

"Here, I'll show you how it works," Mrs. Asaki told the couple. She was proud of her familiarity with modern techniques. "First you pull this," she told them, demonstrating.

But nothing happened.

"Areh?" She turned over the rice ball in confusion.

"Let me do it, Granny," said Momoko. She snatched it out of the old woman's hands and deftly pulled the correct tabs.

"Ara maa," cried Mrs. Kobayashi, "how clever!"

Mrs. Asaki sat quietly. She was suddenly very, very tired.

Mr. Kobayashi took a hearty bite. "Not bad!" he said, surprised.

"Not bad at all," agreed his wife. "The rice tastes quite fresh. Soft and chewy, and salted just right."

"Oh, it's fresh all right," Mrs. Nishimura assured her. "They make them fresh every morning."

They placed one of the rice balls on the Kobayashi gravestone, in between the fresh flower bouquets. Considering the occupants, umeboshi seemed the proper choice. Salmon and mayonnaise was too new; that combination had become popular only in the last decade.

"Well," Mr. Kobayashi remarked as everyone sat eating hungrily and drinking cold tea from a thermos, "It's too late for the cherry viewing, but it's still very nice."

"Yes, isn't it lovely?" said Mrs. Kobayashi. "Yo-chan loved eating here. She used to say it gave her quite an appetite."

chapter 31

The homebound train was almost empty, so they had their pick of seats. Mrs. Asaki and Mrs. Kobayashi settled into the "silver" section. Everyone else took ordinary seats farther back.

The two women were silent as the scenery slid past. Their airy cheer fell away. Today's events, casual as they were, had taken a toll that was only now beginning to make itself felt.

Mrs. Asaki was remembering an incident when she had been a young wife, raking leaves in the garden. A scrawny alley cat was stalking its way across the top of the fence and she had stopped to watch it. The cat, too, came to a wary halt. Ueno cats, which had survived for generations by stealing fish out of open-air kitchens, were alert to mistreatment by irate housewives.

Resting both hands on the rake handle, she gazed into its slit-pupiled eyes. The cat stared back, unblinking.

She had pretended it was a creature of prey, a big cat from Africa. She imagined herself shrinking down in size, becoming more and more at its mercy, until the experiment began to feel real. Suddenly she was afraid. Quickly, roughly, she shooed it away with her rake.

That experience had stayed with her. Maybe she recognized in it some germ of prophecy, the way one does with powerful dreams. She now thought of the exasperated way Momoko had snatched the rice ball out of her hand. Once she would have thought nothing of reprimanding the child, but more and more she regarded her with a kind of fear that was new. This momentum would continue, she knew. It would soon extend to Yashiko, to her own daughter, to her son-in-law . . .

On the seat beside her, Mrs. Kobayashi was absently stroking the folded silk *furoshiki* on her lap. Earlier that day it had been wrapped around her daughter's boxed remains.

"I looked at Sarah-chan's thumb," Mrs. Asaki told her, although in truth she had forgotten all about it until now. "And I do see what you mean."

Mrs. Kobayashi nodded. "Yes," she said simply.

Mrs. Asaki felt a wistful envy for those two, for the closeness and promise still lying in wait for them. How did her sister-in-law manage to go through life never at a loss for a close, passionate relationship to sustain her?

Turning her head, she looked out the window. The hills were close, invigoratingly close. Rice paddies spread out before her; here and there, dirt paths wound away into the hilly terrain. In the corridors of her memory she saw similar roads stretching away: through rice paddies, through canopies of trees. Many times, after a long day in the fields, the locals had ridden home on a wooden cart, facing backward with their feet dangling over the edge. It struck her now, at eighty-three years of age, that this image—a dirt road stretching away behind her—was the most evocative and defining memory of her childhood. She had one early memory—perhaps it had been her first—of such a road stretching away into a blurry sort of greenery. She had seen it from her mother's lap, the back of her head resting securely against her mother's breast. It was so long ago it no longer felt like her own memory but a scene from some nostalgic television drama.

And here she was decades later, a success in life. She knew what her fellow train passengers saw: a well-dressed elderly woman surrounded by a devoted brood. A woman with a secure old age ahead of her. And yet . . .

She tried to remember how it had felt to sit in her mother's lap. She tried to picture herself being held close, being coddled and cared for, and something stirred deep in her core. She felt her eyes blur over with tears.

"Would you like a throat drop?" she heard Mrs. Kobayashi say. She must have noticed something, for her voice was gentle.

Mrs. Asaki nodded her head with a little bow of thanks, not because she wanted one but because it was the easiest thing to do. The candy was an old-fashioned flavor she hadn't tasted in years, brown sugar, and it spread out in her mouth with surprising and comforting sweetness. This, coupled with the unexpected tenderness from her sister-in-law, filled her with a tremulous sense of gratitude.

After a while, still sucking on the throat drop, she turned to the woman sitting beside her. So many times during the war they had come home like this on the train, tired and spent. Once again she had the sensation, as she had at the open grave, of blinking once to find the grieving young woman beside her transformed into a grieving old woman. Who knew Mrs. Kobayashi would lose yet another daughter? Mrs. Asaki, knowing her own guilt in the matter, felt a rush of sorrow.

She said, "Yo-chan was a good child."

"Yes."

"She was happy," Mrs. Asaki persisted. "She loved passionately all her life."

Mrs. Kobayashi nodded her thanks. The corners of her mouth wobbled involuntarily, for it had been a long day. This was a dangerous time for both of them; they were old women and they had been holding things together for a very long time.

"She was a good child," Mrs. Asaki repeated. Reaching out timidly, she patted her sister-in-law's hand. Mrs. Kobayashi did not draw it away. Instead she turned up her palm to meet Mrs. Asaki's hand with her own. At this surprising gesture, long denied her and coming from such an unlikely source, the old woman felt her throat constrict.

"The way you raised that child," she said finally, "was a success." In this heightened moment of compassion and remorse and gratitude, she was moved to offer up the most private, painful part of herself. It was the first time she would admit this to another living being. It would also be the last.

"I could never get Masako to come close to me," she said.

Part 3

chapter 32

Only during the June rainy season did one notice how many hydrangea bushes there were in the Ueno neighborhood. Normally they were invisible, tucked into corners or overshadowed by more imposing greenery. But now, against the backdrop of wooden houses sodden black from the rain and the vibrant green of surrounding foliage, the clusters of pink and blue and lavender glowed with an eerie intensity. Their litmus hues leapt out at Mrs. Nishimura's eye as she walked through the lanes beneath her umbrella.

She was coming home from choir practice. Choir always left her with a euphoric afterglow. It was only when she sang, her voice cleaving the air in powerful arcs of sound, that she felt something rising up within her that was equal to any glory the world could offer. Today they had practiced "Jesu, Joy of Man's Desiring" for an upcoming concert, and its inspired strains had echoed through her head during the bus ride home.

Now that melody faded as she attuned herself to the outdoor world: the intimate hush of the lanes, the somnolent drip, drip, drip as light rain made pinpricks of sound on the umbrella and on the surrounding foliage. Bach's grand surges didn't fit, somehow, with the peaceful domesticity of these lanes. Mrs. Nishimura was content to leave him behind in the practice hall.

As she breathed in the warm, earthy smells of wet wood and moss, a more fitting melody stole through her head—a child's ditty synonymous with rainy days. It was about your mother waiting for you after school with an extra umbrella because it was unexpectedly raining. She hummed it under her breath: *pichi pichi chapu chapu* (that was the sound of splashing water), *lan lan lan.*

It was a catchy tune in its own way, and just as hard to get out of her head. It was from a past time, a past generation. The lyrics mentioned *janome*—traditional umbrellas made of heavy oiled paper—which conjured up old-fashioned images of mother and child walking home past frogs croaking in the rice paddies. But certain things never changed: even in Mrs. Nishimura's youth, whenever it rained unexpectedly there had been a cluster of Ueno mothers standing outside the school gate, holding plastic umbrellas for their children. She remembered that split-second moment of concern, shared by all her classmates: Did my mother come? But she had never truly worried, for her mother was there each and every time.

When her own daughters were small, Mrs. Nishimura, too, had waited outside their school gate (umbrellas with pictures of Ultraman and Lion Man were popular with the boys; for the girls, manga heroines such as ballerinas or stewardesses). As they walked home she had sung the rainy-day song to them, just as her own mother had sung it to her. They paused often to inspect the hydrangea bushes: as small children all knew, their broad leaves attracted snails when it rained.

Ara ara, the song went, *see that poor child soaking wet, crying under the willow tree. I'll give her my umbrella, Mother, and you can shield me under yours . . .*

Ever since learning of her own adoption, she had identified strongly with that abandoned child under the willow tree. But oddly, it hadn't taken away from her memories of early childhood. That feeling of being safe and cared for was still clear in her mind—of walking beside her mother and looking out at a wet, dreary world from beneath the tinted shade of a red umbrella. She still had a child's distorted image of the rainy lanes, surreally barren of anything but the pink and blue hydrangea blooms that had pierced her young mind with the beauty of their colors.

She approached the snack shop. Mrs. Yagi, clad in her work apron, was standing under the awning and counting out change to a tall man pocketing a pack of cigarettes. The shopkeeper gave a quarter-bow in her direction, and Mrs. Nishimura returned it with a smile without breaking stride.

Before turning into the lane, she passed the Kobayashis' long wooden wall with the hinged vendor door that opened out onto the street. Nowadays no one used these doors, with their uncomfortably low lintels, except to put out trash on collection days.

Behind this wall was the Kobayashis' kitchen. Every so often, if Mrs. Nishimura walked very close along the narrow cement ditch, she could hear the faint thuds of a cleaver against the cutting board. As a child, playing here on the street, she and her playmates had sniffed appreciatively as unfamiliar smells wafted out into the lane: Chinese aromas of garlic or ground peanuts, a whiff of Western tomato sauce. Back then, before the modernization of Kyoto, such dishes had been redolent of the exotic. Mrs. Kobayashi's ingredients were common enough— she shopped at the open-air market just like everyone else—but she combined them in unusual ways. "She grew up in a port city," the neighbor women said. "She has high-level tastes, that one."

Mrs. Nishimura turned the corner into the narrow lane, feeling instinctive relief at the familiar crunch of gravel under her feet. For as long as she could remember, this *k'sha k'sha* sound had signaled home.

She paused before the Kobayashis' kitchen door. She had been planning to ask Mrs. Kobayashi a question. The Asaki household was replacing their hallway lights; would Mrs. Kobayashi like to add her order to theirs and save herself the hassle of carrying those long, unwieldy tubes? Mr. Nishimura could install them at the same time, and then old Mr. Kobayashi wouldn't have to use a stepladder.

But on this overcast day there was no glow of electricity behind the frosted glass panels. This meant Mrs. Kobayashi wasn't in the kitchen or even the dining room. She must be in one of the formal rooms beyond.

Mrs. Nishimura hesitated. There was an unwritten rule among Ueno housewives: it was permissible to drop in briefly, unannounced, if the lady of the house was in the kitchen. Domestic chores did not count as private time. But if the housewife had climbed up into the house proper, it would be inconsiderate to barge in.

She would go home, then, and telephone instead.

Almost three years had passed since Mrs. Rexford's death, and life on this lane was back to normal. Mrs. Kobayashi's health was greatly improved. It had taken time, but those skittering lights in her eyes had disappeared and she no longer sat down at odd times to rest. "Sometimes," she told people, "it feels like she's still alive in America somewhere."

Mrs. Nishimura, too, was back to normal. She occasionally recalled, with a cringe of embarrassment, her botched overture in the vestibule. But mostly it was as if it had never happened. After all, the older woman didn't seem to remember; there had been no hint of awkwardness, not even a slight distance. Maybe she hadn't heard it. So, while Mrs. Nishimura hadn't exactly forgotten, the hurt and resentment had faded from her day-to-day thoughts.

After all, such feelings were nothing new. For much of her life they had slid in and out of her mind like slow, dark fish, often disappearing for months at a time. But they never broke the surface; they were nothing like those hungry koi one saw in traditional restaurant gardens, the kind that erupted from the water with mouths gaping and hard bodies sticking straight up into the air. No, her fish were a quieter sort. They were bottom dwellers; they made no sudden moves. In rare moments, when things were slow, she let them rise up and circle about. But most of the time, there were better things to do and she went on about her business.

"Do you ever get angry?" her best friend in college had asked. She was the only person outside her family with whom she had discussed her adoption.

"Yes . . . ," young Masako had replied thoughtfully, "but not in the way you think. Not in a way that's really *personal*."

"Not personal? Against the mother who gave you up?"

"It's like I have two versions of her," she had said. "There's the one in my head and there's the actual woman who lives down the lane. The one in my head is who I get mad at or sentimental about. I talk to her in my head sometimes. But it doesn't really count, because it's almost like she's imaginary."

The truth was that Mrs. Nishimura felt physically incapable of the kind of anger she had seen in her big sister. She had seen Yoko stand up to bullies and back them down. Where did that intensity come from, that overpowering rage that blotted out everything else? It simply wasn't in her. Besides, her own situation didn't warrant it. Or did it? She was too close to have perspective. She sometimes wondered if her reactions were normal; this was another dark secret that she kept to herself.

But today, such thoughts were the last thing on her mind. Still humming—*pichi pichi chapu chapu*—she reached her own house and rolled open the slatted gate.

The mind is mysterious. Sometimes, when people feel buoyant and their insecurities are farthest from their minds, their guard goes down and they are even more susceptible.

In Mrs. Nishimura's case, singing had a lot to do with it. She had joined this municipal choir only a few months ago. She had a rich, strong alto—all the Kobayashi daughters were blessed with good voices—but she had never done much with it. For a year or two, when her girls were small, she had sung in a short-lived choir consisting of fellow mothers on the PTA committee. Lately, with Momoko about to leave for college and Yashiko not far behind, she had felt a nameless yearning to sing again. On a whim she auditioned for Akimichi, a female choir known for its high standards. She told no one; she was embarrassed by her own audacity. But luckily there was an opening for a second alto and she was accepted—on the condition that she work hard to catch up.

The practices were rigorous, nothing like the PTA chorus in which the housewives had pleasantly passed the time. This choir director made them repeat, and repeat, and repeat a note until they got it right. Such intensity of effort did not allow for holding back, for being self-conscious. Soon Mrs. Nishimura forgot herself in the process of becoming a conduit for something larger than herself, something pure and exhilarating and rich and joyful that surged through her and dislodged tiny fragments that stayed swirling in suspension for hours afterward.

With this constant outpouring of emotion, something within her began to shift. There was an imperceptible loosening of that airtight seal that had surrounded her feelings.

It was a subtle disequilibrium of which she was unaware. Now, still dressed in her outdoor clothes, Mrs. Nishimura stood before the telephone alcove in the dim hallway. Her lungs still enlarged from singing, she dialed the Kobayashis' number.

"We're all set for lights," Mrs. Kobayashi told her. "We just replaced them a few months back. But thank you, it's kind of you to ask."

"*Soh?* You already replaced them?"

"We had Teinosuke do it while he was here."

"Ah, well, that's fine then," said Mrs. Nishimura. "I just thought I'd ask."

And it *was* fine. Truly . . . although there was just the slightest disappointment that Mrs. Kobayashi hadn't made a similar offer to them. But that was silly. Mrs. Nishimura preferred not to indulge in petty thoughts.

But this little pang—which should have been no more than a pinprick, or at worst a vague sadness soon muffled on impact—shot past its proper stopping point with a force that alarmed her.

"I thought I heard your footsteps on the gravel a minute ago," said the older woman. "Did you just get back from somewhere?"

"I was at choir practice. Remember? I have choir every Tuesday." That pang was building in her chest, fierce and forlorn and extravagant. She vaguely recognized this sensation from choir: the gathering, the escalating, in preparation for a sublime launch of sound. But it had never happened in real life, and certainly not in anger.

"I tried to catch you, but you'd already turned the corner," the older woman said. "*Ne,* I have a good cut of snapper I've been meaning to give you. The two of us can't eat it all, and with this rainy season it won't keep long."

"You don't have to bother," Mrs. Nishimura said.

"What's that?"

A small part of her mourned what she was about to say even before she said it.

"You never wanted me," she whispered. No sooner had she said it than she was gripped with fear. Fumbling, she hung up the receiver before her mother could respond.

chapter 33

W hen Mrs. Nishimura gathered up her handbag from the telephone alcove, her hands were trembling. Her ears registered no sound, as if she were underwater.

What had she done? Who could have guessed that today, of all days, would mar the long tradition between the houses, so carefully and faithfully upheld over the years? And her gauche outburst was as distressing as the act itself. Over the phone! In between talk of light fixtures and fish! It was nothing like the secret fantasies of her childhood. She had pictured a formal, civilized exchange in a parlor, like the one with her adoptive mother. She had imagined herself speaking with dignity and (since this was fantasy) sharing her deepest feelings with eloquence. Instead she had struck and run, like an ill-mannered child.

Aaa, she was nothing like her sister Yoko.

But somewhere in the back of her mind—behind this feeling of shame, behind the dread of facing Mrs. Kobayashi again—there was a curious sense of . . . not anticipation exactly, but wonder. She had always believed there was nothing new to discover about herself.

How long she stood there she didn't know. Her words seemed to echo in the empty hall as if she had screamed them. She hoped her mother, upstairs taking a nap, hadn't heard.

From force of habit, she headed into the kitchen.

She was immediately aware of a dark outline behind the frosted glass panels of the kitchen door. Someone was outside on the doorstep, holding a dark umbrella. As Mrs. Nishimura paused, the figure tapped gently on the glass.

It was Mrs. Kobayashi.

Never, in Mrs. Nishimura's lifetime, had she come to the back door.

In the split second before hurrying to open it, Mrs. Nishimura felt a relief so great that her knees almost gave way. Only then did she realize she had been waiting for this her whole life.

Her mother had come. This was what mattered, whatever might happen in the next few minutes. Her child had needed her and she had come, at the risk of meeting Mrs. Asaki and putting herself in an impossible position.

Mrs. Nishimura rolled open the door, and her mother's eyes met hers with an expression so tender and regretful she had to look away. She noticed Mrs. Kobayashi wore socks on her feet and plastic gardening slippers; she must have been in a big hurry.

Reaching out her free hand, Mrs. Kobayashi drew her daughter outside onto the doorstep. Mrs. Nishimura stepped into a pair of plastic sandals lined up outside. She rolled the door shut behind them; even in this charged atmosphere, they were aware of Mrs. Asaki's presence.

They stood beneath the hanging eaves, which extended far enough to shield them from the rain. Mrs. Kobayashi closed her umbrella and turned to face her.

"Ma-chan," she said.

The rain was steady, not so much a force but a slow, languid dripping. The scent of loam rose up from the earth, mingling with the clean, sharp smells of ozone and greenery. It occurred to Mrs. Nishimura that smells were just as heady as music.

"I did a terrible thing to you." Her mother's voice had a quiet fervor, the same fervor with which she sometimes talked about Yoko. It surprised Mrs. Nishimura that she, too, could merit the same passion.

"I had a choice to make," Mrs. Kobayashi said. "I chose wrongly. I've regretted it all my life."

Mrs. Nishimura said nothing. She could not.

Mrs. Kobayashi began to talk—about wartime, about the occupation. She spoke quietly and steadily, not requiring her daughter to answer.

She talked of watching her grow up over the years. "Sometimes, when you were a little girl," she said, "I'd hear you running past the house and you'd be sobbing, you'd call out, 'Mama,' and it took everything I had to stay put while you ran home to somebody else . . ."

With one part of her brain Mrs. Nishimura was taking in every word, knowing she would sift and resift through this for years to come.

But now that the moment had come, she found she couldn't respond. That's right, she kept thinking, you chose wrongly. War or no war, no one made you do it. It was your own choice. For the second time today, she felt a rise of anger.

But it wasn't the sudden, wildfire anger of before. A legitimate space had been cleared, permission had been given, and now it was widening out, claiming its rightful territory with a sureness that felt like luxury. Her mother's gentle remorse incited it even more, like an old-fashioned housewife coaxing the hearth with a paper fan and a bamboo blowpipe.

"At the time, I thought it was the right thing to do," Mrs. Kobayashi was saying. Mrs. Nishimura had occasionally wondered if there was a private story behind that official version. Did people really offer up their children because of altruism? But of course they did. The history of Japan was one long story of sacrifice for the common good. Mrs. Nishimura understood duty. But a tiny part of her, the selfish part left over from childhood, still clung to the irrational question: How could you give me up? There was simply no answer for a question like that.

"I've always wanted to talk to you about it," Mrs. Kobayashi said. "All these years, I've wanted to ask your forgiveness."

It was unfair. Mrs. Nishimura wasn't the one who had chosen wrongly. But now, at the peak of her resentment, she had to give absolution. She couldn't do it. She wasn't ready.

And now the full extent of her loss washed over her, all the self-pity she had never allowed herself. Like a wave, it crested. Her windpipe squeezed shut. She felt her face contort in the moment before tears came.

"Ma-chan, Ma-chan." Her mother sounded as if she, too, was crying. Mrs. Nishimura couldn't see; her eyeglasses had fogged up. She pulled them off with one hand and wiped at her eyes with the other. She could smell her own tears, a scent as primordial as the wet earth and rain.

She felt her mother stroking her back over and over, her hand warm through the thin cotton of her blouse. The comfort of it made her feel like crying forever. But eventually her sobs subsided. They stood side by side, gazing out at the rain falling on the hydrangea bushes and the sodden black planks of the fence.

"The whole time I was pregnant with Yoko, I was terrified." Mrs. Kobayashi's voice was faraway and musing. "But the sec-

ond time, when I knew I was pregnant with you, I wasn't afraid at all. I remember saying to your father when we left the doctor's office, 'I'm so happy. I'm really looking forward to having this one.'"

Mrs. Nishimura would treasure these words for years to come.

chapter 34

That night, Mrs. Kobayashi had a recurring nightmare. She was running lost through empty streets, searching in vain for the bomb shelter where everyone else was hiding. The streets were dilapidated, with ghostly forms floating in and out of slatted wooden doorways.

Mr. Kobayashi shook her awake, and as she came to consciousness she heard her own high-pitched moaning. "You were dreaming," he said.

For a long time afterward, she lay listening to the rain splash against the cement floor of the laundry area. She thought of other nightmares she'd had over the years. More than once she had dreamed Shohei was outside in the night, standing silent in the lane. She couldn't see him but she knew, as one does in dreams, that he was wearing a white suit like a Cuban musician. In her dream she would scream out, "Take me with you! Please! Don't leave me here!"

Many times she had woken in the dark and realized, as if her brain was in slow motion, that she had given her child away.

Nighttime reminded her that life, at its core, was fraught with danger.

As soon as Kenji Kobayashi had returned from Manchuria, he had come to the Asaki house with his baby boy. Mrs. Kobayashi avoided his eager, hopeful eyes. She had always known, in a vaguely scornful way, that he carried a secret torch for her. But she felt no respect or admiration. He was a charming ne'er-do-well, a wild card, which appealed to some women but not to her. And he was short. She would never feel safe and protected again, being married to a man no taller than herself.

"Look at the little darling!" cooed Mrs. Asaki, cradling Teinosuke in her arms. "Look, Yo-chan. This is your baby brother."

They sat down to a simple meal of noodles and broth, garnished with nothing but seven-spice, chopped chives from their garden, and three slices each of hard-boiled egg. "There's no meat," said Mrs. Asaki. "I'm sorry . . ."

"It tastes fine," her brother insisted. "It tastes like Japan." His voice choked up a little. "It's good to be back. It's so good to be back."

Mr. Asaki cleared his throat irritably. "You should have worn something else," he said. "We don't need a constant reminder of our humiliation." Everyone looked at Mr. Kobayashi's belted khaki uniform with its stiff standing collar.

"Yes, sir." The young man gave a half bow of apology. "Of course."

They lingered over tea in the parlor. Little Yoko retreated to a corner, where she played quietly with the flat Chinese marbles her uncle had brought her.

Masako, who had been napping in a nest of floor cushions, began to stir. "Here," said Mrs. Asaki, handing Teinosuke to her sister-in-law. She hurried over to pick up the baby girl, who was parting her tiny mouth in a yawn. "Two babies in the house!" she marveled to the group at the table. "What good fortune!"

Teinosuke was all sharp angles, with none of Masako's plumpness. His oblong skull was bald but for a layer of fuzz. It was like holding a tiny, querulous old man. Mrs. Kobayashi set him free on the tatami matting and he crawled slowly under the table, like a dying insect.

"How precious!" said Mrs. Asaki. "He's crawling!" She bounced her daughter-to-be on her lap, and Masako gurgled with joy. Mrs. Kobayashi hated to admit it, but her sister-in-law had a knack with babies. Her own child wouldn't even miss her when she was gone.

"This is a good cigarette," said Mr. Asaki, exhaling slowly.

"Have another, sir," said Mr. Kobayashi. The men inhaled with deep satisfaction as if, now that the war was over, the worst was behind them.

Mrs. Kobayashi felt hysteria rising up within her.

"Yo-chan," she said quietly, "come sit at the table." The child came willingly, clutching her marbles in one hand and dragging her floor cushion behind her with the other. She hesitated as she approached, as if sensing the force field of her mother's emotions.

"Put the cushion here," said Mrs. Kobayashi, patting the floor beside her.

While everyone continued chatting, she rested her hand on her daughter's back where no one could see. She ran her hand up and down over the small shoulder blades. The child smiled up at her, with a soft look in her eyes that was exactly like Shohei's.

Mrs. Kobayashi's hysteria subsided a little. I can do this, she thought. I'm getting through it, one minute at a time. She forced Masako out of her mind. Over and over she stroked this small person beside her, the only person whom it was safe to love.

Afterward, she and her husband-to-be went for a short stroll to Umeya Shrine. They chatted pleasantly of China's history, of people they knew in common, of the crayfish she and Mrs. Asaki had caught in the Kamo River. At one point he cleared his throat. "I know I can't fill my brother's shoes," he said. "But I'll do my best for you and Yoko."

"I'm in your debt," she murmured demurely.

He said nothing about the child she was giving up. For this she was grateful. During their long marriage, it would never come up between them.

Growing up by the sea, Mrs. Kobayashi had heard tales of tsunami as tall as skyscrapers, looming over villages for several moments before crashing. *Life's destructive force,* said the grown-ups with hushed reverence. *So heartless, it's majestic.*

That night she lay upstairs in the Asaki house with a sleeping child on either side. There was a faint roaring in her ears. She thought of villagers looking up at a wall of water, a split second before their annihilation.

This new life ahead, this feudal arrangement straight out of history books, had been beyond her ability to imagine. But now, for the first time, she saw how it would be. It would be *ordinary.* That was the shock of it. They would eat noodles and play with babies and talk about the new restaurant on the west side of town. No one would acknowledge the brutality of it. No one would even notice.

How would she survive? She had no inner resources; she had been rich and pampered all her life. What defined her? Nothing but frivolous memories from her old life. Picnic parties in the mountains with friends from work . . . the first time Shohei had asked her to tea . . . one lovely evening when she had glimpsed a star through a hole in her oiled paper umbrella . . . little Yoko taking her first steps, in a pair of pink kidskin shoes.

Sometimes, if she remembered hard enough, the old romance and possibility and joy bubbled up in her once more like ginger ale.

If this feeling was all she had left, then she would curl her whole being around it. Like a barnacle, she would hold tight while the tsunami crashed over her. I will protect my core, she thought. I will not become a hard, bitter woman.

chapter 35

After that rainy-day incident, what was the right way to act? There was no rule of etiquette to follow. It was as if a large stone had dropped into their pond, and no one dared move until the ripples died down.

Mrs. Nishimura and Mrs. Kobayashi occasionally crossed paths at the open-air market. They paused for a brief chat, as usual. But they never lingered, and they never walked home together.

Mrs. Nishimura went about the busy life of a housewife. Each morning she woke at sunrise to prepare breakfast before her husband's long train commute. Her breakfasts were less elaborate than those at the Kobayashi house, but as long as Mr. Nishimura had his miso soup and his bowl of rice, he was happy. His underlings, he told her, ate hurriedly prepared, overly sweet breakfasts like toast and jam. "How could something like that possibly hit the spot?" he said, shaking his head and taking a deep, long swallow of broth. Mrs. Nishimura was touched by his awkward gratitude.

Afterward she saw him off, standing by the outer gate just as her own mother had done decades ago. But Mrs. Nishimura, being of a different generation, gave a cheerful wave instead of a formal bow.

Then it was time to head indoors for the second breakfast shift. Mrs. Asaki and the girls were not picky eaters, so she served modern fare like butter and toast or healthy—if nontraditional—fresh vegetables such as tomatoes and lettuce. There was plenty of hot rice left in the cooker. And if the leftover miso soup was slightly bitter after a second heating, no one minded. In fact, her mother ate most of it. Although Mrs. Asaki gamely ate the same dishes as her grandchildren, she supplemented them with old-fashioned condiments like miso soup or pickled vegetables.

One morning, a week after the incident with Mrs. Kobayashi, the household was finishing breakfast. Mrs. Nishimura was already in the kitchen, packing the girls' lunches for school. After this many years, she had it down to a science. Half of each oblong container was packed with rice, still warm from the cooker and topped with an umeboshi in the center (this combination was called the Japanese flag). The remaining space was filled with an assortment of *okazu,* or side dishes. Today they consisted of sweetened egg loaf left over from breakfast, miniature sausages, sliced green peppers, sweet *kabocha* pumpkin stewed in soy sauce (from yesterday's dinner), a dollop of expensive mattake mushroom preserves purchased by Mrs. Asaki, and sliced oranges. Each item was separated by strips of jagged green plastic that resembled grass. A perfectly fine lunch, though nothing like the lunches the Kobayashi children used to bring to school. Mrs. Nishimura still remembered those: shredded meat glistening with mouthwatering glaze and sprinkled with sesame seeds; cabbage leaves shaved as fine as baby hairs; homemade Chinese steamed buns, each with a different filling.

Once, many years ago, Mrs. Nishimura had vowed that her

daughters, too, would have lunches like that. But she had no knack for the complex alchemy of flavors. She had to content herself with presentation, arranging the *okazu* with an eye for color and texture that rivaled her skill with cut flowers. The way she rationalized it, Mrs. Asaki's expensive condiments made up for any shortfalls in flavor. As the widow of a government official, the old woman received a generous lifetime pension, most of which she spent on shopping sprees for the family. Their modest meals, budgeted on Mr. Nishimura's salary, were mixed with disproportionately decadent treats such as liqueur-filled European chocolates or rustic tofu made from scratch by artisans.

More than once, in a moment of pettiness, Mrs. Nishimura had thought how much more helpful it would be if her mother just pitched in that extra money toward the household budget. Then she was ashamed of herself. They were already living in this house rent-free, and she knew how important it was for her mother to surprise and delight in her role as benefactor. Now that Mrs. Asaki was too tired for shopping sprees, she increasingly relied on money envelopes. Every so often she slipped one into someone's hand, stuffed with bills earmarked for a specific indulgence: new bicycles for the girls or an afternoon of golf for the man of the house. But this was no longer done from a position of strength, and Mrs. Nishimura felt sad for her mother.

In the adjoining room, the girls had risen from the low table. She could hear them bustling about, shoving books into their schoolbags and throwing remarks back and forth. "Where's my science report?" wailed Momoko. The girls' voices grew loud and excited as they prepared to enter the real world.

Mrs. Asaki, still seated at the low table, was reprimanding someone about something. Mrs. Nishimura couldn't make out the words, but she knew that tone of disapproval. Her heart sank. Why did her mother have to choose such inconvenient

times? As it was, the girls had a short fuse when it came to her
constant meddling. It wasn't such a problem with Yashiko, but
there had been several skirmishes with Momoko. "Let it go,"
Mrs. Nishimura once told her daughter in private. "She just
wants to feel like she's still relevant in your life. I know she's
controlling, but that's just her way. She's not the type to beg."

"Why are *you* so protective of her feelings?" Momoko had
asked. It was a peculiar question, so peculiar that Mrs. Nishimura knew her daughter was referring to the adoption. She had
almost forgotten that her daughter knew. The girl had shown so
little interest at the time—as Mrs. Rexford had said, a grandmother wasn't the same thing as a mother. And when Yashiko
was told, several years after that, she had been more concerned
about her upcoming field trip.

Now Momoko's question opened up a strange new dimen-
sion between mother and daughter.

Mrs. Nishimura did not say what she felt. Her daughter, at
seventeen, might be old enough to know the facts, even shrewd
enough, in some misguided way, to draw conclusions that made
her feel protective of her mother. But she lacked the life experience to understand gray areas. She couldn't put herself in her
grandmother's place and know what a mother might feel, year
after year, when her only child didn't cleave to her—*truly* cleave,
like Mrs. Kobayashi and Mrs. Rexford. It was something Mrs.
Nishimura could never make up to her adoptive mother, no
matter how much she tried. This remorse, perhaps more than
she realized, had shaped her own choices in life. She had per-
suaded her husband to keep living in this house. She had kept a
slight emotional distance from her girls so they wouldn't be
burdened with a sense of obligation. The less she expected of
them, the less chance she would suffer her mother's fate. But
none of this was Momoko's business. Not yet.

"Because," she had replied, "she's my mother, and I honor her. What a question."

Now Mrs. Nishimura slid the flat steel lunchboxes into their embroidered bags. Hoping to forestall any bickering, she hurried out to the informal dining area.

"Here you are," she said a little breathlessly, holding out the boxes to the girls. "Go now, go. You're going to be late."

"Masako, take a look at this." Mrs. Asaki's face was grave with disapproval. She gestured to the girls' buckled canvas bookbags, the wide straps of which were slung across their navy jacket uniforms. "The material is starting to fray. Girls, why can't you be more careful with your possessions?"

"Everyone's bags are like that, Grandma," said Yashiko cheerfully.

"When I was a young woman," Mrs. Asaki said, "we never left the house unless our *furoshiki* cloths were in perfect condition. No loose threads. No tiny rips. It was a point of honor."

"It's not so bad, Mother, really," said Mrs. Nishimura gently. "People nowadays don't hold schoolbags to the same high standard as *furoshiki*. Besides, it's just not economical to keep replacing them."

"If you'd come to me," said Mrs. Asaki, glancing at Momoko, "I would have bought you as many bags as you needed."

Momoko held her tongue.

In less than a year, the girl would be leaving home. How quickly the time had gone! Mrs. Nishimura wished her child's last year could have been more carefree. It occurred to her that in all these years of keeping the peace, of avoiding conflict and assuaging her private guilt, she had never stood up for her daughters and her husband.

"Girls!" she cried. "You'll be late for school! Now go!" The girls fled down the hallway, calling out a formal *"Itte kimasu!"*

in farewell. Stepping out into the hallway, she sent them off with a wave and the formal response: *"Itte rasshai!"* A few minutes later the heavy outer door rattled open, then shut. And the large house was silent.

Mrs. Nishimura returned to the dining area, where her mother sat at the low table swallowing the last of her miso soup. Drained, she sank down onto a floor cushion. Drawing out a clean pair of chopsticks from the container on the table, she reached over in a gesture of companionship and picked an eggplant pickle from her mother's condiment dish.

"They have a nice clean taste, don't they," said Mrs. Asaki. Mrs. Nishimura nodded in agreement. She munched silently.

Later today she would catch the bus for choir practice. Her heart lifted at the thought. She wished she could feel this same kind of lift at home. She thought of the afternoon with Mrs. Kobayashi, when deep, powerful emotions had risen to the surface. She wanted to feel that again . . .

But first there was something she had to do. "The girls are at such an awkward age," she began.

"*Maa maa,* they're fine children!" said her mother brightly.

"A really awkward age," Mrs. Nishimura repeated gently. "They're so combustible. They don't mean to be, but . . . Sometimes they just need a few minutes to themselves. You know, to let the steam out." Something in her voice must have alerted Mrs. Asaki, for she looked up with a wary expression.

Mrs. Nishimura charged on, her mouth dry. "It might be best," she said, "if you stayed upstairs during certain periods, just when they're most easily provoked . . ." She forced herself to hold her gaze. In her mother's eyes was an odd expression: not sadness, not hurt, but the weary relief of someone who has fought hard and lost. That look, Mrs. Nishimura thought, would haunt her to her dying day.

"Like maybe . . . the half hour right after breakfast," she continued, choking a little. "And the half hour . . . right when the girls come home from school. It might be easier on everybody."

Mrs. Asaki did not argue. "*Soh,* perhaps that's best," she agreed crisply. She rose to her feet and headed down the hall to do the laundry. No one expected her to do housework, but the old woman liked to be useful. On sunny days she often worked outdoors in one of the utility gardens, crouching over a plastic basin and scrubbing at the girls' canvas sneakers with a toothbrush.

Alone in her kitchen, Mrs. Nishimura began washing the breakfast dishes. It took several minutes for her mind to fully grasp what she had done. Tiny tremors began running along her spine. How had she found the courage? She had to turn off the tap and take several deep breaths before she could go on.

chapter 36

The rainy season drew to a close, and each day the sun shone with ever-increasing strength. The intimate, sodden hush of the Ueno lanes gave way to a bright, bustling energy, a quickening. Sound traveled swiftly and clearly. Children whizzed past on bicycles; alley cats darted through the long, lush weeds.

One sunny morning, Mrs. Nishimura ran into Mrs. Kobayashi at the open-air market. Mrs. Nishimura was coming out of Shinsendo Bakery, a new establishment with Parisian awnings of red, white, and blue. Mrs. Kobayashi was approaching from the direction of the pickle store. She noticed her daughter and her face brightened in recognition. Mrs. Nishimura waited, admiring the older woman's firm, pleasing stride as well as the peach gauze scarf tucked into the neckline of her blouse.

Stepping away from the bicycles and pedestrians, they exchanged small domestic updates. Momoko was still studying hard for her entrance exams. Sarah was interning at a financial consulting firm over the summer.

"In a week or so," Mrs. Kobayashi said, "it'll be hot enough to carry a parasol." She tilted back her head to look at the sun.

Mrs. Nishimura, too, lifted her face to the sky: a strong blue, with the classic cumulus clouds of early summer. They lingered, savoring the bright warmth and the communal lightheartedness of fellow shoppers stepping past in summer clothes.

Mrs. Kobayashi looked over at Mrs. Nishimura's woven straw basket. "So," she said in a playful tone, "what did you buy?" She had never asked such an intimate question before.

"*Saa,* let's see . . ." Shyly, Mrs. Nishimura parted the handles of her basket. The action felt oddly familiar; she had watched her big sister do it many times. She peered into her own basket, just as her sister used to do.

With friendly curiosity, Mrs. Kobayashi leaned in to look. Among the usual items—garlic shoots, ginger, dried whitebait, fried tofu skin—were two loaves of Shinsendo bread and a kimono fashion magazine. Kimonos were Mrs. Nishimura's weakness. In her free time she pored over the fat quarterly glossies, in which elegant women modeled seasonal kimonos with expressions of gentle tranquility.

"This bread's for Mother," Mrs. Nishimura explained. "She tears off little pieces and dips them in sugar. She calls it a nostalgic craving."

Mrs. Kobayashi nodded. "That's right. She told me a long time ago that it used to be a special treat when she was growing up in the country." She opened her own string bag for inspection. "All I have so far is pickled seaweed."

They were suddenly approached by a middle-aged woman from Mrs. Nishimura's choir. "Nishimura-san!" The woman gave two half-bows of greeting, one for each person. "Do you live in this area too?"

Mrs. Nishimura and her mother automatically jerked away from each other, embarrassed to be caught peering into each other's shopping baskets.

"*Maa,* Kimura-san, good morning! This is my . . ." But *aunt* felt wrong somehow, after all that had happened. She had a sudden impulse: How would it feel to stand here on this street, in the bright light of day, and tell the truth? It would make no difference to her choir mate.

"This," she said, "is my mother, Haruko Kobayashi. And this is Mrs. Aki Kimura, who sings with me in the choir." For a brief moment, time stood still.

"How do you do?" The choir woman bowed, unaware that anything was out of the ordinary.

Mrs. Kobayashi, usually such a fluent conversationalist, could not speak. She was deeply moved; it showed plainly on her face. But she had enough social presence to bow deeply, more deeply than the occasion required, in order to make up for her muteness.

Seeing her mother's tremulous mouth, Mrs. Nishimura felt a piercing joy. And a sort of wonder: with a single word, she had turned all her years of yearning into a benediction for her mother.

Part 4

chapter 37

The first day back in her grandmother's house gave Sarah a sense of wavering in time. Her American self dropped away. In its place, long-forgotten former selves came swimming up from the depths: the little girl who had attended school in Japan, the fourteen-year-old who had lived here one summer, the various older selves she had been on subsequent visits. She was twenty-four years old. She had passed the CPA exam and joined the tax department of a multinational corporation.

"This soup is delicious," she said. "Creamy. Very delicate."

Mrs. Kobayashi nodded. "I changed the ratio of white miso to red. That way it won't interfere with the flavor of the squash."

"Look at these colors." Sarah held out her bowl at arm's length, admiring the overall effect. "So nice and autumnal. The orange of the squash, the speckled brown of the mountain potato . . ."

"Against the red lacquer of the bowl," said her grandmother proudly.

"A perfect combination."

Sarah returned the bowl to its proper position in the palm of her left hand.

"No one makes breakfasts like this anymore," Mrs. Kobayashi said. She nodded at the array of side dishes: eel omelette, umeboshi, glazed kelp and beans. "Over at Granny's house, they sometimes eat their rice with nothing but miso soup and fried eggs. Momoko told me."

"Not very satisfying," said Sarah, forgetting that her usual breakfast in America was nothing but cereal and a banana.

They ate contentedly.

Sarah gazed about at the wooden posts and *fusuma* panels of her childhood. She still half expected to hear her grandfather's hammer tap-tapping in the workroom.

"It's quiet with him gone, *ne*," she said. Mr. Kobayashi had died of a heart attack two years ago. Although his loss paled in comparison with that of her parents, Sarah had loved her grandfather and his death had been a shock.

"Yes, it's hard to get used to. It's strange living alone."

Sarah remembered his affectionate, if clumsy, presents: boxes of caramels for her, packets of Japanese radish seeds for her mother, a bottle of processed seaweed paste ("to put on your bread when you get home") or some other impractical thing for them to take home to America.

"Granny Asaki visited me the week he died—did I ever tell you? You'd gone home by then."

Sarah shook her head.

"She rang the bell at the visitor gate. I'm thinking, what's all this? Then she seats herself in the parlor and bows her head to the floor, over and over. She says, 'You were a fine wife. He didn't deserve you. It's humbled me all these years, the way you worked so hard without complaining.'"

"How lovely," said Sarah. "I adore Japanese formality."

Mrs. Kobayashi snorted. "Well, it's true. I gave him decades of exemplary service. It was for my own self-respect." Then her voice softened. "He appreciated it near the end, though. He used to look up from his plate and say, all gruff and embarrassed, 'You were always good to me. Thank you.'"

Sarah nodded.

"I did more than enough for the man," her grandmother said briskly. "I have no regrets."

"Do you ever dream about him?"

"Not really. Do you?"

"No. I still dream about my parents, though. I keep forgetting they're dead. You'd think after six years, it would soak through to my subconscious."

Her grandmother, chewing, nodded with interest and encouragement.

"It's odd," said Sarah, "that they're so *fresh* in my dreams. It's like that part of my brain is frozen in time."

"Yes, the human brain is very mysterious."

Sarah had thought the same thing ten years ago, when the burbling of pigeons brought back her eight-year-old self.

"Where are the pigeons?" she said now. "I don't hear any."

"*Aaa,* they're all gone. The temple ban finally had its effect."

They ate silently. Sarah's thoughts returned to her grandfather. It was a pity that as she grew into womanhood, the scrim separating adult and child had never lifted between them as it had with her grandmother. Now he was gone, and his inner life would always be a mystery. He must have been lonely, she thought. He must have had love to give, though much of it had gone unclaimed.

chapter 38

Sarah and her grandmother were walking to the open-air market. The morning was hushed and gray, absorbing sound and turning the lanes into a silent movie.

"Oh, that *smell*!" she cried, breathing in the long-forgotten aroma of burning leaves. Back home in California, backyard fires were against the law.

"*Soh,* it's that time of year," agreed her grandmother, as if humoring a child.

This was the first time Sarah had visited in November. The pungent smell took her far back in time, to her kindergarten days in the Kyoto hills. During recess their teacher had tended a small fire in the center of the playground and raked out indigenous sweet potatoes, blistered and blackened, for the children's afternoon snack.

They approached Murasaki Boulevard and crossed the intersection. "*A! A!*" Mrs. Kobayashi exclaimed. "Good thing I remembered! Remind me, if I forget, to buy *shiso* leaves. You know, to wrap the sashimi in."

The open-air market had changed since the seventies. There was a new supermarket, where they bought a small bundle of *shiso* leaves. The store wasn't as big as the supermarkets in California; the aisles were too narrow for shopping carts. But it was just as well, for once-a-week shopping was still an alien concept for Ueno women. The supermarket was popular for its cheap produce, mass-farmed and shipped in from distant places. Women had stopped buying locally grown vegetables; they were too expensive during the economic recession. Vendor carts were a pleasant rarity. The sun-browned farmers in their old-fashioned garb seemed like relics from another era.

"This street's so quiet!" said Sarah. Vendors no longer hawked their wares with loud, exuberant bellows. Cash registers had replaced abacuses and jingling money bags.

"Remember how quiet the weavers' alley was just now?" Mrs. Kobayashi said. "That's the way it was in wartime, when I was a young woman."

Sarah remembered her mother's comment about looms moving in tandem with the stock market. "It's odd," she said, "that even in this bad economy, there're all these new buildings. So many things changing."

"Not everyone's hurting, I guess."

They approached the "expensive" fish store. The open-air market had two seafood stores: the expensive place with the good-quality seafood, and the cheap place with affordable seafood, mostly imported.

"You're visiting at the perfect time," her grandmother told her. "The fish right now, the big heavy cold-current ones, they're at their fattiest this time of year. Sashimi is at its prime!"

Sarah noticed there were no customers in line. Plenty of people were bending over the crushed-ice display, but no one was buying.

One of the vendors, a shrewd older woman, came out from behind the counter to show Mrs. Kobayashi her most expensive items. "Madam!" she said by way of greeting. "After your granddaughter goes home to America you'll be kicking yourself, with all due respect, for not letting her taste this highest-quality roe! At its absolute prime, madam, this time of year!" She waited, with a complacent smile, as Mrs. Kobayashi wavered. Reaching out a hand, she let it hover dramatically over a display of enormous scallops. "Sashimi grade," she said simply. "Flown in a few hours ago from Hokkaido."

It occurred to Sarah that she hadn't heard her grandmother bargain in a long time. That practice must have gone out of style.

In no time at all, the woman was wrapping up their fatty sashimi plus several other unplanned purchases. She rang up the total on a cash register. "It'll be good for the young miss," she reassured Mrs. Kobayashi, "to eat good-quality seafood prepared properly in her granny's kitchen. In America"—her eyes slid over in Sarah's direction—"those people eat their fish cooked in *vegetable oil*."

Sarah laughed, tickled by her expert salesmanship. The vendor responded with a homey smile, revealing a gold tooth.

"You have your mother's laugh, don't you," she said wonderingly. "Startles me every time, miss, coming from that American face."

Sarah, who had long ago outgrown her insecurity over her Caucasian features, could appreciate this paradox. "She's right, you know," she told her grandmother as they walked away. "I don't resemble anyone on my Japanese side."

"You have *lots* of family characteristics," Mrs. Kobayashi said firmly. She counted them on her fingers: a widow's peak, a thumb that joined her hand at exactly the same angle that her grandfather Shohei's had, a floating cyst on her neck that had been passed down through several generations of Kobayashis.

"And let's not forget your voice." Sarah's voice was identical to her mother's. In the early days, whenever Sarah said *"moshi moshi"* over the telephone, Mrs. Kobayashi had felt a wild lurch of hope that her daughter's death had all been a big mistake.

"And on top of all that," the old woman concluded, "you have the same open presence your mother and your grandfather had."

Sarah pondered this as they turned homeward. She wondered what her grandfather Shohei would think if he could see them now: an unlikely pair! She imagined his shock and bewilderment at seeing his own wife walking alongside an American, channeling to her all the love that had once gone to him.

Walking abreast, they turned off the main street. They passed the Kinjin-ya teahouse and entered a narrow residential lane that headed west toward So-Zen Temple. On Sarah's last visit this lane had been gravel; now it was paved. Their shoes made flat slapping sounds against the blacktop, and Sarah missed the gentle *k'sha k'sha* that had so often reminded her of walking on new-fallen snow.

The sun broke through briefly, its pale light slanting tentatively into the lane. Many of the rickety doors had been replaced by sturdier models with slats of brown plastic instead of traditional wood. One corner house had been torn down altogether and replaced with a Western-style model home, complete with white aluminum siding and a door that opened with a knob. Hanging from the knocker was a painted wooden cutout of a puppy, holding in its smiling mouth a nameplate spelling out THE MATSUDAS in English letters.

A bicycle bell tinged behind them. They backed off to the side, careful not to bump into a motor scooter parked beside one of the doors. A straight-backed housewife rode past with a bow of thanks, her wire basket filled with newspaper-wrapped groceries.

"We'll have this sashimi for lunch, with hot rice," Mrs. Kobayashi said as they resumed walking abreast. "You're not here for very long, so we need to plan the menu carefully. We can't afford to let a single meal go to waste." Energized by this task before her, she walked briskly. "Do you have any cravings?" she said. "If you do, tell me now."

"Grandma?" Sarah asked. "Whatever happened to the little lane that hadn't changed in generations?" That summer day, when she and her mother had strolled home after eating azuki ice, already belonged to a different lifetime. "You know, the lane with the thatched roofs?"

Mrs. Kobayashi gave a short, puzzled laugh as Sarah described it to her.

"I have no idea what you're talking about," she said. "They've torn a lot of those down." Then she suddenly stopped short. "Sarah-chan," she said, "do you remember if we locked the kitchen door when we left?"

A few more years, Sarah thought, and these lanes would be unrecognizable. She imagined a day in the future, perhaps when her grandmother was gone, when she might walk through these lanes with her own daughter—a child with even less Japanese blood than she. And a certain quality of reproach in the slant of sunlight would remind her with a pang, as it did now, of her mother's confident voice saying, "It's never going to change, I'm sure."

"Once, when I was a girl," Sarah would tell her daughter, gripping her hand tightly, "I walked these lanes just like you, with my own mother." Saying these inadequate words, she would sense keenly how much fell away with time, how lives intersected but only briefly.

"Thank goodness I remembered the *shiso* leaves," Mrs. Kobayashi said now, leaning over and peering into Sarah's string bag.

"When you were little you refused to eat your sashimi and rice without it, remember? *Maa,* I never saw such a particular child!"

"That wasn't me, Grandma," Sarah said. "That was Mama."

"Oh . . ." Mrs. Kobayashi was silent for a moment. "Well, that would make more sense, *ne,*" she said finally. "Poor thing. Autumn *hiramasa* was her favorite. But we couldn't afford it during the postwar years. Then just when things got better and she could have eaten her fill, she moved away . . ."

Sarah looked over at the old woman beside her. Mixed in with her sympathy was a certain satisfaction: here was someone who still mourned, who still hurt deeply and had not forgotten.

"Grandma," she said, in the gentle tone she had often heard her mother use. "There's no use thinking like that. It doesn't matter anymore."

Mrs. Kobayashi quickened her pace, as she sometimes did when she was feeling emotional. "People don't always get the luxury of timing," she said.

chapter 39

One day Sarah noticed that her grandmother had bought more roasted eels than the two of them could eat.

"Do you want me to take some over to Auntie's?" she asked.

"No, no. There isn't enough for everyone in that house. This isn't cheap, you know." She lowered her voice to a whisper. "The extra portion's for your auntie's anemia. What I do, *ne,* is flag her down sometimes when she passes by the kitchen door. I sneak her in for a quick bite, and no one's the wiser. Or sometimes I give her liver—you know, the kind I always make for you with ginger and soy sauce. Of course it's a secret."

This was the first Sarah had heard of her grandmother keeping secrets with anyone but her mother and herself.

A few days later, when she complimented her grandmother on the miniature rosebush in the garden, she learned it had been a gift from Mrs. Nishimura.

"Oh . . ." She was puzzled. The two houses sometimes exchanged cuttings, but never brand-new plants from the nursery. That had been Mrs. Rexford's style—many times, after one of her outings, she would come home saying, "Mother, look!" and holding out a pot of bluebells or fragrant jasmine.

"Oh," Sarah said again. "Well, that was really nice of her."

It occurred to her that her mother's name had been coming up in conversation much less than it used to.

One night the two women were sitting at the *kotatsu* in the family room. The *kotatsu* was a small low table with an electric heater attached to its underside, and a heavy quilted cover that extended down to the floor and covered their laps. Like most traditional homes in this neighborhood, the Kobayashi house had no central heating. One stayed warm by huddling around a *kotatsu* while chatting or watching television. Sometimes, since it was just the two of them, Mrs. Kobayashi and Sarah ate their meals there as well.

"You two had a *spat*?" Sarah was saying. "You're joking!"

"It was completely one-sided," Mrs. Kobayashi said. "We were talking on the phone about something . . . I can't even remember what . . . then all of a sudden, she got upset and said, 'You never wanted me anyway!' And she hung up."

"What!"

"I know! I couldn't believe my ears. She's never said anything like that in her entire life."

"So what happened?"

"I rushed over there. I didn't even stop to think. I just knew I could never live with myself if I didn't make it right. I said to her, 'I've done a terrible thing to you.' God knows where Granny was that whole time! And I told her, 'There hasn't been a day in all these years I haven't regretted it.'" Mrs. Kobayashi nodded, her eyes watering at the memory. "It was surreal, like jumping off a cliff. But you know how much I've always wanted to tell her that."

"I know." Sarah remembered her grandmother saying to her mother, "I wish I *knew* if deep down, behind that face, she's all right. I wonder if deep down, she hates me."

"Your aunt was such a reserved girl," Mrs. Kobayashi said now. "There was that coolness about her, not like your mother or your aunt Tama. But now she's starting to blossom. Little by little, she's turning into the person she was always meant to be."

"Really? I hadn't noticed."

"Well, it might be something only a mother notices."

Just then, someone tapped on the kitchen door.

"Who could that be, so late?" Mrs. Kobayashi murmured.

It was Yashiko on her way home from her college prep session. She couldn't stay, she told them. She had brought a box of piping-hot octopus balls, a classic cold-weather snack. "Mother said to pick these up for Aunt Mama," she said, referring to the tradition of offering the deceased's favorite foods at the family altar. "I have to run—I'm late for dinner!"

This was typical of Mrs. Nishimura's thoughtfulness. She remembered little things, like how her big sister used to eat these octopus balls standing up like a man, in front of the vendor cart with its red cotton flaps. Even now, on winter nights, that same old-fashioned cart set up shop in the same place: the sidewalk next to the vermilion gateposts of Umeya Shrine. Octopus balls were a nighttime commodity, geared toward college students or salarymen on their way home from work. Since Mrs. Kobayashi never ventured out after sunset and discouraged Sarah from doing so as well, Mrs. Nishimura's gesture was doubly considerate.

After Yashiko hurried home to her dinner, Mrs. Kobayashi carried the box directly to the altar. She lit the incense, struck the gong, and with a good-humored "Eat up, Yo-chan!" placed the Styrofoam box on the slide-out shelf beneath the altar. Then the two women, having finished their own dinner several hours ago, sat back down at the *kotatsu.* After a suitable amount of time, Sarah got up and retrieved the box from the altar. The contents were still hot. The balls of dough were generously studded with octopus chunks, green onions, and pickled red ginger; their tops were drizzled with savory sauce and dried bonito flakes and green seaweed powder. Mrs. Kobayashi took one but ate only half. "You have a young person's digestion, so you might as well eat it all," she said, pushing the box toward Sarah. "They'll be no good once they get cold."

Sarah began working her way through the octopus balls, spearing them one by one with a toothpick. "So why now, do you think?" she asked, returning to their earlier conversation.

"*Saa* . . . who knows? Strange things happen to women in middle age. Emotions rise up from quiet places. They realize life is short, and it makes them act differently."

They were silent.

"Can I tell you something?" Having broached this subject, her grandmother seemed eager to keep on talking. "A few years back—right before your grandpa had his heart attack—we ran into each other at the open-air market. She introduced me to someone she knew. And you know what she said?" Mrs. Kobayashi paused dramatically. "She said, 'This is my mother.'"

Sarah speared another octopus ball and said nothing.

"She said, 'This is my mother,'" Mrs. Kobayashi repeated. "As cool as a cucumber, right in public. She said, 'This is my mother.'"

Sarah looked up and saw her grandmother's face transformed with happiness and wonderment. Something about that expression reminded her of her own mother, long ago, when they had held hands.

"I never thought I'd live to see it!" Mrs. Kobayashi said. "She was always such a cool little girl, she could never say what she felt . . . and there she was, saying, 'This is my mother.' Right in public."

Sarah's vague unease now funneled into a sinking feeling in her stomach. She didn't fully understand it, but its physical effect was real.

"I'm glad for you both," she said gently. "It's very lovely, almost like a romance."

"I know, don't you think so? Listen to this. On Mother's Day I found a little bouquet of hand-picked violets in the milk delivery box. There wasn't any note. But I knew it was her."

"Well," said Sarah, "I guess it's a good thing Auntie doesn't hate you after all." She took a hard pleasure in being so direct. Then she was instantly ashamed of herself.

But her grandmother didn't seem to notice. "I'm sure her feelings are complicated. But it's the start of something, don't you think? It's more than I ever expected."

Sarah nodded, pulling her legs out from under the heated quilt. "Let me go snuff out that incense," she said, "before I forget."

She walked over to the altar. She stood there for a moment, looking at the aged, indecipherable tablets and at her mother's tablet, still brand-new. She was reminded of her early childhood when she would stand in this very spot, sulking or feeling sorry for herself after some imagined slight. She remembered how she had consoled herself by peering into this alternate world, inhaling the odor of incense and thinking fiercely that dead people were nicer than the living.

After a while she snuffed out the incense sticks and swung shut the black lacquered panels for the night. For the first time in years, she sensed her mother was gone—truly, finally gone.

chapter 40

NOW that Mrs. Kobayashi belonged to the ranks of the elderly, she patronized the bathhouse as soon as it opened: 3:30 P.M. on the dot. The other old women in the neighborhood were just as punctual. If they arrived even an hour or two later—Sarah remembered this from her own childhood—the clientele would be completely different. There would be young housewives. There would be small children with flushed faces, immersed in the scalding water bearable only to a Japanese adult, their treble voices counting to one hundred as fast as they could go.

Within this group of old-timers, Mrs. Rexford's legacy lived on. Naked, dripping women still sighed by way of a conversation opener, "Such a pity, *ne*—"

Sarah, seated on a plastic stool, was washing her grandmother's back. Proper etiquette required a person to be fully scrubbed and rinsed before entering a communal bath.

"*Ara,* how nice," said a bent old woman, pattering past on her way to the bathing area.

Sarah and her grandmother, still seated, smiled and returned her half-bow.

She resumed her gentle soaping. At first, she had often pretended it was her mother's back she was washing. It had eased
her ache to give her grandmother the tenderness she had never
given her mother. Even now, she couldn't forgive herself for the
way she had acted as a child.

After their summer in Japan, things had improved. It wasn't
noticeable at first, for their closeness fell away in America. But
as the months passed, that indefinable chemical change within
Sarah asserted itself. She still struggled with her mother for free-
doms and privileges, but their arguments weren't as frequent or
as personal. For Sarah had seen her mother at her strongest and
most admired, and her mother knew she had.

Their arguments became less about Sarah wanting to fit
in with her peers, and more about her wanting to try new
experiences—something that her mother could understand.
Over time, her outsider anxiety dropped away altogether, giving her much more in common with her mother. This took
years, of course, and Mrs. Rexford didn't live to see the full
effect. But before her death there had been the start of a true
womanly friendship between them. For the first time, Sarah
had looked into the future and seen the full-fledged bond
theirs would become.

She knew this now: her relationship with her mother hadn't
been a bad one. But back then, the only yardstick they had was
the closeness between her mother and her grandmother. It was
a source of regret for Sarah, as she knew it had been for her
mother, than they hadn't been able to replicate it.

"Look!" said Mrs. Kobayashi. She was pointing down at their
feet on the tiles. "You and I have the same toes." It was true; the
first three toes of Mrs. Kobayashi's feet were all the same length,
just like Sarah's.

"*Maa,* she takes after her grandma!" a nearby bather commented kindly. It touched Sarah to think of her grandmother eyeing her body so discreetly, so hopefully, searching for the smallest of connections.

They rinsed under the showerhead, then walked over to the bathing area. The enormous tub took up the entire room; through the heavy steam, they could glimpse several heads rising from the surface of the turquoise water. Echoes bounced off the high domed ceiling. On the other side of the tall dividing wall, they could hear the occasional burst of male voices.

They straddled the side of the pool-like tub and stepped into the steaming water. Gritting her teeth to keep from yelping, Sarah descended the steps until the hot water was up to her neck.

"*Aaa . . . ,*" sighed Mrs. Kobayashi, holding a soaked washcloth up to her cheek in order to absorb even more heat. "Nothing feels more luxurious than soaking in an old-fashioned communal bath."

"Isn't that the truth, madam," agreed a woman several meters away. "Those new houses with the baths added on, they have such tiny little tubs. There's no way you can get the water truly *hot,* like it is here."

"One of my daughters lives in a house with a private tub," Mrs. Kobayashi told her. "She's never bathed here, even though she passes by every day on her way to the market. Such a pity. I often think how much she'd enjoy it here."

Sarah felt a flash of anger. This was her mother's special place, not her aunt's. With a queer feeling in her stomach, she remembered how loyal her mother had been, as loyal as Benkei. *Don't you dare hurt my mother,* she had said. And she had cried . . .

Now an unfamiliar woman, treading water with her hands, made her way over to Mrs. Kobayashi. "This must be Yo-chan's daughter?" She turned to Sarah, her face flushed from the heat.

"Your mother," she said, "used to light up a room. She was so full of life."

"Thank you," Sarah replied. Gratitude welled up, making her voice unsteady. "It's so kind of you to remember."

"And this one here's becoming more and more like her mother," Mrs. Kobayashi told the woman. "Sometimes I almost forget who I'm talking to."

The woman nodded and beamed with approval. Sarah, somewhat mollified, smiled back modestly.

Her grandmother was correct, to a certain extent. Sarah had adopted many of the social mannerisms that had endeared her mother to the public—her habit of clapping once when she had a bright idea, or her sunny demeanor and facility for easy chatter. She had internalized her mother's attitude of taking others' approval for granted. It hadn't come easily. She had blurred their identities, as she had once learned to waltz by standing on her grandfather's feet. No one was going to call *her* a blancmange pudding.

Yet there was a difference: these qualities were learned, whereas in her mother they had been instinctive. Sarah knew, and realized her grandmother knew, that she would never have the true spark of the original.

chapter 41

For the next two days it rained continuously: sometimes a downpour, sometimes an invisible mist. According to the weather report, a typhoon was blustering up near Hokkaido and affecting the main island.

Today the rain had stopped, but it was still overcast. Sarah and her grandmother were walking home from the open-air market. The air was damp and warm and hushed.

"Let's cut through So-Zen Temple," Sarah suggested.

"Good idea," said her grandmother. "The pines will smell nice."

The lanes near the temple had hardly changed. Prewar wooden houses still stood behind their rustic fences, the same fences Sarah had admired as a teenager. "Thank god for zoning laws," the neighbors said. After all, So-Zen Temple was an important historical attraction.

They entered the temple grounds through an unassuming back entrance. So-Zen had multiple entrances because it was such a sprawling complex, one of the largest in the country. They walked down a path so narrow they could feel the clammy moisture of the stone walls on either side. Above them towered a profusion of trees—bamboos, flaming red maples, gnarled pines that housed the largest crows Sarah had seen anywhere. Their guttural *cah-cah*s broke through the cheeping of smaller birds.

"You know what Mama told me once?" Sarah gestured up at the trees with her free hand. "She said when she was little, some boy climbed all the way up one of these pine trees to get a nest of eggs. And the mother crow swooped in and pecked at his head . . ."

"*Soh soh!* And he fell and broke his leg," supplied Mrs. Kobayashi with relish. "I do remember that."

It was odd to think of neighborhood children having free rein in what were now official grounds. But when her mother was little, children had pattered up and down the wooden verandas of temple buildings that were now fenced and roped off and labeled like museum exhibits. On this hushed autumn morning, with the grounds empty now that the autumn tourist season had drawn to a close, Sarah sensed for the first time what So-Zen must have been like when Japan was a poor country. The temple buildings seemed to deflate, receding into the foliage and taking second place to the living creatures emboldened at having the grounds to themselves: crows flapping heavily from branch to branch; smaller birds bursting into the air in groups of two or three, their wings sounding like a deck of cards being shuffled.

"This is where Mama used to catch snakes when it rained." Sarah gestured to a ditch running alongside the lane. It was a ditch from a bygone century: narrow and deep, lined with granite blocks. "She said she once found a white one, but she put it back because, you know, white snakes are supposed to be holy."

"Really, she caught snakes? She never brought any home . . ." Mrs. Kobayashi peered down into the mossy ditch. Leaves and rainwater flowed swiftly past. "She was always a thoughtful child," she said, "thinking ahead to spare me trouble."

The pathway dead-ended. They could turn left toward the main part of the complex or else go right, down a long cobbled walkway shaded year-round by the overhanging branches of *donguri* trees. They always took the latter path because it led toward home. The walkway was strewn with small black *donguri*—indigenous acorns that generations of small children had picked off these cobblestones and brought home for their mothers to roast as snacks.

They passed more temples, their wood weathered to a velvety aged brown that was almost black. They were unadorned and timeless. Their simple lines sank into her soul in a way the cathedrals of Europe never could, reminding her of the eternity that lay beneath temporal emotions.

"I wonder if it's going to rain," said Mrs. Kobayashi. The sky seemed grayer now than it had an hour ago. A *donguri* dropped down onto the walkway behind them. This part of the path was always less crowded, since the temples petered out here and there was nothing to see. Today it was utterly deserted. The only other person they had seen all morning was a shaven priest clopping by in the opposite direction, dignified and austere in his dark robes with tan-colored tassels. Above high wooden geta, his *tabi*-clad feet gleamed white. But now he was nowhere in sight.

"Grandma, let's sneak in and see the baby Jizo," Sarah said impulsively. "I didn't get a chance last time, it was summer and there were tourists all over the place . . ."

"Baby Jizo, where? What are you talking about?"

Sarah felt a catch of surprise, for the baby Jizo had been important to her mother. She wondered if she had just made some sort of blunder.

But it was too late now. "Mama used to come here all the time," she explained. "I'll show you. See, you go over this fence . . ." She quickly straddled the low iron tourist railing, looking back and laughing at her grandmother's shocked expression. "Quick!" she said. "There's nobody around. Quick!"

Mrs. Kobayashi's face darkened with disapproval, but curiosity made her follow. Holding down her skirt with one hand, she cautiously straddled the low fence, lifting one wool-stockinged leg after the other. They slipped between the trees, squeezed through an opening in a wall of shrubbery, and there it was: a small clearing with twenty or so crumbling statues of tiny smiling bodhisattvas. They had been rescued after the war from remote country roads up in the Kyoto hills.

Mrs. Kobayashi stood in the clearing and gazed about her with a look of dawning dismay. "You realize, don't you," she said finally, "these aren't ordinary Jizo. They're markers for real-life babies that died in bad circumstances."

Sarah knew. In past centuries, illegitimate babies had been drowned. Orphans had starved during famines. There was even an ancient tradition of putting twins to death if they were born of opposite sexes. Some of the stone markers—so old and weathered they looked like lumps of rock—had two figures etched side by side. None of these children had had a proper burial. Since there was no family to chant sutras and push the children safely into the next world, little Jizo were created in their memory. The sadder the circumstances, it was said, the sweeter the smile a stoneworker would carve. The Jizo would stand on roadsides and protect travelers from harm.

"When Mama was sad or upset as a girl, and even when she was in college," Sarah told her grandmother, "she'd come and sit here. She made up stories about who they were and what their families were like."

To her dismay, her grandmother gave a little shudder.

"When she brought me here," Sarah continued, "she'd say a prayer for them, and she made me say a prayer too." She had a flash of memory: standing here next to her mother, eyes closed and palms pressed together. For a moment she could almost smell the sun-warmed stone and hear the comforting rattle of summer leaves overhead.

"If I'd known about this when she was a girl, I would have forbidden it," Mrs. Kobayashi said. "These souls are lost and hungry, like stray dogs. If they sense a susceptible spirit, they latch on, poor things. And they drag down the living."

It was hard to know how to respond. Mrs. Kobayashi was a practical woman with progressive views. But every so often, like now, Sarah was reminded that they came from different generations and different cultures.

"You must think I'm silly," said her grandmother.

"No," said Sarah. "I think it was a different time. A much scarier time." The crumbling stones, with their aura of tragedy, did look rather sinister in the still gloom of November.

"I told her to stay away from these sorts of things." Mrs. Kobayashi sounded hurt. "I made her promise."

"Well," said Sarah helplessly, "I guess it turned out all right in the end."

"*Soh.* I suppose it did."

chapter 42

Later that afternoon, someone tapped on the kitchen door. It was Mrs. Ichiyoshi, who lived four houses away.

Sarah hadn't seen the old woman in years. She never came outdoors anymore. Once she had been a common sight, hovering over a vendor's pushcart or sweeping the doorstep of her visitor gate. When Sarah and her cousins were small, she would give them green-tea candies from her apron pocket. They accepted politely but unenthusiastically; green tea was an old person's flavor.

Mrs. Ichiyoshi bowed and stepped into the cement vestibule. Waving aside Mrs. Kobayashi's invitation to come up, she perched informally on the raised ledge of the tatami floor, not bothering to take off her shoes: the classic posture of a neighborhood gossip.

"And who might this be?" She looked curiously at Sarah, who had knelt down beside her grandmother on the tatami matting. Mrs. Ichiyoshi had a deep, masculine voice.

"This," Mrs. Kobayashi told her, "is Yoko's girl, all grown up."

"*Aaa,* Yo-chan, of course . . ." The old woman's face brightened with fond recognition. Then she leaned in closer. "Have you heard?" she whispered in her gravelly voice.

Sarah wondered what news about her mother could possibly be so urgent, since she had been dead six years now.

"She's marrying a gaijin!" Mrs. Ichiyoshi told them. "The girl's lost her mind! A gaijin! *Maa,* can you imagine the to-do over at the Kobayashi house!" Her face contorted with a look of scandalous glee that Sarah had never seen. It reminded her of the time she was fourteen, when she had looked up at the Asaki balcony and seen a stranger staring at her through Mrs. Asaki's eyes.

It was the first time she had encountered a senile person. But the greater shock was seeing her mother's past come alive with such ugliness.

Before anyone could respond, Mrs. Ichiyoshi's daughter-in-law came scurrying to the open door. She steered the old woman back toward home, periodically looking back over her shoulder and making jerky bows of apology. Sarah and her grandmother followed them out into the lane, bowing back in polite reassurance and staring after their retreating figures.

"Poor thing, *ne,*" Mrs. Kobayashi said lightly. "Gone funny in the head and still so young." She avoided looking at Sarah. It was unbearably painful that her daughter's disgrace had been witnessed by her child. Sarah would have felt the same way if her grandmother had known of her mother's disadvantages in America.

Later that day Mrs. Kobayashi remarked, with a strange vehemence, "If her real father were alive, he would never have allowed her to marry an American." With this cryptic comment, the subject was closed forever.

There were certain things Sarah never discussed with her grandmother. She never let on that her mother had been anything but a queen bee in America. And she never mentioned their fights.

In turn, she knew her grandmother kept certain things from her. When Sarah was fourteen, her aunt Tama had told her that when her mother left on her honeymoon, Mrs. Kobayashi had dropped her brave face and wept for days afterward, huddled on her knees in the parlor. "I didn't know what to do!" Mrs. Izumi said. "I thought she was going to get sick." At the time, Sarah had assumed this was natural behavior for two people so close. But years later, shortly before she died, her mother had said something surprising.

"It was healthier for me to go away," she said. "We were too attached." That surprising remark had stuck in Sarah's memory like a shard of glass.

She wished she could ask her grandmother about it. But how could she risk hurting an old woman who had suffered so much? The very idea would have outraged her mother, with her Benkei-like protectiveness.

There was one other topic they didn't discuss: the problem of her mother marrying an American. Until now, Sarah hadn't grasped the full magnitude of the situation. "There was a little resistance at first," she was told as a child, "but then you were born, and everyone's heart just melted into a puddle." This had seemed reasonable. In Sarah's generation, there was nothing shocking about a mixed-race marriage.

The Ichiyoshi incident made Sarah curious about her parents' marriage. She had grown up hearing her parents reminisce fondly about their courtship. She had been delighted by the tale of stuffy relatives—a socially prominent branch of the Sosetsu family—who had begged the Kobayashis to stop the marriage. It would impact their children's prospects, they pleaded, referring to matchmakers who dug deeply into family histories.

"But you stood up to those silly people and made them go home, didn't you, Mama?" young Sarah had said happily.

"Of course I did," her mother replied. "And your grandmother backed me up, one hundred percent."

The couple had met while Mr. Rexford was in Japan on a two-month vacation. In the fifties, Japan was still struggling to catch up with the modern world. Students were urged to practice their English on any foreigner they met. Since foreigners were scarce in inland cities, Mr. Rexford was approached by a good many college students. Faces stiff with embarrassment, they would blurt out, "Hello, I have a black pen," or "How is the government in your country?"

One spring day he was standing in a shrine yard, in front of a wooden structure with an enormous rope hanging from the eaves. This rope was meant to be grasped with both hands and shaken, so the large bells overhead would clang and alert the spirits. Then it was customary to drop a coin into the slatted donation box, clap three times, bow, and pray.

Yoko was sitting a few yards away, a sketching board across her knees. She had recently graduated from college with a double major: one in classic Japanese literature and one in English. She was eager to display her skills to someone capable of appreciating them.

"Excuse me," she said. "That rope at which you are gazing is made of the hair of female prisoners."

"It was the best opening line I'd ever heard," Mr. Rexford told his daughter years later.

Their meeting was the start of a tender friendship. After Mr. Rexford went home to America, he wrote her every week. Through their letters, they fell in love.

For many years, Yoko kept their correspondence a secret. After all, Japanese girls from good families did not consort with

Americans. She explained away the letters by telling her mother that Kyoto University had a pen pal program, designed to help alumni maintain the foreign-language skills they had learned. Sarah loved the story of her grandmother innocently saying, "Here's another letter from your pen pal!" as she collected mail from the wooden box at the visitor gate.

"I always had a gut feeling about him," Mrs. Rexford used to tell Sarah. "I just *knew*. There was something in his eyes."

Sarah had never seen beyond those charming anecdotes to the true problem: Yoko had lied to her mother for years. The sense of betrayal must have been especially great because mother and daughter were best friends. Many nights after everyone went to bed, the two had stayed up late into the night, laughing, gossiping, holding philosophical debates. How hurt her grandmother must have been when she learned the truth!

It bothered Sarah that she knew nothing about the most intense and painful time in the women's relationship. What guilt her mother must have felt! How did she reconcile that remorse? Knowing the answer might have given Sarah a vastly different understanding of her own relationship with her mother.

chapter 43

The public bathhouse was closed for maintenance, so Sarah was preparing to bathe at the Asaki house. She padded up and down the hall, collecting clean underwear and socks and a new woolen undershirt from the *tansu* chest in the parlor. Her grandmother was staying home; she would wait until the bathhouse opened on the following day. "You go ahead," she urged Sarah. Even now, old boundaries stood firm: Mrs. Kobayashi never visited the Asaki house except on formal occasions.

It was years since Sarah had bathed at the Asaki house. She had often bathed there as a child; it was quicker than public bathing and it gave the girls more time to play.

Early afternoon seemed the least intrusive time to visit. Her uncle would still be at work, and Yashiko would be in school. Momoko no longer lived at home; she had gone away to college.

"Is it too antisocial, slipping in and out like that while everyone's away?" she asked. She suspected her mother would have chosen a more convivial hour.

"Not at all," said her grandmother, helping to pack Sarah's vinyl bath bag with a washbasin, shampoo, soap, and towels. "It's the perfect time to chat with Granny Asaki."

It was a long-standing tradition for Sarah to sit with her great-aunt and look through her photograph albums. This had originally been Mrs. Rexford and Mrs. Kobayashi's idea. "Why don't you run along to Granny's," they would urge the child, "and ask her to show you pictures from the old days?" It was partly to teach her etiquette. "It makes old women happy," her mother explained, "to have people know how pretty they were when they were young. Remember that."

"She was a real beauty in her day," her grandmother would add. "I remember people always compared her to that famous actress, what's-her-name."

But playing up to Mrs. Asaki's vanity was also the women's way of ensuring that the "half" child, despite her Caucasian features, would endear herself to the matriarch of the family.

Now these visits served a different purpose: to acknowledge that the old lady was important enough, and loved enough, to receive personal visits of her own. Mrs. Rexford's calls had been formal, peppered with deep bows and ceremonial language. But Sarah belonged to a generation awkward with such formality, so this was her way of paying respect.

"Oh, and while you're there"—Mrs. Kobayashi looked up from Sarah's vinyl bag and clapped her hands once, relieved at having remembered—"be sure you pick up our concert tickets."

"Tickets? We're going to a concert?"

"I didn't tell you? It must have slipped my mind. What is *wrong* with me lately? It's your auntie; her choir's performing this weekend at the brand-new Civic Auditorium. You remember—the big building that's been on the news lately."

Sarah had never heard about her aunt singing. Oh, but wait, now she did remember something: a throwaway conversation from the summer she was fourteen.

The three of them—Mrs. Kobayashi, Mrs. Rexford, and

Sarah—had been sitting on the garden veranda one muggy afternoon, fanning themselves with paper *uchiwa* as cicadas droned in the maple branches overhead. Hearing the rapid crunch of gravel, they turned their heads to see Mrs. Nishimura hurrying past along the alley, her slender form flashing in and out of view through the slats in the wooden fence.

"*A!* Late for the bus again," Mrs. Kobayashi said. "It's her choir day."

"Choir? Really!" Mrs. Rexford's voice held the kindly geniality that accomplished people use when praising those with less skill. "*Maa,* good for *her*!"

"It's with some other PTA mothers," Mrs. Kobayashi said. "They've formed some kind of a group." She leaned over and twisted off a dead leaf from a nearby fuchsia bush, placing it in the center of her lap to throw away later. "By the way, I'm thinking of frying up some gyoza for dinner. Or do you think it's too hot?"

Sarah asked if her aunt was a good singer.

Her grandmother had considered this for a moment, gazing off into the distance. "I believe so," she finally said, "but nothing outstanding, I think. It was always your mother they picked for the solos in school."

Sarah now reached over and slipped her clean underclothes into the bag on her grandmother's lap. "The Civic Auditorium, really? They let PTA choirs perform there?"

"PTA?" Now it was Mrs. Kobayashi's turn to look blank. "What are you talking about . . . *aaa,* I see. No no, she stopped that choir years ago, when your cousins finished elementary school." She seemed amused by Sarah's confused expression. "You!" she chided. "*Anta,* it's no wonder we're at cross purposes all the time. Your information's always outdated."

Sarah suppressed a flash of resentment. But her grandmother was right; she lived too far away to be in the family loop.

"Your auntie's in a *real* choir now." Mrs. Kobayashi handed the bath bag over to Sarah and rose up from her floor cushion. "You'll see."

"I'm trying to remember," said Sarah, "if I've ever heard her sing around the house . . ."

But her grandmother had gone away to another room.

She reappeared several minutes later, carrying a loaded tea tray. "I checked the clock, it's still early," she said. "There's time for tea before you go."

They settled into the *kotatsu* and chatted idly over a pot of tea and sugared black beans.

Their talk turned to the Izumis, who still lived far away to the south, where they held prominent positions in the religious community. They participated in various national conferences. Little Jun, now a teenager, was skipping college in order to devote his life to the church. The Izumis had a full life, for they had made many friends in the church.

Reflecting on all this, the two women shook their heads in silent wonder.

"We always thought it would blow over," said Mrs. Kobayashi.

"I know." But it made sense. For now her aunt had the loving family she had always wanted, with herself at its vital center.

Sarah had seen her aunt briefly during her last visit. That was the year of Mr. Kobayashi's death, and Mrs. Izumi had come to pay respects. She brought with her one of those fragrant gift melons that were sold in their own box. Since she couldn't pray at the funerary table, she sat at the dining room table and sipped cold wheat tea.

That was a busy afternoon. A stream of visitors had padded through the dining area on stockinged feet, bowing politely to Mrs. Izumi as they made their way to the parlor. Sarah kept her aunt company at the dining table. They said little. They lis-

tened to the miniature gong in the next room, to the hushed
babble of voices as visitors exchanged greetings with the lady of
the house. Sarah had wondered if her aunt felt any longing to
join that group, to stand for one last time before the altar from
which she had exiled herself.

During a lull, Sarah had placed her aunt's melon on a dish
and taken it into the parlor. But the table was already full, cluttered with orchids and fruits and pastries. She put the melon on
the floor, on the other side of the table, where people's feet
wouldn't strike it.

"Mama and Grandpa used to love those melons," she told her
aunt, going back into the dining room. "Auntie, you're the only
one who remembered."

Her aunt had smiled at her, and the sweetness of that smile
flooded Sarah's heart with a great tenderness. It was her old
childhood crush, refined over the years to something bittersweet. Mrs. Izumi had grown a bit stouter, but she was still
pretty. She had achieved the settled, contented air of a matron,
with nothing left of the old coquettish vivacity.

Sarah now asked, "Does Auntie Tama still wear her hair
swept back in a French twist? The same way Mama did?"

"As far as I know. She still copies a lot of things from your
mother. She looked up to her so much, you know. I think it went
deep." Mrs. Kobayashi shifted position under the *kotatsu* blanket. "This blanket's so hot!" she said. "I'm turning down the
heat switch." In the same breath she added, "She wants me to
come live with them."

"Really!" Sarah thought her aunt had given up by now. But
one never knew about people.

"I told her I'd think about it, but . . ."

The original plan had been for Mrs. Kobayashi to come live
with the Rexfords when the time came. She and Mrs. Rexford

had often talked of the things they would do together: the dishes they would cook, the garden they would tend. Having looked forward to this for so long, it must have been hard for Mrs. Kobayashi to imagine living with anyone else. It was reminiscent, in a way, of marrying for the second time when it was the other sibling she really wanted.

"*Ne,* Grandma, it's not as if you need looking after. I mean, you're still walking around wearing *heels.*"

"Exactly! I plan to stay independent as long as possible," said Mrs. Kobayashi. "I overhear those women at the bathhouse, the ones who live with their children. And I can guess what's going on with Granny Asaki, even though she puts on a public face . . . It's a secure life, to be sure. But secure doesn't mean easy. Human nature being what it is, it's best to think twice before putting yourself at someone else's mercy."

Sarah liked this about her grandmother: the worldliness that surfaced at unexpected times.

"I suppose moving out there is the smart thing to do," continued Mrs. Kobayashi. "It's not as if there's any other . . ." She gave a little sigh.

"But you want to stay near Auntie Masako, don't you."

"Yes. I think . . . I think she'd like me to stay. I mean, she's never asked me outright. But I want to be near her anyway."

"But Granny might not die for a long time. She's really healthy. She'll probably live to be a hundred."

"Yes, I know."

Sarah imagined the women's future: chance meetings in the open-air market, brief stolen moments over a bit of grilled eel or liver. She had been here long enough to see that for all their new closeness, there was little change in their day-to-day routine.

"It doesn't seem like enough," Sarah said. "You hardly even see each other, or talk, or anything. It just doesn't seem fair."

"It's *not* fair," said Mrs. Kobayashi. "But it's enough."

"Oh, Grandma." Sarah felt a great sadness. "Why can't you spend more time together? Those old boundaries can't possibly matter now. You're her *mother.*"

"I gave Granny-san my word. After she's gone—"

"But what if you die *first?*" Sarah's voice rose in spite of herself. "Granny's had all those good years. You and Auntie didn't have any. It's not right."

Mrs. Kobayashi shook her head stubbornly. "I don't agree," she said. "And I know your auntie feels the same way I do." Sarah, sensing that gap of generation and culture between them, knew it was a lost cause.

"It's like a love affair," she marveled. "A sad, beautiful love affair."

Her grandmother nodded. "Romance isn't just between men and women," she said. "It's a state of mind, I suppose. It may be beautiful but it comes with pain. And sacrifice. Not just for yourself, but for others around you. I've often thought that being *in love* is bad for a family. It's much less risky when people merely *love.* There's a big difference, you know."

Sarah sipped her tea, pondering this.

"I've been in love all my life," said Mrs. Kobayashi.

"Your whole life?"

"My whole life. It's the one part of me I always protected."

Growing up, Sarah had thought of her grandmother's charisma only as it related to her mother. With her mother gone, she could see her grandmother had a force of her own. It wasn't the social magnetism of her mother. Nor was it the fetching femininity of her aunt Tama. Her grandmother's charisma went deeper, somehow, than those surface attractions. She made people feel something of the magic and purity and passion that were still possible in this world.

"I admire you," Sarah said impulsively. "I do. Not many people are brave enough to give up security for love." Her vehemence made them both laugh. She felt her sadness lift, replaced by a girlish kind of optimism.

"Your mother, she had that quality too," said Mrs. Kobayashi. "That's why we got along."

Sarah, remembering, nodded. From somewhere outside in the rainy afternoon, there came the muted *pee-poh pee-poh* of a passing ambulance.

"And you got a chance to experience it. But your auntie, she never had much opportunity for romance."

"Not until now," Sarah said.

"That's right," said her grandmother. "Not until now."

chapter 44

After her tea, Sarah slipped her sock-clad feet into an old pair of geta and clopped over to the Asaki house. A drizzle made pinpricks of sound on her umbrella and on the surrounding garden foliage. She lingered in the lane, breathing in the smell of rain and leaves and wet wood.

Alerted by the sound of the garden gate rolling open, Mrs. Nishimura came to meet Sarah at the door. "Go right on up, Sarah-chan," she said. "Granny's waiting for you. I'll bring up refreshments a little later."

Sarah climbed the old-fashioned stairs, which were exceedingly steep and made her feel as if she were climbing a stepladder. She planted her hands firmly on the step above her—partly because there were no handrails, only wooden walls, and partly because her socks had no traction against the aged, slippery wood. Dangerous, she thought. But no one in this family, young or old, had ever had an accident.

Emerging from the dark stairway onto the landing, Sarah slid open the *fusuma* panel and found her great-aunt hunched over a *kotatsu* near the glass panels. All around her, strewn on the tatami floor, were drifts of persimmon leaves. Each year she collected them from the tree in the back garden, while they were still pliable enough to wipe clean with a moist cloth. This she did painstakingly over a period of weeks—she had little else to do—and when they dried out completely, she crumbled them in tins to use as medicinal tea throughout the year. "It's excellent for a woman's health," she always said, though the tea was so bitter no one else would drink it.

"Sarah-chan!" Mrs. Asaki put down the leaf she was wiping. "Come in, come in!"

Reverently, Sarah stepped over the threshold. Nothing had changed since her childhood: the thick *fusuma* panels inlaid with green seaweed; the view from the balcony, now shrouded in mist; caged finches hanging in a corner. The shoji panels had been pushed aside and the spacious room pulsed with a white, watery light.

"Come, come," cried the old woman gaily in her singsong accent. "Don't mind the leaves, just step around. Come, sit down." In old age she was hunchbacked, with a body as frail and insubstantial as a child's. But her spirit was as game as ever. She still dyed her hair the old-fashioned way, using some kind of dried plant sold by Chinese herbalists.

Mrs. Asaki now lifted the edge of the *kotatsu* quilt for Sarah to slip under, as if holding open a door. Sarah acknowledged this with a smile and a half-bow of thanks, feeling a sudden rush of love for this old woman who had filled her earliest memories with nursery chants and games. "Granny," she said. "I'm so happy to see you healthy and thriving each time I visit."

"Tell her hello too," Mrs. Asaki replied. "Tell her that when all this rain passes, I'd love to pay my respects to the altar."

There had been several such moments lately, for Mrs. Asaki was losing her hearing. But she was a proud woman, too proud to say "What?" She faked her way with aplomb, and only occasional slips betrayed the effort with which she hid her infirmity. Sarah never let on that she knew. She merely spoke as little as possible, relying on smiles, nods, and comments that were easy to lip-read.

She reached for one of the albums lying on the *kotatsu* in preparation for her visit. Mrs. Asaki picked up her persimmon leaf and commenced wiping. They sat in companionable silence while the finches ruffled their feathers and pecked contentedly at their feed. Every so often Sarah slid the book toward her great-aunt and remarked, "So pretty!" or "Auntie was so cute!" Her great-aunt gave a pleased cackle and replied: "That was a high school field trip." Or, "That was two years after I got married."

Here was a photograph of Mrs. Asaki as a young woman: tall, unrecognizably beautiful, standing under a tree. She wore a white fur draped around her neck and down the side of her silk kimono. She had grown up in the rural outskirts of Kyoto, the daughter of a town mayor. Despite this unremarkable pedigree, she had married into a fine old family in the city on the strength of her looks. In this picture she was tilting her head demurely to the side, but her sloe-eyed gaze held that gleam that beautiful women have when they know they're invincible.

Sarah knew that Granny had been asked to stay upstairs to make things easier on everyone. It was too bad; social activity had been her lifeblood. Mrs. Kobayashi sympathized too. "Poor thing," she had said. "It would be so much healthier if she could chatter away in a public bathhouse, instead of being cooped up there all alone." But theirs was more of a philosophical pity, for they also understood Mrs. Nishimura's position. As Sarah's mother used to say: What can you do? There was no perfect solution, and right now it was Mrs. Nishimura's turn to bloom at the expense of someone else.

The old woman never let on that her circumstances weren't

ideal. "Who wants to run about at my age?" she bragged. "I'm perfectly happy in my little kingdom upstairs. Surrounded by family, waited on hand and foot, *maa maa,* I'm incredibly lucky . . ."

Sarah scrutinized the photograph again. Mrs. Asaki, glancing over to see what was taking so much time, gave a little laugh of recognition. "I was young then," she said.

In college, Sarah had learned that history was the study of power rising and power falling. Sitting here, leafing through the pages of another woman's life, she felt the truth of this and was humbled. It occurred to her that her own past—the trio of her mother and grandmother and herself that had once seemed so extraordinary, strong and shining like the sun—was hardly unique. Countless other suns, like her great-aunt's, had risen and fallen as a matter of course, each with its own forgotten story, its own poignance.

chapter 45

Sarah found her aunt alone in the kitchen, making preparations for dinner. "I'm just finishing up this side dish," she told Sarah, in apology for cooking in the presence of a guest. She was sautéing a combination of julienned carrots, hijiki seaweed, and fried tofu skin. It looked identical to the dish Mrs. Kobayashi often made, but this would have much less soy sauce and sugar. Mrs. Kobayashi disparagingly referred to it as "Kyoto flavor."

Before going off to undress, Sarah leaned against the kitchen doorjamb and watched her aunt. The radio was on, a plastic Hello Kitty model long outgrown by Momoko and Yashiko. For years now, it had been tuned to the same classical station that played everything from the Western melodies of Strauss and Puccini to the elegant notes of koto, punctuated by a shamisen's bitter twangs.

In general, Mrs. Nishimura seemed unchanged. Under her apron she wore a blouse of pastel yellow, with a round collar that had embroidered daisies on it. She still wore the short bob, although Sarah could see it was professionally cut at a salon, with graduated layers and the subtlest of brownish highlights to indicate she was coloring her roots.

But on closer inspection, Sarah did sense something of the change her grandmother had mentioned. That virginal, ethereal quality was gone. As Mrs. Nishimura reached for a bottle of seasoning, she leaned across the counter with an unfamiliar physical brio that reminded Sarah, for an unsettling moment, of her own mother.

She stared, but Mrs. Nishimura made no more surprising moves. Stirring quietly at the stove, she was once again the aunt of Sarah's childhood: a gentle figure who never frowned or grimaced, who hovered with a damp cloth for wiping children's fingers.

An early memory floated up in her mind. She was six years old; they were walking to the park on a winter afternoon. She was in the middle, between her aunt and Momoko—Yashiko wasn't born yet. "Hold on to Big Sister's hand, for safety," Mrs. Nishimura had told Momoko. As young as she was, Sarah knew her aunt was doing this to flatter her; any other adult would have walked in the middle, keeping one child on either side. Little Momoko obediently clutched Sarah's hand with her mittened one, looking up at her with a chubby, trusting face framed by a knitted hood with animal ears. Sarah felt a rush of importance, followed by overwhelming love for her aunt. The three of them held hands and strolled down the sidewalk. *"Ten ten ten— ten koro rin . . . ,"* Mrs. Nishimura chanted softly as they swung their joined hands back and forth.

It had struck Sarah, with a small child's intuitiveness, that no one but her aunt could have been capable of such sensitivity. Looking back now, she wondered if even then she had sensed a kinship between them, for they both knew how it felt to be on the outside.

"Sarah-chan," her aunt said, "are you finding this Japanese weather too chilly?"

"Not at all, Auntie. Today's quite warm, I thought."

"Yes, you're right!" said Mrs. Nishimura. "It's unseasonably warm."

Talking to her aunt was slightly awkward, as always. On a purely technical level, she wasn't used to making allowances for Sarah's simple Japanese vocabulary. Mrs. Kobayashi had the knack for putting complex ideas into simple terms. Nuclear physics, for instance, became "the rules of science involving—" followed by an exploding sound, with both hands outlining an enormous H-bomb mushroom. "Right, right!" Sarah would say, laughing and nodding. But her aunt would use the term *nuclear physics,* then be at a loss if Sarah didn't understand. So she usually stuck to the simplest of conversational topics.

But language aside, direct emotional entry was difficult. Mrs. Nishimura had a particularly traditional sensibility, with an oblique quality Sarah recognized from historical films. She had to remind herself that her mother, who had married a foreigner, was the unusual one. Mrs. Rexford had little patience for old-school Japanese opacity. "I have a cosmopolitan soul," she used to say, only half joking.

"Auntie," Sarah said, "I'm really looking forward to attending your concert."

Mrs. Nishimura glanced up from the stove and laughed, waving her free hand before her face in a no-no motion as if the very idea of her performing in a concert was absurd.

"I feel bad that I never even knew about your choir."

"You mustn't feel bad," her aunt said mildly.

After some more small talk, Sarah went off to undress behind the cotton curtain. It seemed odd that the informal dining room should adjoin the bathing room, but this was common in traditional Japanese homes where private baths had to be added on. It made more sense, she thought, than the

Western custom of placing the bath in the same room as the toilet.

Fully naked, she slid open the glass door and entered the steaming bathing area. The tub was deeper than it was wide, with a lid to keep in the steam. Directly above the bath, mounted on the tiled wall, was a digital water temperature monitor (she was amused by this modern gadget, which was out of place with the rest of the house). At the other end of the room was a waist-high shower nozzle. Retrieving a low plastic stool from a stacked pile, Sarah drew it up before the nozzle, sat down, and soaped herself. As she shampooed her hair, she could hear faint clattering sounds in the kitchen, the energetic chatter of a commercial on the radio. Then the commercial ended and music came on. She recognized Pavarotti's soulful tenor launching into his classic rendition of "Ave Maria."

"Ave Maria"! There was a family story . . .

"She learned this new song in middle school," Mrs. Asaki had once told the children. "And every day, when she went upstairs to hang up the towels and handkerchiefs, I'd hear . . ." The children waited eagerly as she placed her teacup deliberately onto the saucer with an elderly hand that, even back then, trembled. "Ave Maria!" She said it ominously: *Ah-beh-mah-lih-ah!* "All those strange foreign words—" Mrs. Asaki threw back her head and trilled an affected operatic tune. "Aaah . . . lalalaah . . . So loud! All over the neighborhood! I finally had to make her stop. *Maa,* what the neighbors must have thought!"

Sarah and her cousins had sprawled on the tatami floor, shrieking with laughter at Granny's operatic performance. It was a bizarre anecdote. Neighbors here did not shout out to each other, or argue in public, or burst into song on balconies. Such activities were more in line with florid, excitable countries like Italy.

"Mommy did that, really?" Momoko gasped, and the image of gentle Mrs. Nishimura singing at the top of her voice made the girls burst anew into giggles. "She must have been really happy, to sing like that!" little Yashiko said.

Sarah turned off the shower and sat still, listening. This time, as an adult, she understood what she was hearing: a prayer, a pouring forth of something intense and mournful.

Now Pavarotti's voice swelled in volume, reawakening her childhood remorse for her aunt. A random remark flashed through her mind: her mother (or grandmother) saying, "Let's not mention this to Ma-chan. It's just easier." She was ashamed— partly on behalf of her mother and grandmother, but also for the eager way she had complied, proud of her place in their golden, laughter-filled circle.

Her remorse wasn't just for her aunt. It was also for herself, for the change that had started when she hid the cream puffs behind her back. From that day on, she had followed the trajectory of that choice. Not that she regretted it. She had grabbed at life, as was her right; she had grabbed at a place in the sun. But she had always felt a vague regret for that side of herself she had left behind, that side akin to her aunt. Her memory of the winter day, when she and her aunt had held hands against the world, glowed with an innocent purity that seemed lost to her forever.

But with her mother gone, maybe things could be made right.

That day, for the first time, Sarah let go of a penance she had carried so long she had almost forgotten its weight. With a feeling of relief that was almost luxury, she felt herself relax into second place.

chapter 46

The radio was playing "Tea for Two" when Sarah emerged from behind the curtain. The informal eating area was fragrant with soy sauce and ginger, and a small plate of seasonal chestnut dumplings was waiting for her on the low table. In the kitchen, her aunt hummed along to the lively *cha cha cha*s.

Taking off her apron, Mrs. Nishimura sat down at the low table to keep Sarah company as she ate the dumplings.

"Are these the tickets?" Sarah picked up the flowered envelope placed neatly beside her plate.

"*Soh,*" said Mrs. Nishimura.

Sarah peeked inside. The tickets, glossy and professional-looking, showed an unexpectedly high admission price. The title was printed in raised Chinese characters: "Songs That Got Us Through: A Wartime Retrospective."

Mrs. Nishimura was eying Sarah's untouched cup of tea. "Oh—do you not drink Japanese tea?" she asked.

"Of course I do!" Sarah felt a twinge of her old insecurity. "Auntie, don't you remember?" She took a sip of the tea and, after a suitably appreciative silence, asked, "Are you a soprano?"

"No—I sing with a low voice," her aunt replied. Mrs. Kobayashi would have given Sarah credit for an easy word like *alto,* considering it was a Western term to start with.

The large house was silent. The rice cooker bubbled in the kitchen.

"But your mother," continued Mrs. Nishimura, "she used to sing with a high voice. A beautiful high voice. I can still remember her singing 'Days of Yore' at our middle school graduation."

"Really? Tell me . . ." Now they were on secure ground. Sarah relaxed and listened with quiet pride. Even in death, her mother could fill up a conversational vacuum.

At one point she looked up and saw pity in the older woman's eyes. It resonated sharply, even unpleasantly, for this was how she had always regarded her aunt. Now she realized, with dawning embarrassment, that her aunt was dwelling on her mother's singing for no other reason but kindness.

"Auntie?"

"Yes?"

"I'm glad you're here for Grandma." Sarah plunged awkwardly into the heart of the matter. "When she talks about you, her face lights up. She's so happy. I'm glad, and I know Mama would be glad too." Truthfully, she wasn't completely glad. Not yet. It struck her that siblings everywhere must face such ambivalence, and she was thankful she had been spared this as a child.

"No one will ever be like your mother," said Mrs. Nishimura. "But I'll do my best to take care of your grandma while you're away." She refilled their teacups with a no-nonsense briskness that reminded Sarah, once again, of her own mother.

Later, sated with tea and dumplings, Sarah got up to leave. She had probably held up her aunt's dinner preparations. Gathering up her bath bag, she maneuvered carefully around the low table so as not to poke a hole in the shoji panels behind her.

Her aunt walked her out.

"You must really love singing," Sarah said as she followed her aunt down the hallway, past one *fusuma* panel after another.

"*Aaa,* I know," said Mrs. Nishimura sorrowfully, as if admitting to a bad habit.

Sarah had a deep sense of futility. We're *family,* she wanted to say. Don't use such good manners.

They came out to the front gate. Darkness had fallen, though it was still early. The drizzle had stopped, and the air was sharp with the smell of wet pine. It was indeed warm for November; the typhoon in Hokkaido had altered the air pressure.

Sarah rolled open the slatted gate and paused on the stone step. A faint breeze wafted against her skin, still overheated from the bath.

Caught in the knobby branches of the Ichiyoshis' pine tree, heavy with white light and almost touchable, was a full moon. "Oh, look!" Sarah said. "The moon."

"*Aaa,* isn't it pretty."

They were silent awhile, looking up.

"I look at the moon a lot," Mrs. Nishimura said, and a certain quality in her voice made Sarah take notice. "Like this, with the branches silhouetted on it. In traditional art, you know, the moon's never bare. It's always half-hidden behind branches or clouds." Sarah knew the art to which she was referring. She, too, had been affected by those old Japanese tableaus, by the sorrowful beauty of a shining thing glimpsed, only partially, through a layer of impediments.

Halfway down the lane, she looked back. Her aunt was standing by the gate as she had since Sarah's childhood, waiting to return her wave.

chapter 47

Mrs. Nishimura's concert took place on a still, overcast Sunday afternoon. Sarah and her grandmother took a taxi to the matinee. Mr. Nishimura was working and Yashiko, having already attended the opening concert, had somewhere else to be. Mrs. Asaki was too old for these kinds of outings.

They sat quietly while the seats filled up around them. The orchestra made discordant notes as it warmed up. The audience was mostly middle-aged and older since the concert was a retrospective, held in honor of a songwriter who had written many of the classic tunes of the postwar period. War nostalgia was popular now. There was always something on television about a restaurant serving some wartime dish or a middle-aged person being tearfully reunited with a childhood friend from the occupation era. Sarah, who remembered how fondly her mother used to say "our generation, growing up after the war," understood this need to look back.

She wondered what her mother would have thought of this state-of-the-art auditorium. She could picture her alert eyes looking about, taking in the high acoustical ceilings, the discreet spotlights built into the walls. "They didn't spare any expense, did they," she would have said, "but I still liked the small, dark building from my childhood."

Not so long ago Sarah would have shared this thought with her grandmother, tossing out her mother's name as if she were still one of them. But it felt unnatural now, even forced. She was beginning to like having her mother to herself, like a private talisman. Her grandmother had her talisman too, and the two versions would become less and less alike as the years wore on.

She flipped idly through the program. Her knowledge of Chinese characters was spotty, so she recognized only the title— "Songs That Got Us Through"—as well as the words *Paris, Berlin,* and *New York.* Mrs. Kobayashi had mentioned that the choir performed abroad on occasion, though not everyone went. Many of them were homemakers with children, and their domestic duties came first.

Sarah put down her program and glanced over at her grand-mother, who looked demure and poised in her mink collar. "They didn't spare any expense, did they?" she said.

"*Soh,* they certainly didn't."

The spotlights caught the instruments down in the orches-tra pit, bringing out the expensive gleam of polished wood and brass. This *is* a real choir, thought Sarah, a choir to be taken seri-ously. Her aunt must have worked hard—and kept it to herself, so as not to give her family the impression of neglect. Not that it stopped Mrs. Asaki from saying things like, "It's a nice life she has. Singing like a bird while her old mother eats leftovers. But *maaa,* she loves it, so what can you do?"

Now the instruments died down and the lights dimmed overhead. Sarah leaned forward in anticipation of her aunt's entrance. And in that moment, she knew with certainty that she was going to be all right on her own. Her mother had even said it: *Once you've come first, it stays a part of you.* This moment, right now, was the strongest she had ever felt: being secure enough in her own powers to enjoy someone else about to have her day in the sun.

The choir began filing onstage, one by one, unassuming and matronly in their navy-blue dresses. They lacked the seasoned stage presence of professional performers; one sensed these were ordinary women who, like the rest of the audience, had been personally affected by the songs they were about to sing. From the rising power of the clapping, Sarah knew the audience sensed this, too, and was responding to it. The choir flowed smoothly into its assigned lines, like a marching band. "Front row," Mrs. Kobayashi whispered, leaning over to point her out. "Over there, third from the left." And there indeed was Mrs. Nishimura, looking small but composed.

The conductor strode in swiftly to the center of the stage, bowed deeply, then turned his back to the audience. He raised his baton and waited. The clapping died down. Someone coughed. Sarah turned her head to look up at the audience: row upon row of pale faces rose up in the darkness, waiting. On this threshold, she felt a deep, sharp joy for her aunt and also a fore-shadowing of what lay ahead for the three of them: not the shin-ing, laughing summers of her mother's time but a tender new season that would resonate, like those bittersweet Japanese tableaus, with all the complexities of time's passage.

The first soprano was a lone voice, barely audible. Then the others—second soprano, then first alto (that was Mrs. Nishi-mura's section)—joined in with steadily gathering force, and finally the second alto, its heft overtaking all the others. Their voices swelled to a crescendo, then paused, the notes spreading out like ink in water.

They sang of yellow rapeseed flowers, blooming by the road-side in spring. Sarah's mother had sung this song to her when she was little. Sarah hadn't learned until much later that it was about a bomb site in Nagasaki. Today, transformed by the orchestra and the sheer power of voices, its familiar childish words were elevated as she had never heard them: rich, omniscient. *Small flowers are nodding,* they sang out with one voice. *Cheery and bright . . .*

Sarah thought of young Aunt Masako standing alone amidst flapping laundry, singing out to an empty sky. She thought of the strange power of thwarted emotions. She thought how pervasive thwarted love was, how it lay beneath so much of life's beauty. *We let them ferment,* her mother had said, *till you can't tell them apart.*

chapter 48

On a hushed, sunny afternoon when the last of the red maple leaves were drifting down from the trees, Mrs. Asaki came tapping at the kitchen door. As always, she had an official excuse for coming: to pay her respects at her ancestors' family altar. According to Mrs. Kobayashi, the old lady paid her respects quite regularly. "She looks forward to coming here," Mrs. Kobayashi had confided to Sarah. "Poor thing."

While her grandmother made preparations in the kitchen, Sarah readied the *kotatsu* in the family room. She brought over an extra floor cushion from the stack in the corner—it was autumn, so the cotton covers were a warm shade of rust—and turned on the heat switch under the table. She glanced at Granny Asaki, who stood hunched before the altar, murmuring under her breath and massaging her tasseled prayer beads with practiced, efficient hand movements that spoke of a lifetime of prayer.

"A little offering for your mama," she said afterward, nodding at the envelope on the altar.

"Thank you, Granny! Thank you so much." She lifted the

kotatsu blanket. "It's a beautiful day, isn't it?" she asked as her great-aunt lowered her frail limbs onto the floor cushion. "So sunny and warm."

"Oh no, it's not too warm," the old woman said brightly, reaching under the table to feel the heater. "The temperature's just right."

Sarah smiled and settled the quilt around her great-aunt's bony hips. Mrs. Asaki watched her, nodding imperceptibly.

"You're a good girl, *ne,*" she said. "Your mama in heaven is happy with the way you turned out."

Mrs. Kobayashi entered the room with a tray of covered ceramic bowls. "You've picked a good day to come!" she told her sister-in-law. Placing the heavy tray on the table, she walked over to the frosted glass panels and slid them all the way open; they rattled in their wooden frames. Sunshine poured in, catching glints of gold in the straw of the tatami mats. With sunlight came the smell of burning leaves and the vague sadness of a season nearing its end.

Mrs. Kobayashi stood there for a moment, gazing out at the laundry courtyard. Above the fence the sky was deep blue, with that high dome of autumn described in classic Japanese poetry. "How long has it been," she said, "since we had such beautiful weather?"

This, Mrs. Asaki heard perfectly. "*Soh,* it's been forever!" she replied. "Ahh, how good the sun feels! Like warm hands on my body."

This mystery of selective hearing had been explained to Sarah by her grandmother. "It's only certain pitches she can't hear," Mrs. Kobayashi had said. "You and your cousins, you all have high-pitched voices because you're young women, so she can't hear what you're saying. But my voice has low tones, so we never have a problem. Now, your auntie has high tones, which makes things difficult. You wouldn't think it, would you, with her being an alto and all. But there you are."

Settled into the *kotatsu* with her elders, Sarah did nothing more than smile and nod. She wanted Granny to have this hour free from auditory strain, so she could relax and have a lively chat without shame and disability hanging over her. She remembered how carefully and correctly her own mother had once spoken English.

"Would you care for some *ten-don*, Granny-san?" Mrs. Kobayashi lifted the lid from one of the ceramic bowls. Steam rose into the air, along with a mouthwatering aroma. *Ten-don* was a humble dish of day-old tempura, reheated in a flavorful broth and poured over rice and eggs. It was hardly the thing to serve a guest, but as Mrs. Kobayashi had once explained to Sarah, old people secretly craved comfort food over tea and fancy confectionery. Besides, this dish was easier on the teeth. Broth turned the crispy crust into a soft, flavorful mush that melted in the mouth, and the vegetables—sweet potatoes, carrots, eggplant—turned as soft as pudding.

Mrs. Asaki's aged eyes gleamed, and she hunched over her bowl with a little sigh of pleasure. With hands that slightly trembled, she lifted a chopstickful to her mouth. "Granny-san, it's delicious!" she said. She had always freely acknowledged that Mrs. Kobayashi was the better cook of the two. "It's been *years* since I tasted this dish."

Mrs. Asaki's reprieve was not just auditory; she rarely received such warmth and attention at home.

"That's why she fritters everything away on money envelopes," Mrs. Kobayashi had once told Sarah. "You watch, there won't be anything left for them to inherit. She always thinks of herself first."

"She thinks smart," Sarah had said. For in a traditional world where women had little power, Mrs. Asaki had used her wits. She had married well, strategically leveraging her physical beauty. And in adopting a child in her forties, she was surely motivated by more than the simple desire to love a child. There must have been an awareness that, in a society without nursing homes, a childless woman was doomed. A son would have been preferable to a daughter, but once again Mrs. Asaki had shown foresight by moving her son-in-law into her own home, ensuring her place within their family unit. And through shrewd use of her monthly pension, she still maintained a degree of control. All in all, she had played her cards well. She had achieved the security she sought, if not the full loving spirit that might have accompanied it. Sarah thought her great-aunt would have been an interesting woman to talk to, if she had known her as a fellow adult instead of a one-dimensional granny.

"Has Sarah-chan been telling you lots of stories about America?" Mrs. Asaki asked.

"Yes indeed. The child's a hard worker," said Mrs. Kobayashi proudly. "She tells me she works long hours. Large companies are very demanding, you know."

What Sarah had not mentioned was how disillusioned she was by her career, how little it had lived up to her expectations. She remembered her view of life as a child: a maze in which a perfectly good path sometimes veered off in an unexpected direction. She wondered now if that was the norm rather than the exception.

"*Maa,* you have a good appetite," Mrs. Kobayashi said. "That's very healthy. Old people like us, we have to keep up our appetites or else we're done for."

Mrs. Asaki, who had been greedily focused on her bowl, came to with a little start of embarrassment. If her wrinkled skin could have blushed, it would have.

"It's good to eat," Mrs. Kobayashi reassured her. "Don't worry about appearances, Granny-san. We're past that, you and I." She covered the old woman's gnarled hand with her own. "We're the only ones left. We have to keep on living, with all our might. *Ne?*"

Mrs. Asaki nodded her head, like a child.

"Let's enjoy our food to the fullest, Granny-san," Mrs. Kobayashi said. "Let's not leave a single bite."

Sarah watched them. Both women, in their different ways, had forged through life as best they could. Mrs. Asaki had used foresight and strategy. Mrs. Kobayashi had followed a linked chain of great loves. In the process, they had caused damage— to each other, to innocent bystanders. And although they would never be true friends, each understood what the other had gone through. Each understood the nature of the journey. Life was difficult. Safe havens were few and impermanent.

Something of that hardship and peril transmitted itself to Sarah. Life will be hard, she thought, harder than I know. She wondered how she herself would make her way through life.

Was she equal to it? She thought so. For she could feel the women's reserves passing down to her, reserves she would draw on in years to come. She felt a dim premonition of her power, similar to what she had felt the summer she was fourteen. Her mind flashed back—instinctively, as if fingering a talisman—to the summer day when her mother had held her hand in hers.

"You're right, Granny-san," Mrs. Asaki said in the singsong accent of old Kyoto. "We have to keep on living, with all our might." Nodding her aged head, she looked over at Sarah. *"Ne?"* she said.

And Sarah affirmed it with vigorous nods of her own.

About the Author

MARY YUKARI WATERS has been anthologized in *The Best American Short Stories, The O. Henry Prize Stories,* and *The Pushcart Prize.* She is the recipient of an NEA grant, and her work has aired on BBC and NPR. Her debut collection was a Discover Award for New Writers selection, a Book Sense 76 selection, and a Kiriyama Prize Notable Book. She received her MFA from the University of California, Irvine. She currently teaches in Spalding University's Brief Residency MFA program.